A NOVEL BASED ON THE LIFE OF
ST. AUGUSTINE OF HIPPO

THE
FLESH
AND THE
SPIRIT

Sharon Reiser & Ali A. Smith

THE
MENTORIS
PROJECT

The Mentoris Project
745 Sierra Madre Blvd.
San Marino, CA 91108

Copyright © 2022 Mentoris Project
Cover photo: VTR / Alamy Stock Photo
Cover design: Suzanne Turpin

More information at www.mentorisproject.org

ISBN: 978-1-947431-45-4

Library of Congress Control Number: 2022936032

Names: Reiser, Sharon, author. | Smith, Ali A., author.
Title: The flesh and the spirit : a novel based on the life of St. Augustine of Hippo / Sharon Reiser & Ali A. Smith.
Description: San Marino, CA : The Mentoris Project, [2022]
Identifiers: ISBN: 9781947431454 (paperback) | 9798201571849 (ebook) | LCCN: 2022936032
Subjects: LCSH: Augustine, of Hippo, Saint, 354-430--Fiction. | Spiritual life--Fiction. | Church history-- Primitive and early church, ca. 30-600--Fiction. | Catholic Church--History--Fiction. | Religious thought--To 600--Fiction. | Spiritual warfare--Fiction. | Flesh and spirit antithesis (Pauline doctrine)--Fiction. | Faith and reason--Fiction. | Christian philosophy--Fiction. | LCGFT: Historical fiction. | Biographical fiction. | Christian fiction.
Classification: LCC: PS3618.E5675 F54 2022 | DDC: 813/.6--dc23

The Mentoris Project is a series of novels and biographies about the lives of great men and women who have changed history through their contributions as scientists, inventors, explorers, thinkers, and creators. The Barbera Foundation sponsors this series in the hope that, like a mentor, each book will inspire the reader to discover how she or he can make a positive contribution to society.

Contents

Foreword

First and foremost, Mentor was a person. We tend to think of the word *mentor* as a noun (a mentor) or a verb (to mentor), but there is a very human dimension embedded in the term. Mentor appears in Homer's *Odyssey* as the old friend entrusted to care for Odysseus's household and his son Telemachus during the Trojan War. When years pass and Telemachus sets out to search for his missing father, the goddess Athena assumes the form of Mentor to accompany him. The human being welcomes a human form for counsel. From its very origins, becoming a mentor is a transcendent act; it carries with it something of the holy.

The Mentoris Project sets out on an Athena-like mission: We hope the books that form this series will be an inspiration to all those who are seekers, to those of the twenty-first century who are on their own odysseys, trying to find enduring principles that will guide them to a spiritual home. The stories that comprise the series are all deeply human. These books dramatize the lives of great men and women whose stories bridge the ancient and the modern, taking many forms, just as Athena did, but always holding up a light for those living today.

Whether in novel form or traditional biography, these

books plumb the individual characters of our heroes' journeys. The power of storytelling has always been to envelop the reader in a vivid and continuous dream, and to forge a link with the subject. Our goal is for that link to guide the reader home with a new inspiration.

What is a mentor? A guide, a moral compass, an inspiration. A friend who points you toward true north. We hope that the Mentoris Project will become that friend, and it will help us all transcend our daily lives with something that can only be called holy.

—Robert J. Barbera, Founder, The Mentoris Project
—Ken LaZebnik, Founding Editor, The Mentoris Project

"I see in my members another principle at war with the law of my mind, taking me captive to the law of sin that dwells in my members. Miserable one that I am! Who will deliver me from this mortal body?"

—Romans 7:23–24

"May I not be my own life."

—St. Augustine, *The Confessions* XII.x

Prologue

IN THE BEGINNING

November 13, 354
Thagaste, North Africa

The midwife appeared from the doorway of the stone house and placed the bundle down at Patricius's feet, according to Roman custom. The old woman then stepped back.

Patricius stood outside in the morning sunlight. Rough brown mountains and trees circled his farmland, and the morning sky was a brilliant blue. But his focus was not on his surroundings—rather, his eyes were fixed on the crying infant before him. He bent down, picked up the newborn, and looked into his son's dark eyes. He had no desire to do anything else. He had no desire but to claim the child as his, even though Rome gave him the choice not to.

It was a long way from Rome to Patricius's small farm in northern Africa, but Rome's influence extended far. The Roman Empire stretched from Africa to Britain, from Gaul to Constantinople. To most men, it was the world, and it surely was to

Patricius. Rome was stability and tradition. It told a man what his place was in the world and what he should do. And in return for granting this order, Rome claimed the authority to enforce it, extending authority over life and death.

As Rome was to the Empire, so a man was to his household. This baby, this newborn Patricius now held in his arms, was his son. He fully intended to rear him as well as he could, to give him everything he was able to give. He wondered why that couldn't be a responsibility he really did choose, rather than something that was required of him.

It was a useless question. In this matter, someone else in his household held the final authority.

Patricius pushed aside the curtain that opened to the room where Monica lay exhausted on a pallet. Monica—her dark hair now wet with sweat—looked up at her husband and baby with a wan smile. She looked peaceful even now, after giving birth. This was the trait Patricius appreciated most in his wife—except when he was very angry, and then it seemed to him a kind of obstinacy that could throw him into a rage.

He stared down at her now, returning her smile. He was moved to hold their fine son in his arms, and relieved that Monica's ordeal was over. But he could not resist asking the first question that came into his mind: "Shall he be baptized?"

This question that troubled Patricius also troubled scores of others. Baptizing infants was not unknown at the time, but it was more common to wait until adulthood. The delay came mainly from the great reverence in which the power of the baptismal water was held. Baptism was considered a complete cleansing of sin, and a person could receive it only once. Wasn't it better, argued many people, to wait to cleanse the sins of a lifetime all at once? Surely, that was better than to be cleansed too early and then fall back into sin. Others asked a different question: How long should a man wait to have his sins washed away?

Patricius knew Monica had asked herself these questions. Sometimes he wondered whether she had thought about anything else in all the months of her pregnancy.

Monica was a Christian in every thought and task; Patricius did not appreciate this about her, and he let her know his feelings often. A wife should consider her husband her sole lord, and Monica never let him forget that she recognized a higher lord. Of that she was sure, and she often suffered her husband's anger for it.

So, Patricius was surprised when she replied to his question with one of her own.

"Would you permit it?" she asked. She instinctively formed her words to keep her husband's violent temper from erupting.

Patricius wanted to be gentle as he held his newborn son, but his smile faded. "Much you would care if I did not," he said with a sarcastic grimace. His wife was quiet and determined, and he was suddenly ready to argue with her.

He wished she would fight, but instead she remained as calm as ever and said, "I obey you in everything I can, and I will obey you in this. I ask for permission to make him a catechumen. The rest can wait on his own choice."

Patricius was dimly aware of the catechumenate rite. The sign of the cross on the forehead, the laying on of hands, the murmur of some words, the touch of salt on the tongue—harmless enough. "Very well. I grant it," he said.

"Thank you." Monica's gratitude was real, and she lifted herself to a sitting position, leaning against the bedroom's sturdy wooden wall. After a moment, she asked quietly, "May I hold him?" Whenever she spoke to her husband, Monica kept her tone even and quiet.

Patricius placed the baby in her arms. Monica wondered briefly whether she should have insisted on baptism. It was easy in the abstract to say she would obey her husband in everything that did not conflict with the law of God. In practice, though, it was not always so clear where the conflicts might lie. But right now she had everything she needed, and it was enough. She was a mother. She cradled her beautiful son in her arms. Her Augustine.

Part One

THE FRUIT OF THE GARDEN

Chapter One

It was not easy to remain sleeping with the hot morning sun in his eyes, but during his sixteen years Augustine had practiced this skill. At home, he filled every chink in the shutters. But he was traveling now, and the morning light found its way to his face and shoulders.

He was traveling to Carthage, the great Roman city on the shore of the Mediterranean Sea. In this hub of art and culture, he could receive an education that would prepare him for a great career.

Many times, he had tried to imagine Carthage, one hundred and fifty miles east of the town of Thagaste in Northern Africa, where he'd been born. Augustine had never ventured from home before now, and he'd never seen the sea. Growing up on his father's olive farm, he'd watch as workers pressed and poured oil into jars before it made its journey to vendors across the sea.

Whenever traders came to the farm, he had listened intently when they described what it was like to stand on the deck of a ship and adjust your footing to the rocking waves. At first it seemed impossible, then was soon done with as little thought as drawing breath—and after that, walking on land felt unnatural.

Young Augustine was intrigued by the traders' stories and couldn't wait to test his balance on a ship at sea. Some days he stared into a cup of water and tried to imagine what it would feel like to float on it like a boat. After today, he would not have to imagine. He lifted his head and looked around the small room, squinting at the brightness of it.

He'd been traveling for nearly a week, and today would be another day on a horse, with the hot, white road stretching out ahead toward the horizon under the African sun. It would be another day in which his senses told him they were not truly advancing, despite what the road markers indicated. By the fourth day, he had begun to wonder if the road markers lied.

"Up!" commanded Priscus, the leader of the merchants with whom Augustine was traveling. By now, all of the merchants knew his aversion to morning light and had learned that strong measures must be taken. Without a chance to protest or obey, Augustine tumbled onto the hard dirt floor as three young men yanked the cushion from beneath him.

"All right, I am up!" Augustine shouted in mock indignation. "You have no respect for a person's need for sleep!"

"If we didn't pull you out of bed, you'd languish there all day! We need to get to Carthage, and according to your father, so do you." The merchants teased Augustine mercilessly. He didn't mind.

Augustine shook his head and ran his fingers through his dark, curly hair. Evidently, it was time to get up.

Late that afternoon, the travelers sat up in their saddles at the sight of large stone tombs—now they knew Carthage was close. The dead of Carthage greeted Augustine and his party before they even reached the city gates.

Augustine and the others understood that though a man's breath did not last and his words were fleeting, stone could grant a kind of eternal life that Romans valued. Outside cities throughout the Empire, inscriptions on mausoleums seemed to call to travelers with words about justice and piety and courage. These words carved into stone at least gave a man life by entering the thoughts of the living as often as his name was read.

Priscus, the most talkative of the merchants, sidled up to Augustine on his horse and leaned over to give the teenager's shoulder a teasing shake. "Have you started writing your inscription?" Augustine gave him a long, skeptical look. Priscus persisted, "Come, Augustine, what will your inscription say?"

This passed for humor during the days of counting road markers. Augustine's body was not all that ached after a day in the saddle; his mind longed for intelligent conversation. Still, he liked Priscus, a stout man, older than the others, with a face that seemed to naturally break into a smile. He managed to joke even during the dullest or most tedious stretches of travel.

But instead of answering, Augustine returned the question to Priscus: "What will *yours* say?"

Priscus laughed at the challenge. "More than will fit on a column—if they could print any of it. I have lived for the spirit—I do not say I haven't—but more often than not, the flesh has claimed my attention. There is a good deal more of it, you will agree, and it cries to be fed. The first time I came to

Carthage . . ." He grinned. "Have I told you of the first time I came to Carthage?"

You have, thought Augustine, who now avoided looking directly at Priscus. No use in answering. It would not matter.

"Even if I have, you should have it fresh in your mind. How else will you know what mistakes are worth the making? The first time I came to Carthage . . ."

Oh, thanks be to God, Augustine thought. *The gates.*

Already he felt the cool ocean breeze Carthage was known for against his hot skin. Excitement rose in his chest—he was in Carthage at last!

The city had loomed large in Augustine's boyhood imagination ever since he learned its history from his father, who was well-informed, having regular contact with merchants from other countries who bought his olive oil. Augustine reflected on the stories he remembered of Carthage and how it came to be.

Here it was before him, this famous city: stone buildings, wide avenues with people coursing through, and glimpses of the sea. Yet, his father had told him, Carthage had once been entirely destroyed. Centuries before, the Phoenicians had built a colony on the site; the inhabitants, the language, and the city itself came to be called *Punic*, from their Phoenician origins. The city grew to dominate the western Mediterranean, and its ships ventured through the straits and down the coast of Africa.

"Legend has it that a Trojan prince named Aeneas came to the city in his wanderings, and when he was welcomed by Queen Dido, he contemplated more than a political alliance,"

Patricius once explained to Augustine as they walked through the olive trees. Patricius had glanced at his son to see if he'd said too much. Augustine had not reacted to the sexual reference, so Patricius went on. "But his gods did not will it. They commanded him to leave, and their commands had to be obeyed. So, Aeneas left Dido, left her to the fire, and sailed away toward the city he would found, the city that would one day put all of Carthage to the flames."

"Was that really the reason Rome and Carthage were enemies?" Augustine had asked. He was an inquisitive boy with a developed sense of logic.

"Ah, you are right to ask!" his father said happily. "There were indeed other reasons for the rivalry of Rome and Carthage—sea lanes, trade, strategically placed islands, and the other concerns of outward-looking people."

Augustine nodded, for these were reasons he understood.

"Still, it gave men a comfortable feeling to believe the gods were on their side," Patricius said. "In those days, there were many gods to choose from. Each man could confidently choose his favorites." He was proud of his son's intelligence and fed it as much as he could. He added, "You will be interested to know that the Carthaginians—heirs to the Phoenicians, who had first claimed the Mediterranean as their trade route—thought the sea would be their battleground and were greatly surprised by how remarkably able Romans were in learning from their adversaries how to build their ships."

As they traversed the grove of olive trees, stopping now and then to inspect their leaves, Patricius explained that, stalemated on the sea, Carthage determined to take the long road, led by a man who possessed both endurance and audacity.

"Who was that?" young Augustine asked.

"His name was Hannibal," Patricius said with reverence. "He conquered the Alps and brought his elephants within sight of Rome. In the end, he failed to take the city, but he had come close enough to require more than defeat. Carthage had to be punished."

And so, Augustine learned, Carthage was defeated, sacked, despoiled, and burned. Carthage was no more, and Rome rejoiced.

"The city was gone, but the land remained a strategic peninsula with a harbor within easy sailing distance of Rome," Patricius said, explaining that within a generation, Rome attempted to colonize the area. But most of the Senate preferred to consolidate power closer to home and let Africa run wild.

It would take another century for Roman influence to be established there. And it would take another man of endurance and audacity to do it: Julius Caesar. Augustine knew this name—all boys did. On African soil, Caesar defeated his great rival, Pompey, and the native chieftains who were loyal to him. "The men of his victorious army saw African land and African women, and Caesar was pleased to let them claim both," Patricius said angrily. Clearly, he did not enjoy this part of the history.

What Caesar did not have time to complete, Patricius said, his nephew Augustus accomplished. A statesman and military leader, Augustus sent his surveyors to Africa, and from the top of Byrsa Hill, the heart of the Punic city, they laid out a new Carthage in a grid of east-west and north-south streets.

"Carthage became Roman," Patricius said matter-of-factly. "The port was restored and the grain of Africa sailed to Italy. The city acquired a forum, a temple to Jupiter, libraries, baths—everything that, to its colonizers, comprised civilization . . ."

Suddenly, Priscus's shouts roused Augustine from his reflections on the long history of Carthage. "The gates! We have arrived!"

Augustine looked up at the city now within view and halted his horse while the others trotted for the gates. He wanted to take in the full implication of the city before him.

Here was Carthage. The city that was given a new birth by the conquerors who had taken its first life.

Augustine was acutely aware that he'd come a long way from Thagaste. The air was thicker here, laden with a moisture and fragrance that Augustine learned was the sea. He was used to breathing a higher air, half a mile above sea level and seasoned with pine, not salt.

The air was not the only difference. From his first moments in the city, Augustine compared himself to the citizens and recognized he was just a provincial, the son of a poor farmer from a small town.

Patricius had saved and sacrificed everything he could, without giving up the name of a free man, so his brilliant boy would not become a poor farmer. Indeed, Patricius had seen to it that both his sons—for after Augustine, Monica gave birth to their second boy, Navigius—received the education of free Romans.

Patricius was proud of their family name, Aurelius, which indicated their Roman citizenship.

The heart of such an education, as any Roman or African knew well, was rhetoric. The use of words mattered more than the thoughts they expressed, and schools held contests and offered prizes for recitation. Even as a child, Augustine had suffered agonies in memorizing Juno's wrath at the coming of Aeneas to Italy in Virgil's *Aeneid*. When it was his turn to declaim, his pure, young voice filled the square with the poem's hexameters:

> *"Then am I vanquished? Must I yield?" said she,*
> *"And must the Trojans reign in Italy?*
> *So Fate will have it, and Jove adds his force;*
> *Nor can my pow'r divert their happy course.*
> *Could angry Pallas, with revengeful spleen,*
> *The Grecian navy burn, and drown the men?*
> *She, for the fault of one offending foe,*
> *The bolts of Jove himself presum'd to throw:*
> *With whirlwinds from beneath she tossed the ship,*
> *And bare expos'd the bosom of the deep;*
> *Then, as an eagle gripes the trembling game,*
> *The wretch, yet hissing with her father's flame,*
> *She strongly seized, and with a burning wound*
> *Transfix'd, and naked, on a rock she bound.*
> *But I, who walk in awful state above,*
> *The majesty of heav'n, the sister wife of Jove,*
> *For length of years my fruitless force employ*

Against the thin remains of ruin'd Troy!
What nations now to Juno's pow'r will pray,
Or off'rings on my slighted altars lay?"

Everyone present heard the heart of the goddess herself coming from the body of the quiet boy who always stood at the edge of the crowd.

Patricius did not understand his son Augustine, but he recognized that here was the material from which lawyers were fashioned, and from lawyers came the officials of the Empire. The Empire was the world. The man who served the Empire might, to one degree or another, command all the world had to offer.

So Patricius had denied himself and his family all but what was strictly necessary to sustain life. They patched their own clothes and let the embers sink low in the braziers. Patricius had called in every favor he could claim, from distant kinship to the local landowner, Romanianus. It pleased Romanianus to be the patron of talent, and he was generous enough to do so without demanding the debt be paid in land. Patricius might be left with nearly nothing, but whatever was not nothing remained his.

When Patricius sent Augustine to Carthage to further the boy's education, Augustine was especially sad to leave his brother behind in Thagaste. Navigius was bored by books and content with tending the olive trees. But in moments when he was not content, he envied his brother for being sent to distant Carthage.

Yet Augustine felt the pressure—his success would be his family's success; his failure, their failure. So, as soon as Augustine found his school in Carthage and settled into his room, he applied himself to his studies with a fervor that sought to avert failure by sheer will.

Here in Carthage, I have every advantage of civilization and culture, he reminded himself. *Here, if success cannot be achieved, the fault lies with the one who cannot achieve it. Here begins the rest of my life, here at the edge of the world.*

Still, Augustine was a teenager and enthralled by the city's people, architecture, and landscape—particularly the harbor, where the Mediterranean sparkled in all its magnificence. In the afternoons when classes were done, he walked the dusty streets toward the waterfront. He passed grotesque mosaics of men without mouths, or of men with no heads who kept their eyes in their shoulders, or of men with two feet protruding from a single leg. He paused and marveled, but these curiosities were only the prelude.

At the harbor, he watched men load ships with silver and tin to trade in faraway countries. But the light dancing on the water fascinated him most of all, even as it nearly blinded him. He stood and stared, with the world behind him, and before him the infinite that turned a man into nothing but a glint on the tip of a wave.

When he had dreamed of the sea as a boy, he imagined it as he had seen it on maps: bounded, enclosed. Yet this sea that was beyond the measure of his mind was itself only a part of the world.

He had often spoken to his mother about the sea, wondering aloud what it looked like and what he would do if he saw it. "A man should do what was set before him to do," his mother would say. Monica had little use for speculation. While Augustine lived in the past in order to shape the future, she dwelled in the present with a fervent hope for the future.

Though she was far away at home, Augustine's mother seemed to be lodged in his mind. She was a quiet but forceful and intelligent woman.

Augustine thought about his parents' relationship. Patricius could be kinder than most men when he was not angry, and Monica had learned that when he was angry, she was wise to remain silent. In Patricius's calmer moments, Monica would explain to him her Christian viewpoints. And always she prayed.

Patricius practiced the old Roman ways, not out of religious conviction so much as hallowed custom. Ancestors and gods were to be respected. These gods had served Rome well enough thus far.

Augustine was well aware that his mother was a Christian, less because she talked about it but more because of the principles that guided her actions and her kindness toward others. He could tell his mother felt that her husband's soul was in her care, and she felt even more responsible for her son's soul. Augustine had been sped on his way to Carthage with Monica's prayers and exhortations and admonitions and supplications, and then more prayers.

Augustine did pray. His earliest prayers had been made with

great fervor: he pleaded to his mother's God to save him from the constant beatings of the schoolmaster who taught him his first grammar and arithmetic. It was hard to pay attention to those subjects when there were games to be played, and the schoolmaster clearly did not consider it part of his job to give games any kind of allure. It was enough for him that the boys should learn their letters and numbers, no matter if it be under the rod.

Those prayers had not been answered, but Augustine still prayed—when he remembered. He had watched his mother's devotions, morning and evening, continue as the years passed, despite the fact that Patricius's views remained unchanged.

The Christian God had held sway in Monica's household, but in Carthage, Augustine encountered men and women with quite different, even bizarre, beliefs. Many who found Roman religion—with its abacus-like delineation of duties and cold stance on questions of life, death, and life after death—unfriendly turned to Eastern cults, of which Christianity was only one. The god Mithra and goddesses Isis and Cybele, for example, all claimed devoted adherents—and Augustine would soon encounter them.

In the glow of the moon shining high in the night sky, Augustine held his breath and tried to hide his shock at the scene he faced. He'd been wandering alone through the streets of Carthage on a warm evening when he turned a corner and encountered an agitated crowd. He tried to see what they were looking at, but there were too many people pushing to get to the center.

Augustine heard the name Cybele and the word *initiation*, and he remembered boys at school talking about this cult. Could this be one of their rites? He drew closer, though he was wary, for he sensed an explosive energy in the crowd.

It was a ceremony unlike anything Augustine had ever seen. Some participants shouted, laughed, and shook their heads in an ecstatic trance. The ceremony was at once intimate—the men and women seemed to let their emotions flow freely—and public, with many spectators. Augustine soon realized this was indeed an initiation rite. The chosen man—a youth with handsome dark features—descended into a deep pit covered with rough planks, arranged with gaps between them.

"Step aside! Step aside!" called a priest. He led a steer, garlanded and gilded, through the crowd and onto the platform, then positioned it for sacrifice. The priest pulled from his robe a long, sharp dagger and violently stabbed the animal, which jerked and groaned. From the pit the young man strained up, his head and chest thrown back to offer as much of his body as possible to the cleansing rain of blood.

Augustine knew the followers of the Cybele cult believed the man was now reborn to eternal life—for a period of twenty years, at least, after which this gruesome ceremony could be repeated.

Fascinated, sickened, and shocked, Augustine watched until the carcass had been drained and the new man emerged from the pit. He was impressed by the fervor of the people around him, but he did not share in their awe. After all, his mother had raised him with stories of a sacrifice greater than a steer.

Augustine rushed away from the scene and found his way back to the room he rented from his school. That night in bed, the brutal ritual he'd witnessed kept him up awake. Surely, the rebirth of a man's soul must come from within that man, he thought, not from the blood of a beast.

September in Carthage brought cooler temperatures and ripe pomegranates.

"What are you doing, coming to lessons with your hands stained red from pomegranate seeds? Go wash them immediately," reprimanded the teacher to three of Augustine's fellow pupils. "And look at your tunics—you've ruined them!"

"The sweetness of the seeds is worth the caning," whispered one of the boys to Augustine.

"We will be beaten today for some fault anyway, if not for this," said another boy with a laugh.

Augustine watched with amusement, and considering the general laziness of the offenders, he privately agreed. But he was at a loss to understand how a fleeting sweetness could be worth public dishonor.

His family had been poor, so food was nourishment, and that was all. It could be pleasing, the pomegranate as much as other fruit, but it would be gone in moments, leaving only its juices behind, the enduring mark of a trivial—Augustine thought pathetic—sin.

Sin. That was a word from his mother, from the stories she told him when he was a boy. Augustine's attention drifted as he stared out the small classroom window onto the dusty street. He had given little thought to his mother's stories in these past months, and suddenly Augustine missed her very much. He wanted to do something to please his mother and her God.

Between lessons, as he strolled out into the school courtyard with other boys, one of them asked, "Are you going?" Augustine looked at the boy quizzically. The boy explained that the next evening everyone would attend a Christian celebration for the beloved Bishop Cyprian, who had been martyred in 258 during the persecution commanded by Emperor Valerian. Augustine already knew the great basilica he passed each morning was built over the site of Bishop Cyprian's burial spot—and this is where the celebration would be held. He readily agreed to meet his classmates there.

But he never found them—throngs of men, women, and children flocked to the basilica the next night, cramming the forecourt and spilling into the street. Once or twice he caught a glimpse of a classmate, but before he could reach him, the crowd pushed him in a different direction. Augustine was surrounded by such a press of people that he could barely pass around the platters of food and amphoras of wine that circulated through the crowd in great numbers. The light of the stars and torches was not enough for him to distinguish one person from the next. In place of sight, though, his other senses were stimulated by the intense fragrance of food, the warm taste of wine, the touch of cool cobblestones, and the shouts of men and women singing praises of Carthage's patron, the bishop who had not deserted his flock. The throng extolled Bishop Cyprian's courage, praised his continence, and proclaimed his skill as an orator as a gift of heaven.

Stirred by the voice of a man who stood on a wooden box reading the Psalms, Augustine closed his eyes and prayed. He prayed to possess the holy bishop's virtues, though he hesitated and quickly amended *continence* to *chastity*. Augustine resisted the idea of renouncing the flesh altogether.

Next, an old man stood on a bench above the crowd and told of Cyprian's generosity and how he had sold his inheritance to provide for the poor. Tonight, in his name, the man said, the poor were fed.

"We are all poor in spirit, so the Gospel tells us," laughed someone nearby as he refilled Augustine's cup from an amphora.

The people's singing was becoming less coherent. As the wine warmed his blood, Augustine found that his own feet were becoming less steady. He was pulled by the ebb and flow of the crowd. He put out a hand for balance, though he had a small chance of finding anything steadier than himself. His hand found the curve of a woman's hip. He pulled his hand away. "My fault," he said at once.

The woman turned to face him, her dark eyes glittering in the torchlight. "A man should be sorry for his faults," she said, her voice youthful. She smiled. "Are you sorry?"

It would be easy to say yes, to own the fault and turn away. But there was a warmth in his blood that was not wine, and a stirring that had nothing to do with psalms. It reminded him of a few years earlier, when he was at the baths with his father, who shouted with delight to the other men present that he looked forward to his son making him a grandfather.

Augustine shook his head—he had come here tonight to please his mother. It seemed that he might end the night by pleasing his father instead.

"That depends," he told the girl. "It has been said that there are many poor people here tonight. To answer your question, I must first inquire into the nature of poverty."

"Must you?" Her fingers brushed his. She did not understand the game, but she was willing to play it.

"Poverty, surely, is a lack—a need unmet. If either of us had such a need, then we would be poor. And if we each had a need the other could meet, then we would be poor together, for so long as we were unsatisfied."

She took his hand and returned it to where it had so briefly rested. "I am poor," she said.

"Then I am not sorry."

With her hand over his, they sought a path through the crowd, intoxicated with wine and psalms. As they stepped out into the street, Augustine made a further emendation to his prayer: "O God, give me chastity and continence . . . but not yet."

Chapter Two

"What have I done?" Augustine spoke out loud to his empty room the next morning. He reflected on the night with the beautiful young girl—it had all happened so fast and unexpectedly. He'd been drunk, but he remembered the night with pleasure and with shame.

In the days that followed, Augustine tried to banish the girl's name from his mind as quickly and lightly as she had departed his bed. He succeeded to some extent, but he found that appetite fed upon being fed. It was not that woman he desired, but she had shown him what it felt like to desire a woman. He desired that desire, and he longed for a woman who would satisfy it. As his thoughts turned more and more to women, it was easy to give up thinking of God.

While he searched for love, he found that the theater provided an amusing fulfillment. He attended performances with fellow students, and the bawdy scenes they watched day after day prompted them to recount their own tales of conquest.

"Yes, I've done that with several women," one boy said as they reviewed a particularly lusty scene. The boys walked toward their homes, going over the show's particulars.

"Liar," another said. "You don't know any women."

"Augustine, what do you say—are you a seducer or seducee?" another classmate teased.

"I will not tell," Augustine said with a smirk he hoped would convince them of his experience. Several boys burst into a song from the show, while another shouted out details of a recent sexual exploit, making Augustine wonder what was true and what wasn't.

He kept quiet during these conversations, for he learned a great deal from them. Some of his companions spoke of being with girls in ways that seemed to be common knowledge. He was embarrassed by his ignorance and wondered if his friends would desert him if they realized he was just a country innocent.

He was already at the top of his class in school, and now he used his talents as a student to learn about the ways of women. He listened to his friends, storing away ideas and words for future encounters, and as occasion offered, the budding rhetor contributed a story or two that were quite true.

But more than carnal knowledge, he longed for romantic love. He wondered, *How does love begin?* A pity it could not be had simply for the asking. Some boys said they paid an astrologer to find out what the stars told them of love in their future. Augustine considered this, but as it turned out, he didn't have to—for love would come into his heart quite soon.

One day in November, when it was too cold to go to the waterfront, Augustine explored the streets of Carthage instead. He found himself walking beside the workshops of the silversmiths, and he lingered to watch them work. It was like assembling a puzzle made of metal and fire. Each man performed a task on a piece, then moved it down the line—it was shaped here, augmented there—until at the end the item was complete. Each link that was made helped determine what it would be.

Turning a corner, he heard the loud clang of hammering—coppersmiths shaping bowls and vases. Next door came a woman's voice, one accustomed to making itself heard above the neighboring clangor.

"A compliment is not silver," she said.

"Neither are most of our coins," replied a man with a crooked smile. He leaned over a shop counter, facing the woman—she was young, perhaps sixteen or seventeen, and her curly dark hair was pulled back from her face beneath a striped kerchief. She was a Berber, and that in itself was no uncommon sight in Carthage, for the Berber tribes had been in Africa long before the Romans had arrived. The sight of a woman doing business, however, was novel enough to draw a small crowd. Augustine joined it.

The woman was not the lone worker in the shop. At the back, between piles of copper pots, an older woman with a marked family resemblance sat on a narrow staircase that led up to the room above the shop, where the owners slept. Standing beside her was a slave who watched the others with a sharp eye. He was not allowed to participate in the bargaining, but he served as a symbolic male presence.

The object of the bargaining was a copper lantern, elegantly embossed and studded with holes arranged in a pattern of interlocking diamonds. The young woman kept her hand firmly on it. "If your money is worthless, you should feel less of a pang at parting with it," she said, unsmiling.

"Pretty lady," the customer said, putting his hand over hers. She glanced at it coldly but allowed it to remain. "When you have lived as long as I have, perhaps you will know the copper market as well as I do. In fact, I am offering more than the piece is worth."

Augustine pushed his way to the front of the crowd and plucked the lantern out from under their hands. "How much?" he asked loudly.

The woman turned to appraise this new customer. Taking in his dark curls and open smile, she quickly named the price.

"Sold," Augustine said, reaching for the purse at his belt.

The other man spun around angrily, releasing the woman's hand. "Sir, a negotiation is taking place," he snarled.

"So I saw," Augustine said. "And I observed that you and the lady were not agreeing." He smiled at the woman. "Whereas I think she and I might agree very well."

He inwardly thanked his school friends—their stories of flirting with women and how they'd won their favor were finally of use. Augustine had now put the situation on a different footing. If the lantern was not his true object but merely a means to an end, then the other man could afford to be magnanimous. It was the part of a gentleman to smile upon a young man's conquests.

As if on cue, the man smiled. "By all means, my friend. May the flame be bright and lasting." He bowed to Augustine, who returned it with due deference. The man's departure caused the crowd to disperse.

"Thank you," the woman said, holding out her hands. Augustine realized she was waiting to take back the lantern.

"No, no, I meant it." Augustine placed coins on the counter. "I said I would purchase the lantern. I will purchase it and . . . and nothing more. I mean, not that anything else is for sale."

The woman laughed. "I have any number of kettles." Behind her, on the stairs, the older woman snorted. "But in truth, sir, there is no cause for you to purchase it. Thank you again for your assistance. Let that be all."

Augustine was not willing to let that be all. He glanced around the interior of the shop. "How do you come to be selling copper?" he asked. "These are not your work, are they?"

"No. My father is the smith. But he is ill upstairs, so today I tend the shop."

"And tomorrow?" he asked. She shrugged. Augustine nodded to her mother, who watched the exchange closely. Then he said to the young woman, "I wish your father a speedy recovery. Good day."

He walked away, carrying the lantern close to his body.

The Berber girl, whose name was Titrit, scooped the coins off the counter. She was not sentimental. She knew now there were two options. First, Augustine would not come back. A handsome, well-spoken young man, almost certainly a student with a career ahead and family obligations to accompany it—he would have better people with whom to spend his time than a coppersmith's daughter. It was probable he had been amusing himself as much as protecting her. Students were like that. He had bought the lantern, perhaps because he was rich enough for that to be part of the fun. But his tunic had not been rich, she had observed. It was plain cotton with no adornments.

The other possibility was that he would return. That would not and could never mean marriage—but it could mean a liaison similar enough to marriage to make no difference while it lasted. Titrit could not remember when she had first known she would be either wife to a smith's son (marriage between trades was not forbidden, but it was rare) or concubine to . . . someone. The title of wife had much to recommend it. But so did the young man of the lantern. It was different to consider a life as it related to herself, then to consider it in relation to the man who would lie beside her.

She thought this imaginary man in her future might have a face, if he came back.

On the stairs, her mother cleared her throat. "Congratulations. You sold a lantern," she said.

"What did you want me to do?" Titrit asked.

"Sell lanterns, of course. That's what we're here for, no matter what the customer looks like."

Titrit was not surprised her mother had seen so much, but she could not see the future or know if this encounter with the handsome young man was a beginning or merely an anecdote. She returned to her work with her mind on the young man. He was handsome, yes, and though that was pleasing, it was not unusual. What had been unusual was that she had understood him. Titrit had not been exaggerating her deafness. The ring of her father's hammer never quite seemed to leave her ears, yet she had heard that young man's voice clearly. She neither knew nor cared why it should be so, but hoped only to hear his voice again, for as long as she was allowed.

She carried this hope with her through the rest of the day, more than once glancing out to the street to see if he might be coming back. At the end of the day, as she closed up the shop, she thought about him. As she fetched water from the fountain, she thought about him. And as she went out to buy their evening meal because the smoke of cooking in their one room was too much for her father at present, she thought of him again. She carried the hope of seeing him again into sleep.

The next day, he came back.

As it turned out, Augustine's fear did not come to be. He had gone searching for love, knowing full well that love meant fidelity. He believed fidelity was a price that must be paid for love—worth enduring when it was all set in the scales. He expected love to be a comparison, a "this over that." But he was finding that it was an absolute. It was not that he wanted Titrit more than he wanted other women. He wanted Titrit. And each time she allowed him to learn more about herself, he was more attracted to her.

As the months went by, he was pleased to discover he wanted Titrit and no other.

"My love, do you see?" she said one morning to Augustine as they lay in bed.

"See . . . ?" he asked, not quite awake. She pulled the covers away from her body and he saw: her stomach appeared to have grown.

"A baby?" he asked, though he knew the answer by Titrit's sly smile.

"A baby. *Our* baby," she said, stroking his cheek.

Augustine looked down. "I am happy, but unhappy too," he said softly. "I want you all to myself, and a baby will claim your body and your love."

"But you will be the father, and you hold claim above all others."

Augustine was not yet eighteen, and until now the word *father* had been a distant idea, a role for which there would be plenty of time when he was not the person he now was—whenever that might be. Suddenly, it was to be now.

He tried to picture his child, but this too was only a word. As days passed and Titrit's belly grew and she was ill nearly every morning, Augustine worried for their future. Many days she could not leave their apartment or even their bed, and Augustine dashed up and down the three flights of stairs in their building, dodging the other tenants to bring her water, food, and the latest news of the city.

One day, he brought her a gift. It was spring, and he had been out to the waterfront again, entranced by the scene of ships at the docks. The sun was bright, as usual, and the sky was completely without clouds. It looked more blue than the sea, a blue you could almost touch. Why should the sea be so frightening when the sky, which was much vaster, felt like an embrace?

It had been a little more than a year since he had come to Carthage. When he and Titrit first got to know each other, he told her about his journey, about how strange and wonderful Carthage had seemed at first. Then he had grown used to breathing the fragrant air. "Yes," she had said, "the jasmine." At the time, he thought it was an odd remark. He recognized the scent of jasmine, but it hardly seemed worthy of comment, nor would he have thought the conversation worth remembering. How strange memory was!

As he climbed the stairs that afternoon, his arms were full of jasmine. Titrit sensed the fragrance in the slight movement of the air from the open door. It pulled her out of bed and into his embrace, then to the chest in the corner, to find a suitable amphora to hold the sprays.

Over her shoulder, she said, "You have a letter today."

While she worked at her arrangement, Augustine took up the letter on the table and broke the seal. It was his brother's hand, but inside was his mother's voice.

Titrit, her eyes still on the flowers, felt the change in Augustine's mood. "What is the news?"

"My father has died," he said. Four words, and now it was real, true. It had happened in Augustine's mind and heart, not in the outside world alone. To speak it, to put it into his own words, made it his. A breeze brushed his face as he turned to look out the apartment window, across the rooftops.

Titrit did not know how to react. Augustine understood; he did not know himself. Was his father really gone?

He said that soon I would make him a grandfather, thought

Augustine. *He was right, and it did him no good. He wanted this, not I—yet I will have it and he will not.*

He returned to the letter in his hands. The bare fact had been quickly told. Monica had devoted most of the parchment to what was, to her, of far more interest: Soon before he died, Patricius had come to Christ, she explained with evident joy. He had been a man very much of his world, proud, open-handed, jealous of his dignity but accepting the responsibilities of that dignity along with its privileges. He had been a Roman, with a Roman's place and a Roman's plans.

Perhaps knowing that he would soon leave this world made Patricius wish to enter the next one in peace. Augustine could not imagine the path his father took to his sudden new belief, but Monica did not dwell on how it happened. It was enough that her God had answered her prayers.

Augustine inferred from his mother's letter that she hoped he might follow the same path to Christ. Her grief and hope were entirely genuine, but she wanted to drive home her point: her husband had been saved, but her son's future was still in doubt.

The letter then turned to the present. Augustine was to continue with his studies, she wrote. It had been his father's wish, and Romanianus would stand as his patron. Monica was confident he would do honor to both his parents.

"Will you have to go?" Titrit asked in a wavering voice that betrayed her fear he would leave forever.

Augustine put the letter aside. Titrit suddenly needed to hold on to the chest, and she perched there, precarious and awkward and sickly pale. Right now, she hardly resembled the pretty, confident girl bargaining for a lantern, and she knew it. She knew her pregnancy had not been what he desired. Augustine realized sadly that Titrit expected him to leave, and she expected him to be relieved.

He crossed the room to her, shaking his head and holding out both hands. "My brother is better able than I am to take care of the land," he said. "There would be nothing for me to do. My work is here, and my mother says I am to continue just as I am." Her hands found his. "And that is what I intend to do."

His answer had been true insofar as it answered the question in Titrit's heart, and she was satisfied. They both knew he would not really continue just as he had done.

The weeks went on. Titrit's sickness ebbed, but as they each resumed their normal roles, an unexpected silence grew between them. Titrit continued to help her mother in the shop as much as she could, and Augustine buried himself in his studies. Each noticed the distance between them grow, but neither seemed able or willing to cross it. They knew a baby would soon fill that distance with its demanding presence.

Augustine did not love Titrit any less. When he read late into the night because he could not sleep for the ache of his desire, the desire was all for her. How, then, could his love have so little joy left in it? Was this the love he had sought so long?

There came a night when, shortly after he'd fallen asleep, he was awakened by . . . What was it? All was quiet, yet something disturbed him. He realized Titrit was not beside him, and a candle was burning in the main room. He rose and followed the light to find Titrit clinging to the edge of the table, a shattered cup on the floor beside her.

She had not heard him, and when he touched her, she gasped and shivered. Then she clung to him, trying to summon the air to form words, but none were needed for him to understand the situation.

"Now?" Augustine asked.

"Now," Titrit answered, her face set in pain.

"Why did you not wake me?"

"I would have, when I was sure." She clenched her teeth and hissed. "More sure."

Augustine settled her as comfortably as he could, then quickly swept up a handful of shards from the broken cup.

"I will run and be back as soon as I can," he said, and then he was gone. He raced through the silent streets, stopping for a precious minute to explain his errand to the night watchman, before pounding on the midwife's door.

Then there was waiting, and Augustine trying not to listen. Titrit's screams woke the neighbors, and for a time Augustine was busy explaining the situation to them. The woman from the second floor stayed to help. She vanished into the bedroom, and then there was more waiting.

I wanted her, Augustine thought. *Was that so much?*

The night stretched on, seeming to approach the day without actually getting closer to it. He began to think the answer was yes. He had wanted too much, and now what he had wanted would be taken from him. What was there that was worth being desired, if it could be snatched away? Snatched away screaming, so that the last memory would be of agony on the other side of a curtain.

He paced because he could not bear to stand, then he sat because the pacing was clearly futile, then he stood because it seemed wrong to sit, then the whole cycle began again.

He was on the floor, searching for the last tiny shards of the broken cup, when he sensed a shift in the sounds from the bedroom. An instant of total silence seemed to stretch longer than all the hours that had gone before, then he heard a scream, but not the scream he had feared. It was not the last; it was the first.

He waited. He had been told with great clarity on which side of the curtain he was to stay. Now the midwife lifted the curtain and came out, a bundle in her arms.

"Titrit . . . ?" he asked the midwife.

"She is resting. She will be well. It was a simple birth." The midwife saw Augustine did not believe her, but she did not care what he did or did not believe. Her duty was well defined, and it was nearly done. Now she placed the bundle at Augustine's feet and took a step back.

Immediately, Augustine dropped to one knee and took the infant in his arms. He had not the slightest doubt in his mind that he would claim . . . him. He was holding a boy. *His* boy. His son.

Ever since he had learned Titrit was pregnant, Augustine had wondered how he would feel or should feel at this very moment. He knew what his responsibilities would be. The difficulty was that one of those responsibilities was a feeling—the obligation of a father to love his son. But how could love be love if it were an obligation? Love was supposed to be a choice. How, he had wondered, could he choose to love a person without knowing him? How could he choose without knowing what he chose?

The baby squirmed and kicked. Augustine's hand, unsure where it belonged, slipped a bit. The midwife, patient with the ignorant new father, positioned his arms to provide the proper support. The baby squealed at the adjustment, but after a cry of outrage decided the new arrangement was to his liking.

Augustine's choice had been made without his knowing it. Or no choice had been involved. Indeed, this love was far beyond his control, yet it felt no less like love. Perhaps it should best be called a gift. If so, it was a gift of God.

They called him Adeodatus.

Chapter Three

Adeodatus was indeed a gift. His father enjoyed nothing more than spending hours observing his son's every tentative grasp and frustrated grimace, but life did not stand still.

Augustine left their apartment each morning and felt a tiny shock of dislocation. The world outside was the same as it had been, and so, despite being entirely changed, was his own life.

He went to class and read the works he was given—the very same works his teachers had been given to read: Virgil, Terence, and Cicero.

"Augustine, will you read?" the professor asked one morning. He had set the day's lesson on Cicero's *Hortensius*.

Augustine took the book and read: "'If we have souls eternal and divine, then must we needs think, that the more these shall have always kept in their own proper course, i.e. in reason and in the quest for knowledge, and the less they shall have mixed and entangled themselves in the vices and errors of men, the more easy ascent and return they will have to heaven. We must bestow all our labor and care upon these pursuits.'"

As Augustine read, his voice grew quieter and his tone more even. In fact, his quietness drew a rebuke from the professor, who stopped his recitation and gave the task to another pupil. For perhaps the first time in his life, Augustine hardly cared. He did not want to recite these words; he wanted to think about them.

A soul eternal and divine, he pondered. The eternal soul had, of course, been the subject of teachings he'd received from his mother and the priests, but here was the way to eternity through the natural faculties of the mind.

The quest for knowledge. The quest for wisdom. Here was something to which a man might worthily give his life. What was the law? A profession of time, one case succeeding another, each demanding earthly justice only, and each looking for it in laws written by men. Laws written in and for time. But to find wisdom, to seek and pursue and come to love it, that was to escape time.

"What did you think of that reading?" Augustine eagerly asked one of his classmates when the lesson was done and they all adjourned to a nearby place to eat.

The classmate shrugged his shoulders as if to say "Not much" and ran to be the first to claim a seat.

"Wait!" Augustine called. "I want to hear what you think!" But the young man wanted to leave the lesson behind and Augustine found he could not be heard anyway because of the noise of the street.

When the boys later ambled together toward the Antonine Baths near the waterfront, as they did every day, Augustine tried again. "Did you hear what we read today?" he asked his friends. "Weren't the words . . . perfect?" His friends laughed and hurried him through the warm room and the hot room, remarking that Augustine seemed already feverish enough, and what he needed was a good spell in the cold pool.

But once they had all been warmed and sweated and then cooled, and they relaxed at their leisure in the pool, he put his question once again. "No, but answer me this," he said. "Every day, we come here. We spend time and effort and money on the satisfaction of our bodies. Why should we not do as much—or more—for the satisfaction of our souls?"

"This satisfies my soul," someone said quickly, to much laughter.

These young men had a quick answer to everything, of course—that was their training—but surely they could be made to listen somehow.

"It cannot satisfy," Augustine said, his sense of logic now taking hold. "The soul knows tomorrow this will all be done over again. The soul knows this feeling will pass. How can it rest in something it knows to be fleeting?"

"Such questions are a problem only if you ask them," someone said.

"But they should be asked," another voice replied. Augustine looked around, astonished to hear someone else speak his own thought. The speaker, a stranger, was a tall, solemn young man with light brown hair, his brow furrowed in concentration. He saw the young men all staring at him and he seemed to realize for the first time that he had spoken his thought aloud. He flushed. "I ask your pardon for the intrusion," he said, hesitating, "but such questions should be asked."

Augustine smiled and said, "When a man enters the arena on your side, it is no intrusion." He offered his hand. "Aurelius Augustine."

"Lucius Nebridius," the man replied.

In the following weeks, Nebridius frequently visited the baths with Augustine. Eventually, the two learned they could pick up a conversation wherever they had left off, whether that was a day ago or a week ago. Nebridius had not received an advanced education, but he had been well tutored and had a formidable memory, even by the standards of an age that prized memory. What most endeared him to Augustine was that he would not move on from a question until he was certain he grasped the answer. That trait was less endearing to Augustine's classmates. When their heckling grew to actively impede discussion, Nebridius invited Augustine to dinner to continue the class conversation without interruption.

At the baths, Augustine had felt no need to wonder about his new friend's standing in Carthage society. But the invitation now prompted him to speculate inwardly about Nebridius's family. Now, as he followed him through increasingly elegant streets, past fountains and terraced gardens—for Carthage might perch on the edge of the desert, but the city was Roman, and the lifeblood of Roman civilization was water—he wondered more and more.

Nebridius brought him at length to a beautiful villa, such a house as not even Romanianus could boast. Its tall stone walls were adorned with vines of purple flowers, and a mosaic tile path led them to the wide front door. They stepped over the threshold guarded by the good luck charm of an inlaid mosaic fish, and Nebridius identified his new friend to the slave who kept the door.

The two friends passed into the atrium, where more fish were inlaid in the floor and in a raised pool that collected rainwater. Some of the mosaics in the pool were encased in glass. Augustine stopped to sweep his hand through the water. He watched the ripples pass over the glass, making the fish appear to swim.

Augustine was so preoccupied in trying not to be awed by his surroundings that it took him a few minutes to realize Nebridius looked uncomfortable.

"This is my mother's house," Nebridius said. "My father died before I was able to remember him, and she likes to have me with her."

"I too have a mother," Augustine assured him.

"Does yours reach for her fennel every time you cough?"

"She did when she could hear me cough."

"Please do not think . . . I do not want this to . . ." Nebridius searched for words, then threw up his hands. "At the baths, all men are equal."

Augustine shook his head. "No, in fact, they are not. The baths can make some flaws more apparent. It is the same with the life of the mind—not all men are equal." He ran his hand through the pool again. "In neither case does a man's wealth, or lack of it, make him who he is." He shook off his hand, raining water droplets across the tiles. "Though I imagine it makes him more comfortable."

Nebridius smiled. "I know of no reason why philosophy should not be comfortable."

Nebridius's home was larger and more beautiful than any Augustine had ever seen. When their conversation resumed, he had difficulty turning his mind to philosophy. Once he was fairly launched on the subject, however, his surroundings ceased to intrude. He was able to express to Nebridius what would not have been so easy to describe at the baths: his difficulties with the Scriptures.

"I have set the pursuit of wisdom as my goal," Augustine began, "and I believe I know where the road is to be found. The lessons of my childhood made their imprint, and I understood that to speak of wisdom means to speak of Christ." He told Nebridius that he was on fire to leave the mundane world behind and immerse himself in pure light, so he had turned to the books from which his mother had told her stories.

"What did you find there?" Nebridius asked, one eyebrow raised.

Augustine already knew his friend was a pagan. The name of Christ was, to Nebridius, only one among many. Yet he would give every man his hearing, even the Nazarene carpenter, and so Nebridius's question was an honest one, awaiting an honest answer.

Augustine shrugged. "I found the world—a jumble of stories, the worst of mankind and its lusts."

"Do you mean to give up those lusts?" Nebridius knew by now about Augustine's relationship with Titrit and their baby.

"They have nothing to do with the mind," Augustine said. "I am talking about wisdom. If a book is to show us the mind of God, then it should speak divinely. The Christian Scriptures claim to speak of God. They claim to reach heights Cicero never saw. Yet they do not speak half—a quarter—as well as Cicero did. What god would allow himself to be written about in such a clumsy fashion? Or rather, in many fashions, for each book goes its own way, and there is no common style among them. A beginning student of rhetoric could do better."

"Do you mean yourself?"

Augustine smiled and sipped the wine Nebridius had poured for him. He let the question rest unanswered.

"So you say we must look elsewhere?" Nebridius tried again.

"Yes," Augustine said. "But I do not know where that might be."

Augustine repeated these words to Titrit that night while they ate together at their wooden table. Adeodatus played on the floor. Their son had discovered all his limbs, but he was still deciding what to do with them. He didn't seem sure whether he entirely approved of this world into which he had been thrust. His elders seemed to be slow in comprehension and even slower in fulfilling his wishes, and he took his revenge in tears at any and all hours. But in his sleep, he smiled.

Titrit wished for both smiles and sleep right now. Ever since giving birth, she had found that when she was alone, she longed for Augustine and his words to reassure her the world was the same as she had left it. She had also found that when Augustine spoke, she longed for him to be quiet so the baby might sleep. She understood the contradiction and that it was not Augustine's fault, but she was too tired to stop blaming him for it.

"There must be an answer," persisted Augustine, "and if there is, can it be possible no one has found it?"

"An answer to what?" Titrit asked. She took Adeodatus up off the floor and set him on her lap to nurse.

"An answer to everything. To every question."

"There are always two answers: yes or no."

"I do not mean that type of question. I mean the questions that ask who and what we are, why we were made, and what we were made for."

"Most people do not have time for such questions," Titrit sighed.

"Have you never wondered about them?" Augustine asked with surprise.

"Not before you asked them. When you grow up surrounded by hammers and copper, they fill your head, and it is hard to find the silence to wonder in."

Adeodatus was drifting off to sleep. Titrit ventured with great care to shift her arm and relieve a cramped elbow. Her care was not enough; Adeodatus woke and demanded a second course. At least in getting him resettled she could shift him to the other elbow. When she had accomplished that, she realized Augustine had gone silent. She glanced at him and saw he was lost in contemplation, staring into the baby's round face. He did that often, though never for long. His mind seemed incapable of stillness for more than a minute.

Titrit felt uneasy as she looked at Augustine. Sometimes she was acutely aware that their baby was all that bound them together. Still, Augustine could leave at any time. Titrit had been raised to be grateful for what she had and not to dwell on what she didn't. She went into the bedroom and made herself lie down for some much-needed sleep.

The following afternoon, Augustine and his schoolmates, by an unspoken but mutual decision, separated upon their arrival at the baths. Augustine lingered outside to wait for Nebridius, who duly appeared. Augustine remarked upon the dark circles under his friend's eyes.

"The big questions grow bigger in the night," Nebridius said, "especially when you are alone with yourself and your thoughts."

"They grow somewhat smaller when you are alone with a six-month-old infant and his mother," laughed Augustine. "No, I take your meaning. In the night, the answers can sometimes seem closer, but more often they feel farther away. Which was it for you?"

"I hardly know. I suppose that means farther away. But I thought for a long time about what you said, about a wisdom that would leave the world behind."

By now, they were in the warm room. Augustine's fatigue began to seep away, replaced by a pleasant languor that freed his mind. "A purification. A purging," said Augustine.

As steam rose around them, Augustine and Nebridius launched into a stimulating, far-ranging philosophical discussion.

"It came to me that perhaps you were too quick to abandon the Christians and their god," Nebridius said. "Or at least, all the Christians. Some here in Carthage are as serious about purity as you are."

No need to ask which Christians he meant. It had been little more than sixty years since the end of a persecution had brought about what persecution itself could not accomplish: the Christian Church throughout Africa torn in two, a tear that had begun right here in Carthage. The two young men knew their recent history well: Under the Emperor Diocletian, the Church in Africa had gained many martyrs, but it had also discovered in its midst many who chose the life here and now over the life to come. Men and women burned their incense to the pagan gods. Priests became informers. And bishops, by right and by duty the shepherds of all, handed over the Holy Scriptures to be thrown into the fire.

To some, this last offense was worse than all the rest. If a bishop betrayed his office by this, by what right did he keep his office? No man who surrendered the Word was fit to call down the Word Made Flesh—or to consecrate others to do so.

So ran the argument, and it found many champions. None was more passionate than a man named Donatus, elected Bishop of Carthage in 313 as an answer to Bishop Caecilian, who had his ordination from one of the "traitor" bishops.

Every schism requires a name, and while Donatus had not begun the movement, those who believed the man defined the office became proud to call themselves Donatists. Donatists were condemned by Constantine in 314 and hunted by Macarius,

Imperial Commissioner for Africa, in 347. They were tolerated by Julian the Apostate in 362. They had their own martyrs now, as well as their own bishops and their own faithful. Augustine was not one of them and knew he could not be. It might have been Monica's training.

"They are serious," he answered Nebridius, with a laugh he did not quite feel. "But I want purity of wisdom. They want purity of the man. A religion, if it is to be useful, must take into account how a man lives in the world. It must recognize that a man is . . ."

"Divided."

It was not Nebridius who spoke. Augustine recognized the voice and looked around for the speaker. A middle-aged man, whose flesh was clearly accustomed to being fed, sat nearby. "Priscus?" Augustine said.

"Priscus, in very truth," he replied. The merchant smiled and moved closer to the two young men. "Will you introduce me to your friend?"

This was not company Nebridius normally kept, but the baths were communal. Augustine made the introductions, explaining that he had journeyed with Priscus and his fellows from Thagaste two years before.

"Has it been two years?" Priscus mused. "Yes, I suppose it has. Many miles for me. And for you—do I hear rightly? Does the student of rhetoric put his mind to other matters?"

"Do you sell wisdom now, along with your other wares?" Augustine asked.

Augustine's tone was light, but Priscus answered seriously.

"Wisdom is not to be sold or bought." He lowered his voice, just enough to make Augustine and Nebridius lean in closer, and said, "It might be given."

"Tell us," Nebridius said, skeptical but always thorough. No avenue should be unexplored.

"Not here."

"Why?"

Priscus chuckled. "Think a moment. If I could tell you why, then I could tell you all. For now, let us continue to relax. There must be stories enough in the last two years to fill another hour." He turned to Augustine and asked, "How have you taken to Carthage?"

"Extremely well."

"Yes, I thought you would. It is very different from Thagaste, is it not? More to see and do. No doubt that has all had an effect on you. I can remember, as clearly as if I were still your age, what it did to me."

Augustine caught Nebridius's eye in silent apology. Possibly—probably—this would be an afternoon of boredom. Most likely, all Priscus wanted was to spin some tales and drink a flagon of wine at someone else's expense. If that was all, so be it. There could be no great harm in a few hours of boredom and wine. If, however unlikely, it was not all, then the wine and the boredom would be a small price to pay.

But, as it happened, Priscus refused the wine when it was offered.

"On such an occasion, I should not feed the base part of

myself," he explained. This intrigued the two young men, and they suggested a nearby place to eat instead.

"No, I will not eat," Priscus said, shaking his head. "I mean to nourish your souls, and your souls alone." Nebridius and Augustine glanced at each other. "Follow me," Priscus said, and without a thought, the young men did.

Priscus led them through the cobblestone streets to the wide forum, where men and women passed, some carrying bundles on their heads. Augustine never got tired of observing the many different people in Carthage, and he never lost his awe of the magnificent stone structures. Built into the side of the Byrsa, the concrete terrace was a monument to Roman engineering, stretching 175 yards from east to west and towering more than 180 feet above the lower city.

Here they sat beneath a colonnade, surrounded by libraries, the official buildings from which the province was governed, and the temple to Jupiter, which had been built in homage to the god and to the great temple that bore his name on the Capitoline Hill in Rome.

Priscus pointed to the temple. "Jupiter, king of the heavens. They must be crowded heavens, for they also include . . ." Priscus paused to count on his fingers. "Juno, Mars, Venus, Mercury, Diana, Vulcan, Minerva, Apollo, Ceres, Neptune, Vesta. And who can count the smaller deities who watch over our crops and our hearths? Or the emperors who are worthy of worship? Or the gods we have imported—conquered, really—along with the lands they once protected? Though I have never understood what help such gods were expected to be," he said. "In order to pray, a man must first consult a list. Is that how we experience the world? Is that how we experience ourselves?" Priscus looked at the young men.

"How, then?" Nebridius returned the question, for he recognized that Priscus wanted to launch into a speech, and he did not admire speeches as much as Augustine did.

"There are only two powers in the world: the light and the darkness," Priscus replied. "If you prefer, call them good and evil. These two powers are eternally at war, and they work in everything that is, including in every man. At any given moment, one or the other will have the mastery. Which one is in control? For your answer, just observe what a man chooses to do."

Nebridius frowned. "Does the man really choose? You make it sound as if these two powers choose for him."

"Which is the stronger?" Augustine spoke over his friend's question. This talk of an internal war, yes, the echoes of that were there in his heart. Did this explain why he had never felt whole? For as long he could remember, Augustine had felt split. His mind was logical, inquisitive, intelligent, yet he'd often given over to impulses that disregarded all sensible judgement.

Priscus answered Augustine's question. "They are equally matched. How else could the battle have persisted so long, through all times and in all events?"

"It is a pretty story," Nebridius shrugged, clearly not convinced, "but it is a great deal to take on faith."

"On faith? Do not take it on faith," Priscus said. "The divine part of a man is his reason. He should use reason to come to

God. The world is an open book to the man who can see and hear and touch and smell and taste, and who has the wit to understand what he experiences."

"An open book that few people read, apparently," Nebridius countered.

"How many of them wish to read it?" Augustine asked, turning to his friend. "Nebridius, remember how we met. No one else who was with me cared to ask these questions, and they are all scholars. What does the rest of mankind think about?" *Hammers and copper, and coaxing a fretful babe to nurse*, he thought, Titrit suddenly coming to mind. "No, it does not surprise me in the least that wisdom could be at once simple and rarely known."

"There is another reason why it is not better known," Priscus said, clearing his throat. And then he presented the one fact that had been lacking to catch a young man's heart: "It is forbidden."

Chapter Four

Nebridius was skeptical, but Augustine was attracted to these ideas Priscus had laid out so clearly. In a matter of weeks, Augustine became a Manichaean.

Not all at once, of course. He discussed the principles with many men in between his studies and caring for his family, which included a young son learning to walk. No matter how eager he was, Augustine had few hours left for this new world to which Priscus had shown him a door. But whenever he had an hour, he went back to the door and pushed it open a bit further. He wanted to know more.

The sect of Manichaeism had begun in Persia a century before, when the prophet Mani received a revelation: If Jesus Christ was the wisdom of God, in very truth, why did men need authority figures to give them principles that they must believe without understanding? Christ had shown men their own natures, the light and the dark inside them. The light was divine; the darkness was the opposite. No one could deny that darkness existed. And how could darkness come from God? It could not. There must be another power at work, a source of darkness as real as the source of light, entirely separate and equally powerful.

Here was the God Augustine had looked for and failed to find in the Catholic Scriptures: a being of pure light, and an intellectual guide instead of an angry father. Here, also, was the answer to his personal dilemma. Here, in short, was a religion that would allow him to be with Titrit, a lowly woman who would never be his wife. He could live in sin without calling himself a sinner.

Augustine had always known the life he led with Titrit was not of God. In the writings that thrilled Augustine's soul, Cicero, who had awakened him to wisdom, set down uncompromising words about the promptings of the flesh: "The strongest of all, and so the most hostile to philosophy."

Augustine knew it was true. He thought about this often as he lay in bed with Titrit in the quiet night. He would stare at the rough ceiling, feel the sea breeze drift through the window, and listen to the soft breaths of his sleeping son.

The Manichaeans also knew the strength of the desires of the flesh. But—and here was the glorious, all-important difference—the Manichaeans said that dark part of himself was not himself. The impulses of the flesh were inside him, yes, but were not him. It was not Augustine. Augustine could still be pure. This was what he had longed to hear.

As he was drawn more to the Manichean life, he eventually became an auditor, or what the Catholics would call a catechumen. He was not yet initiated into the highest mysteries, but he served those who were: the Elect.

To the Manichaeans, all was material. The soul itself was

material, though of a far higher and purer and finer form of matter than the flesh. All things possessed some degree of the divine matter, each according to its nature. Certain foods, especially melons and other fruits, possessed it to a great degree. This divine element could be freed when consumed by the Elect. It was the auditors' duty to bring such offerings to the Elect so that through their meal they might turn fruit into gods.

The sect had been banned almost as soon as it appeared in the Empire—the Romans did not like extremes in their religions. Far more damning was the fact that Mani's teachings came from Persia, a longtime enemy of the Romans. It was one thing to conquer foreign gods, and quite another to be conquered by them. Driven underground, the Manichaeans formed a religion and a network of followers. Influential members lived in nearly every city in the Empire, and merchants, such as Priscus, kept their eyes out for likely recruits as they traveled the royal roads. To become a Manichaean was to join a brotherhood, and the brothers took care of their own.

Augustine, carrying melons, quickly discovered he was no longer certain he wanted a lawyer's career. So few people in the world understood wisdom. So few even wondered about it. If a man had the skill to awaken that wonder and knowledge of wisdom, should he not bring them to others? Wasn't that the higher path?

So, he would teach. Let the world and its laws go on without his help. Moreover, Priscus encouraged him to go home to teach. There were already so many teachers in Carthage—would one more be noticed? At home in Thagaste, Augustine would be welcomed as the brilliant native son, returned from the heart of the Province to recount all he had discovered there.

In Thagaste, also, he would not have Nebridius constantly by his side, challenging him with skeptical questions. Augustine had become uncomfortable being his friend and even avoided the baths so as not to see him. Nebridius had no interest in the Manichaean doctrines. Augustine's enthusiasm grew, but he could not share it with his old friend—Nebridius rejected the whole premise of equal powers in opposition. The Manichaeans, Nebridius argued, said God was incorruptible. Very well. They said there was a darkness opposed to God. Very well. But if God were truly incorruptible, then how could the darkness harm him? What effect could it have, that God would risk entering into combat with it? Why, if he were untouchable, had God simply not kept himself untouched?

Augustine could offer no answer to the riddle, but he was not greatly concerned. He was a neophyte, so he simply didn't know all the Elect did. Nebridius conceded the point, but he added that if the Manichaeans were appealing to reason alone, it seemed . . . problematic . . . for them to ask Augustine to take their reasons on faith.

Clearly, it was time for Augustine to go home.

"Augustine?" Navigius called.

Summoned by a slave, Navigius had rushed in from the groves to see his brother, whose arrival was unexpected but not as surprising as seeing that Augustine brought with him a woman and child.

The brothers embraced. "And . . . ?" Navigius asked.

"This is my son, Adeodatus," Augustine said, "and his mother, Titrit." Navigius smiled at the attractive woman with dark hair who held the young boy in one arm. Adeodatus looked at his uncle curiously.

If she were his wife, Titrit would have been introduced as such. Navigius felt he needed to talk to his brother urgently. He had long accepted that Augustine was far more intelligent and accomplished than he could ever be. And Augustine had spent the past few years living in Carthage—he surely must have seen and learned so much. But he had not spent the past few years living with their mother, and Navigius feared Augustine had forgotten how strict Monica was concerning Christian rules of life.

"Mother will be sorry not to have been here when you arrived," he said, fixing his eyes on his brother. "She is in church, as she often is."

"Then nothing has changed while I have been away," Augustine said with a smile.

"Nothing here has changed."

Augustine's smile said that his brother's attempt at subtlety had been seen for what it was. "I thought I was sent to Carthage precisely so I could change."

Navigius abandoned subtlety. That was Augustine's ground, anyway—he could always tangle him up in words. Navigius pulled Augustine aside, out of Titrit's earshot, and said, "You know this is not the change mother wanted. How can you possibly think she will accept your . . . ?"

"Titrit?" Augustine said. "I thought I had explained already. Titrit is the mother of my son. It follows, therefore, that she is the mother of our mother's grandson." He made a show of looking around the atrium. "I see no other grandchildren about the place. I think she might forgive the son who presents her with her first, however he came to be."

Navigius thought that might well be true. Monica would dote on the child, that was certain. She would not blame the young boy for his parents' sin. But would she accept the mother for the child's sake? This was less certain, but possible. It grew more possible because she would be so overjoyed to welcome home the prodigal. Navigius was well aware that Augustine was Monica's heart. He could think of nothing she would not endure if it meant having him back under her roof.

"Augustine!" Monica's voice rang. Now they would find out.

Monica flew into the atrium. A hundred concubines could have crowded the room and, for that first minute, she would not have seen them, so blinded was she by the light in her eyes.

"Mother," Augustine said calmly, hugging her.

"It is a long way to come for a visit. I will have your room prepared. Navigius?"

"I will see to it," Navigius said. He was sorry to be sent from the atrium just now, but he would learn the result soon enough. He might even hear it—the house was not large. Navigius went about his business as Monica turned back to her beloved son.

"Now, tell me, what have you brought back to me?" she asked.

As it happened, any conversation that took place was too quiet for Navigius to hear. He was not surprised. Whatever might be said, Augustine would not raise his voice to Monica, and Monica did not need to raise her voice to make herself understood.

Navigius gave his orders to the slaves. He was on his way back to the atrium when Monica found him. She was alone. Navigius might not understand his mother's motives, but he had lived with her all his life and it took no great skill to read her face.

"It was the woman?" he asked.

"No. The woman I was prepared to endure." She managed half a smile. "Mind you, I would have placed her in the room next to mine, so that my grandson might lie close and my son might not."

"But even so, you are not letting them stay."

"No, I am not," she said.

"What has he done? What could he have done that is worse than bringing his concubine to your house?" Wild speculations filled Navigius's mind, though he tried to banish them. He could not imagine what could make Monica look as she did right now: like death—like death without hope.

"He has become a Manichaean."

Navigius waited. Slowly, he realized that was not the beginning of the explanation, but the end of it. "Is that . . . ?"

"All?" Her tone was fire and ice together. Navigius knew he had blundered, but he could not comprehend how. "Yes, that is . . . all." She looked as if she would continue, but then she decided she would regret it. She brushed past him and hurried away.

It was still a day for work. Navigius walked the path to his trees. He'd learned from his father how to tend this olive orchard, how to coax the fruit just to ripeness as it nestled in silver-green leaves. While he worked this morning, he reflected on his brother and mother, wishing he understood them better. He often felt he disappointed his mother.

At dusk, he trudged back toward home through the dry fields. The lamps had been lit and he found Monica in the atrium, staring at the door from which Augustine had been banished. Navigius drew a careful breath.

"Mother, please tell me why you are so angry at Augustine," he said. "I cannot see. I am not your son who sees things. Augustine broke your heart today, but he still has your heart." Navigius felt a stab of jealous satisfaction.

Monica took a step toward him and reached for his hand. In the half light, he noticed she looked older, wrinkled with worry. "I love you, Navigius," she said.

"I never said you did not," Navigius said. "It's clear, though, that you love him more." Her hand dropped away. "You could deny it, except you will not lie, not even in this." Her silence filled the atrium. He searched for a way to break it, but she broke it first.

"I cannot help it," she said. Navigius heard tears in her voice.

"I never said you could, any more than I can help not being able to see. But I might see, if you showed me," Navigius pleaded.

Monica wiped the tears from her eyes and tried to stand up taller. "Come to my room," she said, beckoning for him to follow her down the hallway.

Navigius understood. The house was not large, and the atrium was its center. She did not want the slaves to hear any more of their conversation. In Monica's room, she sat on the narrow bed and gestured for him to take the single wooden chair. He remained standing by the brazier, grateful for the warmth. She stared at the floor for a long moment, twisting her wedding ring on her finger.

"I'm sorry," she began at last. "I've tried to be what each of you needed. Clearly, I have not provided what Augustine needed. Tell me what I should have . . ." She looked up and stopped twisting her ring. "Forgive me. That's not a question for you."

Navigius crossed the room, kneeled by the bed, and clasped Monica's rough hands. She pressed his fingers, then she began crying in earnest. The sobs caught in her throat so that she could hardly breathe. She reached for Navigius and he held her, silently cursing Augustine for creating so much trouble.

Finally, she was quiet. The room had grown fully dark. Navigius was thankful the steward had refrained from announcing dinner.

"You still do not see," Monica said, searching his face.

"I can see he's caused you grief, but I don't see what he believes is so great a matter."

Monica raised her head. Her face was still red but her tone was calm. "Let me say it simply, Navigius. What Augustine thinks will determine what he does . . . Actions begin in the mind. When he took that woman into his bed, he rejected one part of the Christian faith, but if he had held to the rest, there was a chance it would show him his sin. By making himself a Manichaean, he has rejected Christ entirely, everything that would show him what sin is. It is the difference between wandering from the road and throwing away the map."

Navigius considered this. "Worse, surely," he said. "It is trusting a map, but a map that leads you in the wrong direction."

A look crossed his mother's face that he had never seen before. It was a look of happy pride for him, not Augustine. Finally, he had said something right.

Augustine stared at his mother's closed front door while Adeodatus scampered off to search for rocks, Titrit chasing after him. Augustine's first thought was to get out of the street as soon as possible. Their business would be the talk of Thagaste by sunset—but he could face the gossip better from inside walls, no matter whose walls they might be.

It took only a moment to hit upon the obvious place to go. He beckoned to Titrit. Adeodatus had found a rock for each fist and was well content to move on. Augustine led his little family through a maze of streets until they came to a door familiar to Augustine that brought him warm memories.

Romanianus opened his door quickly and raised his arms in happy welcome. Even when Augustine explained their circumstances and introduced Titrit and their young son, Romanianus simply nodded in acceptance. As a man with years of experience and plenty of missteps of his own, Romanianus had an indulgent smile for the ways of women. At once, he gave orders for bedrooms to be prepared. Titrit took Adeodatus and his rocks away to nap, and Romanianus bore Augustine away to the garden for a long talk.

"You must tell me everything you've been doing," he said to Augustine. The garden had a long meandering path through flowering shrubs and large trees that provided pools of shade. Augustine told his old friend what he had seen and learned in Carthage. Romanianus was delighted to hear of Augustine's friends and his studies, and of the questions that had preoccupied so many days and sleepless nights.

"I want to teach here in Thagaste," Augustine said finally.

"Very good. I applaud you," Romanianus said as he swatted away a persistent fly. "I will assist you any way I can. I see I must bid farewell to the young lawyer of my imagination." He smiled forgivingly to Augustine. "I am very fond of you and your family, and I will do all I can for you."

There was something unusual about Augustine's mind that Romanianus had not seen in any other man, young or old. Augustine had the knack of demonstrating what he saw in such a way that even if you could not see it, you wished you could. So Romanianus confidently offered Augustine funds to lease a storefront. He was certain the pupils would come.

When the bargain had been struck, Romanianus summoned a slave. "Bring us wine," Romanianus said.

Augustine was secretly pleased at this, because it gave him the opportunity to refuse it—wine was forbidden by the Manichaeans.

"I will not join you in drinking," he said somewhat pompously.

"And why not?" Romanianus asked. He was surprised, for he knew Augustine had enjoyed wine in the past. He looked closely at the younger man with one eye, watching for the annoying fly with the other.

Augustine made a show of hesitation, then shared the enlightenment he had found as a Manichaean. Romanianus listened attentively, and along with the fly buzzing near his ear, some half-remembered sayings of priests filled his head. "But . . . how can there be two different powers? How can there be a separate force, equal and opposed to the good? Did God not make the world and everything in it?" he asked.

Augustine watched Romanianus shake his head and raise his hand again. "Who made that fly?" Augustine asked.

"The devil," Romanianus answered with certainty. Then he stopped, his hand still in midair. Augustine was smiling.

The pupils came to Augustine's school, a simple storefront. Old friends sought out Augustine and Romanianus offered a hospitable table at his house for them all to gather for dinners. Few evenings went by in which his villa did not ring with the laughter of young men. Many evenings, Titrit joined Augustine and sat away from the men, observing quietly, or she played with her young son in the garden.

On one of the first such gatherings, a young man brought along a friend whom Titrit had not seen before, introduced as Laurentius. He was tall, thin, and had a mischievous smile—he'd known Augustine as a boy.

Laurentius entered the house carrying a pear in his hand. He tossed it to Augustine, who caught it by reflex. His grip was so hard that he broke the pear's skin, and juice dripped over his hand. With barely a look, Augustine threw it out the open window.

"It was from my own tree," Laurentius said in protest, but Augustine, busy wiping the juice from his hand, pretended not to hear. Then the two exchanged a glance and laughed.

Watching the scene, Titrit wondered what their joke meant. It had something to do with the pear, but what? She thought it odder still that as the evening went on, no one mentioned the pear, even though Augustine and Laurentius talked and laughed about nearly everything else under the sun.

That night, when they were alone and Adeodatus was at last asleep, she asked Augustine about it. Augustine was usually willing to address any question at length, but this time he only shrugged and turned away. "It was nothing. Just a pear," he said.

"If it was nothing, then why bring it? Laurentius meant it to be something . . ." Titrit said.

"How am I to know what was in his mind?" Augustine said, suddenly defensive.

Titrit stared at him, perplexed at this evasive reply. "Laurentius thought you would."

"I do not doubt Laurentius thinks a great many things,"

Augustine said condescendingly. "I heard some of them tonight. I think I can win him over. He was eager to hear what I knew about—"

"Fruit?"

Augustine clenched his hands and stepped away from Titrit. He glared at her. "Why does this matter?" he asked. "It is so small a thing."

Titrit threw up her hands. "If it is so small, why will you not tell me? Why lie to me now?"

Unexpectedly, Titrit felt a surge of anger rise up and she could not stop it. Resentment from the past several years burst out of her. "You bore me away from Carthage so I could have your mother's door slammed in my face—"

"My face, not yours," Augustine interrupted.

"I was there on the street with you," Titrit said. "Your fortunes are mine. You have made them mine."

"You did not object," Augustine retorted, ready for an argument. "You knew what I wanted and what I was."

"Yes, I knew. But I don't think *you* knew what you were. At least, what you were then is not what you are now. I gave myself to a lawyer. A future statesman. A man who would someday have power and influence."

"By which you, being a woman, mean money."

The trouble with loving a man for his wit was that Titrit could be the target of it. Well, she was no match for him, but she could give him a fight.

"What if I do?" Titrit asked, looking him in the eye. "It is a more practical goal than all this philosophy of yours."

"Now, there you are wrong." Augustine was on firm ground here. "I know you will say money is more practical because with it you can buy what gives happiness. But have you ever made a wrong choice about what to buy?" He smiled. They both remembered a certain meat vendor near the forum, and the two days of agony that had followed the purchase. "Well, consider all of life that way. How can you know what to buy unless you know first what happiness truly is? It follows that philosophy is not only more important but more practical than the exchange of a coin."

Titrit softened. She saw his logic. "It surely has a better advocate," she said, crossing the room to stand beside him. She stopped short of touching him; she wanted him to touch her first. "The truth is, I did not give myself to a lawyer or a states-man. I gave myself to you. I took your fortunes for my own, whatever they might be, and I have followed them."

"You have," he said, but he did reach out to offer his reassuring touch.

"Then share this with me. This little thing."

For a moment, he looked as if he wanted to. His hand came up, as if without his knowing it, but still he did not touch her. A moment later, his hand fell back to his side.

"It was only a pear," he said.

It was a cold, cloudy morning when Bishop Domitian left through the church's back exit after offering his Mass and saw a woman waiting for him. He recognized her immediately: Monica, the widow of Patricius, mother of Augustine. He felt a twinge of repulsion—he knew her to be a determined woman, and the way she was planted in his path meant she wanted something.

"My lord," she said, blocking his way.

The subdeacon who followed the bishop glanced at his master, but Domitian put up his hand, indicating for him to be still. He stopped next to the cold, dark outer wall of the church and inclined his head to listen to her. He had an idea of what she would say and decided he would hear it.

"My lord, I am—" she started again.

"I know you. What have you to say to me?" he asked.

"If you know me, perhaps you know my son?"

"Of course. A brilliant boy."

"A man grown, my lord, and he has fallen into a man's sins."

"I have heard as much. How long has the woman—" the bishop started, but Monica shook her head. He paused. "It is not the woman who troubles you?"

"No." Monica paused, then added, "Yes, she troubles me, but she is not the principal trouble. If it were only sin of that kind, he would know he was sinning and he might be persuaded to repent. No, he is a heretic, my lord, a Manichaean. As long as he remains such, how can he even know what sin is?"

Domitian took a moment before answering. He looked again at Monica and saw nothing he had not seen before: only a middle-aged woman, her eyes dark and her shoulders stooped. But as the Lord had said to Samuel, "Man seeth those things that appear, but the Lord beholdeth the heart." There was more in this woman's heart than appeared on her face.

"That, also, I had heard."

"He must be shown his error," Monica said. "He must be made to see where he has gone wrong, and then he will turn away. You, my lord, with all of your learning, you must debate him, refute him. Show him that—"

"I cannot."

"You can! Of course you can!"

"Let us say that I will not make the attempt. I cannot show him what he will not see."

"But if it is set before him in plain words—"

"He will prefer his own words. Philosophy is a mistress, not a book. Your son is in love, and he loves the sound of his voice and the thrill of battle when he defends his mistress. Let him be and pray for him."

"Of course I pray for him," Monica said. The tears that had been brimming in her dark-circled eyes now began to fall. The subdeacon's face said that he'd expected this and was grateful not to be a bishop. "I pray for him with every breath. It has not been enough. Someone must persuade him."

Domitian suddenly felt that in his sermons on the parable of the persistent widow in the Gospel of Luke, he had never done full justice to the unjust judge's point of view. "It is likely someone will persuade him, but that someone is not me," he said. Monica's tears continued. The bishop persevered, trying a different tack. "The Manichaean doctrines attracted me too in my youth. I read everything I could find, listened to anyone who would speak. Some of the books I even copied out myself, so as to learn them better, and here is what I found: the more familiar with them I became, the more dissatisfied I was. They were not the truth. If a man looks honestly at words that are not the truth, he will see what they are and what they are not. Our Lord tells us to seek, and we will find. So ask yourself, is your son honest with himself?"

"Yes," Monica replied without a pause.

"Then he will see for himself that the Manichaeans do not have what he desires," the bishop said confidently.

The subdeacon cleared his throat. The bishop was ready to move on, aware of the many others awaiting his attention on this day. "Continue to pray for him," he advised Monica again. "It is cold here—pick yourself up and go home."

But Monica persisted, catching his sleeve. "For how long should I pray?"

Domitian removed her hand. How could she ask such a question? "Leave me," he told her. Yes, the parable spoke truly. "It is not possible that the son of these tears should perish."

She stepped back and was silent. He turned to leave.

Looking back, the subdeacon saw Monica drop to her knees. Her tears were gone and her eyes were closed, as if she had heard the voice of God.

Chapter Five

Monica prayed. She believed the bishop's words and took them for a promise. Now it only remained to hasten their fulfillment with constant prayer.

Weeks went by, and still Augustine was as far from God as ever. Not only that, but he actively took others away with him. He was a born teacher—his infectious enthusiasm for learning made him popular with his students, who brought his words back into their homes.

One of his favorite students, Alypius, an intelligent boy with a quick mind, was pulled out of the classroom when his father heard what he was learning. This was quite a scene, as Alypius had practically worshipped Augustine, who was only a few years older than himself. But many other students remained.

Monica observed Augustine and still prayed, and still wept. The bishop had not meant to speak for God; he had merely intended to rid himself of an annoyance. Now she wondered, had God spoken to her through a man who had not intended the message, or did she herself choose to hear what she longed to hear?

One night, as she fell asleep with tears still warm on her

cheek and her lips still open in prayer, she found herself in a dream, standing on a narrow wooden bridge that stretched in either direction, farther than she could see. A young man was walking toward her, his step light and sure. He was handsome, but what she chiefly noticed was his smile—it was warm, natural, and right. It was the most beautiful smile she had ever seen.

"Woman," he asked her kindly, "why are you weeping?" It was clear he already knew the answer, but he wanted her to speak it.

"I weep for my son," Monica replied. "I fear he will be damned."

"Look where you are," he said. Monica looked and saw.

She awoke with a vision and a promise clear in her mind. As soon as it was light, she rose and said her morning prayers, adding one of thanksgiving to her usual petitions. Then she dressed and left the house, barely disturbing the stray dog who occupied their front doorstep.

She made her way to the center of the town, to the little storefront Romanianus had leased to serve as Augustine's school. It was one room, divided from the street by a curtain. In an hour or so, passersby would hear the pupils reciting. But they had not yet arrived, and Augustine sat inside, preparing the day's lessons.

Monica pulled open the rough linen curtain and stepped inside the rectangular classroom before Augustine had time to look up from the day's text. He set down his book and rose. "Mother," he said.

"Augustine, I had a dream last night."

He was too courteous to show his annoyance, but she knew

him well enough to see it. "So did I. So, I would guess, did many people."

"But their dreams were not visions from God," she said. She hurried on before he could make the retort she saw forming behind his eyes. "No, only listen." She told him where she had found herself in the dream, and of the young man, his question, and her answer. "Then he told me to look at where I was. I looked down, and I was standing on a rule, with the measurements marked out clearly beneath my feet. The young man said I should not be anxious. He told me to look again and see that where I was, there you were also. I looked up, and you were standing beside me. You were there in the flesh, just as I see you now. The vision says you will come back to the faith, and back to me."

Augustine looked at his mother and shrugged. "If this was a vision and not merely a dream, it means only that we will think alike one day. Why could it not be that you will become what I am?" he asked.

"That is not what was said," Monica answered with conviction. "It wasn't 'Where he is, there you will be also,' but 'Where you are, there he will also be.' You will come home."

Augustine turned away, as if to pick up his book. "Well, we shall see. In the meantime, Mother . . ."

"In the meantime, you may come home," she paused, inhaling deeply, "if you wish."

That took him by surprise, more than the story about her dream. It was easy to express certainty but quite another thing to act upon it. She knew the offer was likely to have an impact. She wanted him back. She abhorred this heresy he taught, but this heretic was her son, and she wanted him back in her life, in her home, if he would come. That had been the risk—Monica could ban her son from her house, but she could not force him to reenter it. After she made the invitation, she waited in silence, for she was wise enough to know more words would not help her cause. She took a step away, as if looking around the room—though in truth there was little to see—so she would not look at him. *If he says yes, I must be calm*, she thought.

"I do wish it," Augustine said at last.

She spun around, her arms outstretched to him, her smile written not just on her face but in every line of her body.

He made no move toward her. "I will inform Titrit, and we will be there in time to dine this evening," he said coldly.

Was this her punishment, or simply his terms? It was useless to ask. She let her arms fall. "I will see that your rooms are prepared," Monica said with a grateful smile.

A boy stepped around the curtain into the room, then stopped when he saw his teacher speaking with someone. Augustine waved him inside. "Come in. Class will start in a few minutes!" he called. Then he turned to Monica. "We will see you tonight, Mother. In the meantime," he said with a twinkle in his eye, "please do your best not to dream."

When the day's lessons were done, Augustine returned to Romanianus's house. He was not immediately able to give Titrit the news, for as soon as he entered, he heard screams from small and untiring lungs. He followed them to the lush garden, where he found Adeodatus red-faced and writhing in Titrit's arms.

"What's this?" Augustine asked. He kneeled down, and Titrit gladly relinquished their son to him. It was late in the afternoon and the air was still hot.

Adeodatus was eager to explain. "I want my sword!"

"We watched the gardener pruning the thistles and Adeodatus took a fancy to his knife," Titrit clarified.

"I want my sword!" the boy repeated angrily, his lower lip quivering.

Augustine tried logic. "It is a knife, not a sword, and it is not yours," he rationed.

"I want my sword!"

Augustine decided logic was worth another attempt. "You are too young for a sword, or even a knife. You would only hurt yourself."

"I want my sword!" The boy was adamant.

Obviously, logic was of no use, so Augustine tried authority. "You may not have it, because I say you may not." He picked up the still-screaming boy and carried him inside, resigned, for today, to be the worst father ever.

When Adeodatus's cries finally subsided and Augustine had comforted him, Augustine told Titrit of Monica's visit. "Was I included in this invitation?" she asked.

"You were included in my acceptance of it," he said. Though she was silent, Titrit's thoughts were easily read. "Do you think I should not have accepted?"

Titrit carefully considered how to respond. "We are comfortable here. Romanianus is glad to have us. I doubt your mother's house will be quite so comfortable," she said. "But it is not for me to say. She is your mother."

"She *is* my mother. Please understand that to be loved by her is sometimes a burden too great to bear. But it is love. And I . . . because I cannot give her what she desires above all, I choose to give her what I can." Augustine smiled and, with the hand that was not holding Adeodatus, brushed Titrit's brown cheek. "For the rest, do not worry too much about being uncomfortable. You are the mother of her grandson." He indicated the grimy, sniffling boy in his arms. "How can she fail to be enchanted?"

So Augustine returned to his mother's house with his son and Titrit. Each evening, friends continued to visit him and stay for conversation and laughter that lasted into the night. They had all been carefully schooled, and no words of the Manichean teachings to which Monica could object were spoken while she was in the room.

But she was well aware that after she retired, the prophet Mani was preached in her house. She would go to her room, lay awake, and wonder how she could allow such talk under her roof. And then she wondered how she could possibly put a stop to it. She fell asleep at last with these questions unanswered, but no dream provided the solution.

She felt better in the light of day, when she had many distractions. Her grandson delighted her and captured her attention, and she had the usual work of the household. As long as she attended the tasks that kept the house running smoothly, her worries grew lighter.

With the passing of months, everyone in the household fell into comfortable routines—except for Adeodatus, who seemed to do or say something entirely new each day. His fascination with sharp objects remained a constant theme, so he required constant adult vigilance.

Over time, Titrit began to feel Adeodatus was all she had left of Augustine. She knew he remained faithful to her—when at last he went to bed each night, he did so beside her. And when he was in her arms, they were as loving and familiar as they had been from the start. In the darkness, she could close her eyes and believe she was still his, forsaking all others. But when daylight came, and with it his friends, she opened her eyes and realized she no longer had his mind.

In Carthage, he had talked to her and shared his doubts, desires, and questions. In Carthage, aside from Nebridius, few other men listened to him. Now he filled the house with friends and eager students, and as both friend and teacher, he blossomed.

Titrit was not surprised. At moments when the firelight from the brazier caught the glow in his eyes, she felt truly happy for him. She would never be all he needed, and she knew their relationship would eventually end. But the plea in her heart was always *Not yet*.

Of all the young men who gathered around Augustine, Laurentius was his most constant companion—the two had known each other growing up, but only when Augustine returned to Thagaste did their friendship blossom.

After the very first gathering at Augustine's school, Laurentius had brought no more pears. His parents were pious, faithful churchgoers and conscientious almsgivers, but they proved no match, philosophically or rhetorically, for their son's brilliant new friend. And so it was that Laurentius, under the influence of his childhood friend, became a Manichaean.

The two young men loved to talk into the night. One evening in March, they remained in the garden in Monica's home, long after the other guests had departed. It was the time of the winter rains, and around midnight they ran inside to the sound of drops falling into the atrium echoing throughout the entire house.

Augustine invited Laurentius to stay the night, but he politely declined and laughingly asked what harm could come from water. So he went.

The next night, Laurentius did not visit Augustine in Monica's house. He sent a message saying he had come down with a fever. On the following night, the message was relayed that he was unconscious and could not be awakened.

For the next few days, Augustine stayed at Laurentius's house, though there was little to be done. Someone who had read the works of the physician Galen proposed cucumbers as a remedy, but they had no effect. Laurentius's mother brought in a priest and had him baptized, despite him being unconscious. Augustine cared little for that, one way or another. What harm could come from water? He was certain they would have laughed about it together, if they were given the chance.

On the sixth day, that chance arrived. Augustine was called out of the sickroom to speak with Romanianus, who had come on business regarding the school. Augustine gave answers that satisfied him, and eventually he went away, leaving Augustine free to return to the sickroom.

There, he found Laurentius's mother. She was speaking to Laurentius, for he was awake but very pale. His long, dark hair, still wet with sweat, spread over the pillow. He was too weak to raise his head, but nevertheless his fever had broken.

When Laurentius's mother left and they were alone, Augustine spoke quickly to his friend, his words tumbling out. Everything he had wanted to say in the last six days demanded to be released all at once. Laurentius listened and smiled, occasionally putting in a word of his own. Then Augustine told Laurentius the crowning joke, the one he thought they would laugh at together: "Your mother had you baptized," he said, his face animated.

But Laurentius did not laugh. In fact, he did not even smile. "I know," he said quietly.

Perhaps, like vigor, the sense of humor needs time to be replenished after an illness. "Baptized when you were unconscious—what does that mean?" Augustine still tried to joke about it. "Will you be a Christian when you are asleep? Or out of your mind? How should I—"

"Please." The word was quiet, but Laurentius said it with

enough force to stop Augustine's babbling. Laurentius turned his head weakly and looked directly into Augustine's eyes. "You are my friend. I wish you to remain so. I think you also wish it. If you do, you must never speak to me that way again."

Has the fever completely broken? Augustine wondered. "Of course, if you ask it," he said, rising from the chair. "I will leave you. I am sure you should rest, and equally sure that I should. It has been a vigil of many nights."

"I know it well." Laurentius's smile returned. Augustine gripped his friend's hand where it lay on top of the blanket, then took his leave. He pondered Laurentius's words on the way home; they had startled him. But he shook his head—he had won Laurentius over by argument, and he surely could do so again if need be.

When he arrived home, he found Adeodatus using a stone to sharpen a stick. Evidently, he had spent too much time observing the slaves at work. Depriving his son of the fruits of his labors, and enduring Adeodatus's tearful protest at such rank injustice, Augustine went to find Titrit.

She saw how it was from his face. "All is well?" she asked.

All but a joke that fell flat, Augustine thought. "All is well," he replied.

She took his arm and wrapped it around her waist. Although he allowed it, Augustine held her for only a moment before pressing her fingers and releasing her. "I must sleep," he said, turning away to avoid the disappointment in her eyes.

～

After the first restful sleep he'd had in a week, he awoke to find Titrit leaning over him, one hand gently clasping his wrist.

"Beloved," she said gently.

Whether it was the touch of her fingers, the sound of her voice, or the sight of her face, he was not sure, but suddenly he knew Titrit was about to deliver bad news. In all his life until that moment, he had never wanted not to be told something as desperately as he did not want to be told what she had come to say.

He said it for her. "The fever has returned?"

"The fever returned," Titrit said, nodding. "The messenger just came. It was so sudden that they could not take the time to send for you before." Augustine hurried to rise, hoping somehow there was still reason to hurry, but she put her other hand on his shoulder and ended all hope. "There is no need. He is already gone."

On the day of the funeral, Augustine made sure he was far away from the church. He couldn't bear to see the Christians claim their prize, as if the fact that Laurentius would not laugh at a joke meant anything, really.

Augustine fled to his brother's grove and paced among the olive trees. It was quiet there and he found comfort in the silver-green leaves that seemed to embrace him. Augustine sat down to rest, and the pain came back like a stab.

This was a place without memories of Laurentius, so it should have been a refuge from pain. Every stone of every street in Thagaste spoke of his friend and proclaimed his absence, but these trees had never known him.

How can I feel his absence even here, where he has never been? Augustine thought. *He might have walked with me here someday. Now he never will. I have not lost only all that was; I have lost all that might have been. All I have left is the grief.*

If grief remained, he must accept it. At first Augustine found no relief in crying, but after many weeks of shedding many tears, he began to feel some happiness. To weep was to feel the wound, and the wound was Laurentius. To feel the wound was also to feel alive. Augustine now had a horror of death that the loss of his father, a distant event told in a few strokes of a pen, had never awakened in him. He had not felt diminished by Patricius's passing. After receiving his mother's letter with the news of his father's death, he was the same man he had been before.

But his friendship with Laurentius had been like a safe haven, where he could be himself and express his doubts, fears, and new ideas. Now all that remained of that relationship lived in Augustine's memory.

Thagaste was too full of reminders of death. Augustine had to leave. He would go back to Carthage—he could not stay in a place where every building was a memory and every tree was a pear tree.

Chapter Six

But after making the long journey back to Carthage, the city proved to be little comfort. Titrit was overjoyed to be home, and that was a consolation. Adeodatus had been sorry to leave his grandmother's house—though not as sorry as Monica had been to see him go. But to him, for whom a year was an unimaginable amount of time, Carthage was a new and exciting environment, and he was determined to explore as much of it as his parents allowed. In his child's mind, this was far too little.

Augustine walked through the new apartment he had found for his family, and out the back to a small street. He followed it a few hundred feet, looking around at the stone buildings and listening to voices of people who lived and worked in this neighborhood. As was the case nearly everywhere in Carthage, a cool sea breeze drifted across his face.

Augustine's heart was still heavy with grief for Laurentius. It felt as if a part of him was gone forever. Would this sadness ever diminish? Still, he was glad to have returned to Carthage and to the sea.

Augustine loved his mother, but he was also glad to be away

from her intensity. When he had explained why he needed to leave, he was surprised she understood.

"I know you are grieving for your friend," she'd said kindly. "But for me, grief cannot be avoided. I live in the house I shared with Patricius, in the town where I buried him and where I hope one day to lie beside him." Augustine had looked down sadly. "But I can see how you might wish to," she had added, trying both to understand and to explain herself, "if it is a grief without hope."

Not quite understanding what she meant, Augustine had gone to gather his belongings and prepare for the trip back to Carthage. As he filled his bag, he realized the meaning. For her, Christ was a hope she trusted and believed in. He envied her conviction.

Monica's house was much quieter now that Augustine, Titrit, and Adeodatus were gone. She had time to notice the trees and bushes that had flowered. She had time to see Laurentius's parents, who lived nearby and were mourning their dead son. Hope was often in Monica's thoughts that spring in Thagaste; hope was what she needed always.

Augustine had stayed with her in Thagaste for just a year. Despite Monica's prayers, her not-so-subtle hints, and her example, her son had left her house no closer to God than when he arrived. In fact, he was further away, for he was angry now—angry at the God he did not believe in.

What did I do? Monica wondered as she gathered dishes for clearing. She blamed herself that Augustine still had not come to

Christ. *What did I leave undone? I thank you for the angel's promise. I thank you with all my heart. Without that assurance, I think I would have died when he left me. But your angel did not tell me what I must do to bring it about.*

She eagerly went to bed each night like someone watching for the messenger who would deliver the next book of Virgil. She awaited the next part of the dream. Yet she also watched and listened in the bright sunlight of the day. She knew God spoke not only through dreams. He spoke through his servants, as he had given her comfort through Bishop Domitian.

Now she walked down to the well near her house and recalled with a blush that sometimes God spoke to her through people who had no intention of speaking his words. Long ago, when she was a little girl, Monica had been trusted to fetch the wine for meals. Accompanied by a slave girl named Kahina, Monica would dip her cup into the cask—reaching at first, for it was as tall as she was then—and fill the jug Kahina held.

One day, before she poured, Monica took one tiny sip. The taste was bitter and she decided she did not like wine. But she did like the feeling it gave her—a little flutter of excitement, the thrill of making her own choice in the midst of doing the task that had been set for her. Yes, she liked that very much.

She continued to sip, and after several days, the wine did not taste so bitter. Before long, she was filling and emptying her cup before a drop of wine ever found its way into the jug. The wine made her giggle and feel silly. She knew it was wrong but she couldn't stop. Kahina watched her silently. Monica continued stealing the wine for some months.

Then came an evening—*Was I nine? Ten? Ten, surely*—when Monica was not sent to fetch the wine. Family friends had come for dinner. Their son, a boy of fifteen dressed in a new toga, was named Patricius—he was polite and obviously self-conscious. He was not quite as handsome as Monica hoped he might be, but no marriage decisions had been made. There was time yet for that.

Still, she liked what she'd seen of Patricius. He was awkward at dinner, unsure of how to converse with a ten-year-old girl whom he had never met and whom he would in all likelihood marry. She had not known that a boy of fifteen could feel awkward, and as the evening went on, it became important to her that he not feel that way. She thought the conversation was beginning to go better when she looked across the room and saw Kahina, silent, waiting to serve, and . . . giggling. Monica glared at her. That only made Kahina giggle more, her shoulders shaking with the effort to keep the sound inside her.

For the rest of the evening, Monica struggled to maintain her part in the conversation. Patricius did not seem to mind, though he looked askance at the sudden change in her. Monica seethed. Kahina must be spoken to. She would be the mistress of her own household one day, so she had to learn how to keep order.

At last, the dinner ended. After the guests and hosts had said polite goodbyes, Monica's parents asked how she liked Patricius. She shrugged and did not offer an answer, preoccupied by how she would scold Kahina.

Her speech to Kahina was forceful. She flubbed a few

words, but no matter. Just as she was coming to the part about "the virtue of self-control is the handmaid and the guardian of the other virtues," she stopped. Kahina was laughing. Not giggling silently, but laughing out loud.

Monica lashed out at her. "Do you find virtue a subject for laughter?"

"Not virtue, no. But you, a little boozer, lecturing me on self-control?"

There was plenty Monica could have said in that moment, but it didn't matter. She knew Kahina was right. It was difficult for Monica, just ten years old, to see a painful truth about herself for the first time. She was a thief. The meaning of the word *sin* was transformed in an instant from an abstract notion to *something I have done*. She was horribly ashamed.

Monica wept for much of that night, though she made sure to stop before dawn so her red eyes would not betray her. The next evening, she was again sent to fetch the wine, and Kahina followed with the jug. But this time, Monica did not take a single drop. Soon she would be eleven, too old for such nonsense. And after eleven would come twelve, then thirteen—old enough to be married.

Monica washed the pots with the cold water and her rag, secretly thanking Kahina for laughing. She had not tasted wine after that.

I married. I had a son—two sons. I was widowed, and now all I have are two sons, and one of them is far away. He is far away in Carthage, and I cannot reach him. You did not leave me in my sin, she thought to God. *You spoke to me through a servant. Speak to him. Speak to him through me. But first speak to me so that I may know how to speak to him. I will wait upon your word.*

Monica waited. Temperatures warmed, olives ripened, and lichen began to creep up Laurentius's tombstone. Letters came from Augustine in Carthage—not as often as she would have liked, but they came. Every letter brought news of young Adeodatus growing up. His perfections were one topic upon which mother and son agreed, so Augustine, canny rhetorician that he was, dwelled upon them not only at length, but almost to the exclusion of all else. Adeodatus was a fast runner. Adeodatus had many friends on their street and organized games. Adeodatus was growing taller every day and eating more food than Augustine thought possible.

Augustine's letters often took a personal turn and told more than he intended. Monica studied each sentence and pondered their meaning. She could tell her son was not at ease. This was usual for Augustine, yet his discontent seemed to be more than his typical impatience to do and know everything now. She sensed—or was it wishful thinking?—that the Manichaean answers did not satisfy him any longer. He no longer spouted the Manichaean viewpoints, nor did he mention his meetings with other Manichaean followers—in this absence, Monica's hope grew.

Two years after Augustine left Thagaste, Monica read in one of Augustine's letters about his former student Alypius's safe arrival in Carthage. The boy had prevailed upon his parents to send him there to study, and they agreed on the condition that he avoid Augustine's influence. But before a year was out, Alypius had again become one of Augustine's pupils. His parents sighed. They were not surprised—young men are drawn to fire.

Monica knew Alypius's parents, a couple named Caius and Cornelia. Whenever a letter arrived from one of their sons, the three would visit each other's homes to read and analyze each word and phrase with a focus that would put a student of oratory to shame. It had been six years since Augustine's departure from Thagaste, and Monica missed him sorely.

"Thank you for inviting me," Monica said to Caius and Cornelia at a time when they had two letters to analyze—one had arrived from Augustine the same week as one from Alypius.

After providing Monica with some food and a warm place to sit beside the burning coal in the brazier, Caius and Cornelia told Monica that Alypius had revealed he was going to Rome to study law with men who could assure his career. It was a great distance, but a dazzling chance. They rejoiced, and Monica rejoiced with them. She picked up the letter and read it to the end. After she slowly put it down on the bench, she announced she was going to Carthage. Caius and Cornelia almost laughed, but held themselves in check when they saw Monica's serious expression.

"My dear, why do you suddenly want to go?" Caius asked.

"Augustine has become impatient with his pupils. He writes that they are late, inattentive, rowdy, and impertinent," Monica said. "But he adds, 'Unlike, as I hear, the students of Rome.'"

"Do you think he will go to Rome too?"

"Yes, but perhaps not right away. He has a life in

Carthage . . ." Monica said. It was as close as she had come to mentioning Titrit. "He will have to become more deeply dissatisfied, then he will begin to look elsewhere."

"You think he may become dissatisfied?"

"I know he will, and very soon. Your son, Alypius, has told us so."

Cornelia took up her son's letter again and held it near the lantern. Had she missed a part? "How? When he speaks of Augustine, he speaks only of anticipation."

Alypius had written that Faustus was coming to Carthage. Faustus, the great bishop of the Manichaeans, whose learning in the liberal arts was said to be unmatched—unless it were by his eloquence, which was said to be unmatched—unless it were by his piety. Faustus, wrote Alypius, would answer all the questions that had been increasingly bothering Augustine. The contradictions over which Augustine had puzzled, between Manichaean doctrine and his own observations of the natural world? Faustus would put everything right.

"Faustus is a Manichaean," Monica said firmly, "therefore I know he will not speak the truth. In the end, Augustine will not be satisfied with words that are less than the truth."

Caius considered this, then looked again at Monica. "Yes, but how can you be sure?"

Monica's eyes grew big. "Is faith to you no more than a probability? Will you live in the name of Christ only until a better one comes along?"

"Of course not, but—"

"The rising of the sun is less certain than the God who

commands it to rise," Monica said. "Saint Peter did not stretch out his arms to a probability. Saint Paul did not bow his head to a probability. He bowed to something more sure than the sword. I will go to Carthage."

Soon Monica trotted down the street back toward her home. Augustine would become disillusioned very quickly, she was sure of it. She must be there to help him when that happened.

That night, as Caius and Cornelia prepared for bed, Caius commented on Monica's confidence that Augustine would soon turn away from Manichaean beliefs. "She is more devoted to her god than anyone I know," he said, shaking his head.

Cornelia nodded in agreement. "She is single-minded, certainly, determined that Augustine believe as she does. But she is right—Augustine has a fine mind and an independent heart. He can perceive falseness quicker than most. He will do as he chooses."

It was evening and Augustine's two friends, Alypius and Nebridius, joined him in the low-ceilinged room with a round wooden table for dinner. After, they relaxed in their chairs.

"To a calm sea and a fair wind, and to Rome beneath the sunrise," Augustine said. He raised his glass to Alypius, once his student and now his friend, and drained it. It contained only water—in this he remained an exemplary Manichaean, but there were social rituals to be observed. "And when you have come to the center of the world, may you not forget those who are still at the edges."

"This is a comfortable edge," said Nebridius as he drank his glass of wine. The years had not made him a Manichaean, but he and Augustine had ceased to argue about it. Now, when the subject arose, Nebridius would simply say his religion must have wine.

"It is," answered Augustine, and he smiled at Titrit as she passed through the room on her way to ensure Adeodatus stayed in bed. Alypius took a sip of water so that he might look elsewhere. He had been attracted to Manichaeism by Augustine's fervor, and for the sect's ideal of chastity. He was fond enough of Titrit, but she was a living contradiction in his life that Alypius could not reconcile. This was another reason for his journey to Rome: he hoped Augustine's contradictions would be less troublesome at a distance.

The three men talked into the night, for autumn was coming on, and that meant letters would be long in coming. Few ships crossed the sea in winter; news had to wait until spring. So the three young men spoke together as if words could be stored up, like so much grain against the lean months.

When the sun rose, Titrit and Adeodatus woke and came to bid farewell to Alypius, who had spent the night at their house. Titrit was gracious and Adeodatus was solemn, as only a ten-year-old can be.

Augustine felt he should dispense with lesson preparation in the face of his friend's leaving, but Alypius would not hear of a duty neglected, least of all on his own account. So the friends parted. Alypius and Nebridius went down to the port, and Augustine went to his classroom. He taught the day's lesson, but his mind was distracted with thoughts of Alypius boarding one ship and Faustus arriving on another. He fervently hoped Faustus would provide answers to his questions.

For instance, this one: Wasn't the very act of waiting an admission that he needed someone else to bring understanding? Augustine had been told by the Manichaeans to trust his reason, but it seemed it could not carry him far enough.

Chapter Seven

It was easy to say "I will go to Carthage," but to plan and then make the long journey was far more complicated. First, Monica had to endure a winter of waiting—she needed Navigius to escort her, and he could not leave until after the harvest and the pressing of olives. Winter was not a time to travel, except at great need, and Navigius did not think Monica's case merited the risks.

At last, spring arrived. When she broached the question of a departure date, Monica sensed Navigius had hoped the months of waiting would cool her enthusiasm and make the journey unnecessary. Disabused of that hope, he did not argue long. His role in the family was as the dutiful son, and he played it now with practiced skill.

Once resigned to the journey, he accepted it with a good enough grace. Simple curiosity had never been a strong enough motive for him to visit Carthage, but now that the decision had been made, he looked forward to the journey. He grumbled about being uprooted in order to chase the prodigal, but admitted he was eager to look upon the sea.

But when they finally reached Carthage, he was no longer

sure it was worth the trip. The journey had been dusty, long, and monotonous, and Monica had eyes for nothing except the road ahead. Carthage itself disappointed him too—the city was so dense with people, noise, and stone that Navigius almost couldn't breathe. The maze of narrow streets made him feel closed in. Buildings that rose to three, four, or five stories made him feel small. And everywhere: people. One hundred faces streamed past him each minute, so many that not one face could be truly seen before the next took its place. One thousand voices spoke but none was intelligible above the others. Smells he could neither count nor name bombarded his nose. Navigius had never felt so overwhelmed and alone.

Finally, he and Monica ventured to make inquiries. After following conflicting directions—and getting lost three times—they came at last to Augustine's building. They climbed the steps to the second floor. Navigius kept a careful eye on Monica, sure that in her haste she would trip on the unfamiliar stairs, but she seemed to hardly touch them. While worrying about his mother, he himself missed a step and had to recover his balance. By the time he reached the landing, Monica was already knocking on the door.

First they heard voices inside, then footsteps, then the scraping of the lock. Monica leaned forward, swaying not from weariness but from an inability to be still before the journey had quite ended. Then Augustine appeared on the threshold. "Mother?" he said with surprise.

He had changed in six years. Augustine was not taller, but he stood straighter. He had taught for long enough that now he wore authority unconsciously, as a role taken for granted. But his eyes exuded the same intense energy. Wherever he was, his mind had already moved on. That feeling struck Navigius with particular force today. He smiled at his brother.

"It is good to see you," Navigius said.

"It is good to see you as well," Augustine said softly. Without hesitation, he stood aside, inviting them into his home. Over Monica's head, he glanced at Navigius with a questioning look, as if to say, *How comes this?* Navigius shrugged as a silent reply: *It is Mother.*

Titrit and Adeodatus, who was now a tall boy, stood in the main room. Titrit glanced once at the visitors, then fixed her eyes intently on Augustine. Augustine returned her look, but turned quickly to his son and said, "Adeodatus, you remember your grandmother and your uncle."

Adeodatus was not sure he remembered, but still he bowed properly before them. "Grandmother, Uncle, it is an honor to welcome you to our home," he said.

Whatever had been on her mind, Titrit recovered. "Please, sit down. You must be tired after your journey. If we had known of your coming . . . You see, Augustine was about to step out."

Monica, who was halfway seated in the indicated chair, leaped up. "Then I will go with you," she said to Augustine. "No, no—there is no call to disrupt your life. I did not come for that. But, surely, I can go where you go."

After a tender goodbye to Titrit and his son, and a friendly wave to Navigius, Augustine walked quickly away from his house with his mother at his heels. He dodged and wove through the crowded narrow streets, while Monica struggled to keep up behind him.

"You never wrote to say what had happened with him," she shouted to her son.

"Who, Alypius? He is capable of writing for himself," Augustine replied.

"No, I mean Faustus," Monica said. "Alypius told us of Faustus's coming. I wanted to know—"

"I know your thoughts already," Augustine said without looking back at Monica.

"But . . . why do you keep your thoughts from me? I believe you are wrong, and I believe that it matters, so I tell you so. If you believe you are right about something as important as the nature of reality itself, why do you not tell me about it?"

Augustine stopped and looked down at his mother. She had not changed one bit. She was as relentless as ever, possibly more so. He was not in the mood to hear her, so he turned and kept walking. Monica trotted behind him, still talking.

"Does it matter so little to you that I am mired, as you think, in error? Do you care for me so little that my resistance deters you? I think if you were really sure, nothing and no one could keep you from speaking of it to anyone you met. And so I ask again—what happened with Faustus?"

Augustine's pace slowed. There was no use in trying to avoid this conversation. "I found him exceptionally agreeable. He is a warm and altogether delightful man. He speaks beautifully."

"But does he speak truly?"

A group of boys just released from school raced past them. Augustine pulled Monica out of their way. She gripped his sleeve.

"Did he answer your questions?" she asked.

Augustine had little choice but to answer his mother. "In character, he was everything I had been led to believe," he said. "Indeed, he was more, for he had the humility to understand what he did not know and he refused to speak on subjects he did not understand."

A seagull squawked from a rooftop, and Augustine paused so as not to shout over it. Monica waited, knowing Augustine was merely gathering his words.

"He knows less of the liberal arts than I do," he continued when the squawking ceased. "And as for the mathematical questions that had troubled me, the stories of the movements of the moon and the stars that are found in Mani's books, and the discrepancies between them and what I had myself observed—to these he had no answer." Had he conceded too much? Augustine hastened to add, "This does not mean you are correct, Mother."

"I know that well," she replied. "But doesn't this mean that he—that the Manichaeans—must be incorrect?"

He gently pulled his sleeve away from the clasp of her fingers. He answered so quietly that she strained to hear above the human commotion on the street. "If I admit to doubts, will you refrain . . . for now . . . from pressing me any further?"

She weighed the bargain and decided to accept. "For now," she said, nodding.

They walked on in silence. For the first time, Monica began to look about her. "Where are we going?" she asked.

"To the waterfront."

Monica froze, not hearing the curse of the man who bumped into her. Augustine would have to become more deeply dissatisfied before he began to look elsewhere for answers—perhaps at last to the Scriptures.

Augustine had not stopped walking. She sped on to catch up. "You are sailing?" she asked, her voice high and breathless. "You are leaving Carthage? Let me come with you. We need only to return and explain to Navigius—"

"Mother, stop. Can I not bid a friend farewell without being suspected of a journey myself?" He took her hand. "Near here is an oratory to Saint Cyprian. Let me take you there, and you can rest and pray to the holy patron of Carthage while I go aboard to make my farewells."

Monica looked about. Strangers hurried by, and she was unsettled by the grimaces of the grotesque half-humans trapped in the mosaics. Her son gripped her hand and awaited her reply.

"Very well," she said. "It is always good to pray."

He led her to the place, and she was happy to retreat into the cool, silent oratory. She kneeled and prayed while the wind blew. An image of the tide ebbing came to her mind. The waves flowed back, but Augustine did not come.

Night was falling by the time Navigius found her.

"He has gone?" she asked. The evidence of the past hours was not enough. It would not be true until she heard it spoken.

"He has gone. Titrit broke her silence only an hour ago, when clearly it no longer mattered."

Through the roaring in her heart, she heard herself say, "You took only an hour to find me in a strange city. I am impressed."

"It took no great skill," he said. "A few inquiries and I found this place, then it was obvious where you would be."

"He must have expected that."

"Assuredly," Navigius said sarcastically. "He would never abandon you."

"Enough," she snapped. Then she burst into tears.

Titrit was willing to answer any question she was asked.

Yes, Augustine's journey had been long in planning.

Yes, Augustine would send for her and Adeodatus once he settled in Rome.

"Why are you so calm about all this?" Monica asked. Titrit did not understand her surprise.

"I have always known he will leave me. This way I learn, a little, what it will feel like." Even Monica, in her state of distress, could not ignore the sadness in Titrit's voice.

To Rome's citizens, the city was bread—actually corn, pork, wine, and oil—and circuses. To provincial governors, Rome was the seat of the Empire. To the thousand tribes they governed, Rome was the guarantor of order. To all of them, Rome was the center of the world—or even the world itself.

To Augustine, at present, Rome was a low ceiling, a wall painted to look like a garden, indistinct noises from the atrium of the house, and fire.

Almost immediately upon arriving, he found lodging with

a fellow Hearer of the Manichaeans, but before he could learn the way to the Forum, he came down with a fever. For two days, Augustine lay in bed with delirium. He dreamed of desert mirages and shimmering pools that vanished before he could plunge into them.

On the third day, he regained his right mind, but he was too weak to do more than turn his head and see his host standing beside the bed.

"Help me drink," he whispered. His friend held a full cup to his lips.

Morning and evening, Monica occupied the basilica of Saint Cyprian. The Christians of Carthage quickly grew accustomed to the quiet woman who smiled when she knew someone could see her. The other regulars at the basilica wondered about and occasionally whispered to each other, for surely concern could not be the sin of gossip. More than one of them held her up in prayer. When she did not know someone could see her, she crumpled into herself like a woman who mourned a death. "No," said one, "hers is not the face of a mourner, but the face of the dying."

Monica reviewed the years of her life with Augustine and spoke to God in her prayers:

He had nearly died of the fever. He was only a child—seven, eight?—and he'd had a child's faith. Amid the delirium, there was a quarter of an hour when he knew me. He knew where he was and how it was with him. He begged me for water. I brought him a cup, but he said no—he meant the water that washed away sins.

I had been praying for health of body, Lord. In that moment, my heart stopped. It could not bear such fear and such joy all in an instant. He was leaving me, and I had failed. He wanted you and I had all my desire.

I sent for the priest. The fever broke. I saw then that he would have his life after all! It would be a life filled with occasions of sin. To return to the mire after being cleansed would carry a greater guilt. I spoke with the priest when he arrived and he was in agreement. The sacrament was put off. I told myself that when it was needed, he would still want it. Then I fell to my knees and thanked you for restoring my son to me.

I wanted him to live, and to live as a Christian. But if I could not have both, was his only way to you the way of death?

No. She had received a promise through her dream in Thagaste, and through the bishop's words. Her son would be where she was, however hard that might be to believe now, when he had put the sea between them. She had received a promise, and the one who had promised was faithful. He did not say how the promise would be fulfilled.

She had been promised that her son would live in Christ, but the way to that life might still be the Lord's own way: the way of death.

If it must be, then let it be, she prayed. *Let it be mine.*

Chapter Eight

It was the sixth day. The fever abated, but Augustine was not yet well enough to get up. Just as he considered it, a visitor arrived.

"Alypius!" Augustine called, but did not get up, though he refrained less out of prudence than because Alypius, before he was even through the door, gestured for him to remain as he was.

"Come and tell me anything and everything," Augustine said. "I wander in thought through the streets of Rome, but because my body is confined here, you must be my eyes."

Alypius smiled at his former teacher. Augustine saw he had grown. Alypius was a strong young man with clear eyes and a direct gaze. He made himself comfortable in the recess by the window. "What would you see first?" he asked.

"A minute earlier I would have said 'My friend Alypius,' but you have anticipated me."

"I should have come sooner, I know . . ." Alypius began.

Augustine shook his head. "No, you are here now and that is enough. How fares the lawyer?"

"I am a student, not yet a lawyer. I am . . ." He paused, his face in shadow from the light behind him. "I would have said, 'I am well.' It would not be untrue, and yet it would be. In truth, I too have suffered a kind of fever. Not of the body," he added quickly, "no matter how much it felt like it."

"Explain," Augustine said, fascinated. He struggled to rise. "How did it begin?"

"I was walking home when I met a group of my fellow students in the street. They were going to the amphitheater to watch the gladiators."

Augustine remembered Carthage, and this earnest student who had been always prepared, always docile . . . except when the charioteers were racing. Alypius had been cured of that passion, his eyes opened by the scorn with which his teacher viewed such passing follies. But had he truly been cured, or had the disease merely gone dormant, ready to break out in a more virulent form?

Alypius read Augustine's thoughts. "I know," he said. "I tried to refuse, but it was five to one and my friends swept me along. I swore to them—and to myself—that they could bring my body to the arena, but I would close my eyes and keep them shut, and not allow the scene at the arena into my soul."

He threw up his hands as if to say that plan did not work. "I thought I was strong enough to keep that oath," Alypius said. "I should have been strong enough. And I did, Augustine, I did close my eyes, but . . . I did not cover my ears."

Augustine understood. He could visualize the entire scene as vividly as if he had been present. There were many ways into a man's heart; sight was only one.

"The entire crowd roared as if it were one voice, and before

I knew it, I opened my eyes for just a moment, only to see the vanity that ensnared idle men."

Alypius paused, reviewing his words, finding them insufficient. He hurried on, leaning forward. This is what Augustine enjoyed so much about Alypius—he spoke with precision. "I mean, I thought to observe, no more. And this, also: I thought that if I observed, my friends might afterward listen to me when I explained the dangers of the pastime for them."

"You thought all of that in a moment?"

Alypius replied with a smile. "Some of it I thought after, perhaps."

"So, you looked," Augustine said, nodding his head sympathetically.

"I looked. One man was down. The sand was dark. His opponent's sword was stained almost to the hilt, and yet as he raised it, it gleamed. The blood dripped off the sword and he— he put his head back so that the drops might fall on his face. The crowd still roared. I felt I was no longer surrounded by it. I was part of it—not the crowd, but the sound itself. As if this, here and now, were the reality and everything else were a waking dream.

"After we left and returned to our homes, I felt as if I could do anything, but at the same time that I could do nothing. I have never felt so alone. I wanted to be part of that sound again—to be more than myself." He looked at Augustine, pleading with him to understand.

Augustine did understand, though not by the way of blood. Every man had a base instinct to which reason yielded, some fever that seemed sweeter than health, even as he could see and diagnose the fevers of others. He said simply, "And so you returned."

"Yes, I returned. It was easy enough to find friends who were going there. Then it was only slightly more difficult to make up a party myself. Today, I intended to go on my own after seeing you."

"Without telling me?" Augustine asked.

Alypius nodded. His smile was gone, replaced with a grim look. "I thought we would go about as we used to do in Carthage, and we would talk of philosophy and the delights of the mind, and I would have fewer hours in the day for other diversions. I thought the desire would gradually fade, and I would never have to tell you it had returned at all."

"Alypius, you might not have had to tell me, but I would have seen."

"As to that—"

Augustine put up a hand. "You did tell me. That is what matters."

"Yes. As I walked here, I reminded myself of all I do not tell you. I broke a stylus yesterday. I purchased a new pair of sandals. A thousand such small events make up each of our lives and no one else's. They are not secrets. But when I arrived here, I realized that not to tell you would be a lie."

Alypius let out a deep sigh of relief. His story was done.

"I am glad," Augustine said. Then he went silent, reflecting for a moment. "Now, consider this: Do you think the desire might have faded if you still fed it with occasional visits to the arena?"

"No."

"Do you intend to feed it?"

"No. But I think I would if left to myself. Help me."

"I will," Augustine said. His eyes lit up with excitement. "Because I cannot go out to the streets of Rome due to my fever, you must tell me how everything looks."

Alypius smiled and settled back, pondering where to begin. "At the northern entrance to the Forum there is an arch, and next to it a chapel. Inside is a statue of Janus, the god who can look both ways at once. By tradition, the chapel doors are kept closed in times of peace, but they are opened in times of war," Alypius said, grinning, "lest a closed door should hinder a god from coming to the aid of his city."

As Alypius described the flower-filled gardens, the elaborate fountains, the vendors who sold ripe produce, the people from other countries passing by in strange dress, and his own favorite landmarks, Augustine listened in rapt attention. He was not only captivated by the images Alypius called forth, but by his wonderful use of language in the telling.

All roads led to Rome—a truism that was carved in stone. Markers on all the surrounding roads told travelers their distance to the city. But Rome was no longer the center of the Empire. By the beginning of the fourth century, the Empire's expanding borders were leaving Rome on the geographical margins. Milan, farther north and strategically placed, became the emperors' residence of choice when they were in the west. They may also have found its climate more agreeable than the swampy fogs of Rome. The Senate remained among the fogs, but by now it was a convenient symbol, a stripe on the toga that had been the Republic.

"It's been only a year, but I'm afraid my enthusiasm for Rome is gone," Augustine told Titrit one evening after Adeodatus had gone to bed.

"Is it the weather—the fogs?" she asked. Titrit missed the North African climate, but rarely mentioned it.

"No," Augustine said.

"Do you miss your friends at home?" Again she spoke for herself unknowingly.

"I will tell you. I teach my students rhetoric with great dedication, which is all that is expected of any teacher. In Carthage, the students were disruptive and disrespectful. Here in Rome, I thought they would be better. I was told the custom here is to pay teachers at the end of the year. I thought it was unusual, but I was willing to accept it as the way it is done. But it turns out that most parents conspire with their sons not to pay me at all. When I made inquiries to other teachers, I was told this is quite common."

Titrit usually had little to say when Augustine talked to her about his work, but she understood this. As a woman who had once barely earned a living in her family's business, she was shocked. "That is . . . stealing," she said.

"Yes, it is, and disrespectful of the value of the lessons," Augustine said, shaking his head. "I am thinking we might go north, where I understand students are more serious about their studies, and parents pay."

Titrit was uneasy with the idea of another move. "And what about your friends . . . ?"

Augustine knew she meant his fellow Manichaeans here in Rome. He still kept company with the group, more by habit than by conviction. He found many of their arguments absurd, but he was not prepared to reject them. Sometimes they could be useful.

He looked out the window. He had mixed feelings about Rome—it was certainly an invigorating city, but right now it wasn't serving any purpose for him. "There is someone I will visit," he said. He was thinking of the prefect of Rome in that spring of 384, Quintus Aurelius Symmachus, known as a man of letters. "Perhaps he knows of a position for me somewhere in the north."

In lineage, honor, and sense of duty, Symmachus was a true representative of Rome, a city whose gods were woven into the fabric of citizens' lives. Roman families were attached to their gods, and many resisted the shift to Christianity.

Symmachus and his party did not believe the shift was inevitable, even though Emperor Gratian issued an edict that halted all funding for the rites of the old gods, banning the rites themselves. Worship took money, and suddenly the money was gone.

But Emperor Gratian was no longer on the throne. Gratian's successor, Emperor Valentinian II, might be more willing to allow his people to continue worshipping the gods of his ancestors.

So when Augustine asked to visit him, Symmachus readily agreed. This young African's reputation had followed him from Carthage. A silver tongue, it was said, and a mind of gold. He was a fine candidate for a post at the emperor's court—and he was a Manichaean.

As he waited for Augustine to be brought to him in the atrium of his house, Symmachus stared out the window, his mind churning. Symmachus had an idea to send a Manichaean to Milan. It would very much annoy Ambrose, he thought with a satisfactory smile.

"Ambrose of Milan may be my cousin," Symmachus muttered out loud, "but we have little in common."

Ambrose had been a senator, a rank conferred by his appointment as Governor of the Province of Aemilia-Liguria. He'd taken up residence at the headquarters of the province in Milan, and in late 373 he oversaw the election of a new bishop.

Both the Catholic and the Arian factions were determined to fill the vacancy. They disagreed on a critical point. The Arians claimed Christ was not equal in dignity to God the Father. They claimed Christ had been created, and that though he had the nature of God, he had it in a lesser way. The Catholics were outraged at this diminishment of the honor due to the savior of the world. The Arians were outraged that a "creature" was given equal honor to the eternal Creator. The dispute, which by now had spread throughout the Empire, had often resulted in violence.

Ambrose understood both sides, but above all he wanted peace. He was asked to give a speech at the election of the bishop, and he wanted to use the moment to inspire peace and unity between the two factions. His first words were barely out of his mouth when he was interrupted by the shout of a child's voice: "Ambrose the Bishop!"

He looked up, momentarily disoriented. As a boy, he had pretended to be a cleric, grandly presenting his hand to be saluted, for one day he himself would be a bishop.

"Ambrose the Bishop!" The chant got louder as more people joined in.

He shook his head—no, no, didn't the people in this crowd know he was not a priest—in fact, not even baptized?

But the people did know Ambrose. Soon after he had taken up the governor's mantle, he'd demonstrated that he was a man of great integrity. Now, they decided, he would be their bishop. Ambrose disagreed, but in this moment, he saw the crowd would not stop.

So, he ran. He forced his way out the back of the cathedral and did his best, in the days that followed, to destroy the high opinion of his character by telling anyone who would listen about the worst aspects of himself. He told them about his unwonted cruelty to criminals years before. He desperately summoned street girls who were paid for appearance's sake in hope of fooling a mob determined to see a miter placed upon his head.

When he attempted to escape Milan by night, Ambrose

became confused in the darkness and took a wrong road—and in frustration finally returned home. When the citizens discovered his attempt, they placed a guard around his residence and would not let him leave. They wrote to the emperor, asking him to release Ambrose from his service as governor so he might become their bishop.

If Ambrose had a hope that the emperor would be reluctant to agree, it was short-lived. The emperor had feared an outbreak of Catholic-Arian strife, so to be presented with a nearly unanimous petition offering a simple end to the business was a cause for rejoicing. Accordingly, he rejoiced, and consented.

Ambrose surrendered to the emperor's will, believing it expressed the will of God. In just eight days, between November 24 and December 1, 374, he was baptized, ordained, and consecrated.

One might have thought, mused Symmachus, remembering those events ten years ago, that such a reluctant bishop would be a quiet one. That had not proved to be the case. In his new role, Ambrose brought every relationship he had formed, every bit of experience, to the service of the Empire. He denied that the edict that took away funds for the rites of Rome's gods had originated with him, but in Symmachus's mind, there was a direct connection between the bishop's devotion and the emperor's zeal.

With a new emperor on the throne who might listen to new voices, Symmachus searched for any way to influence him. By all reports, this young African—a Manichean—might serve that purpose.

So, almost before he had made his bow to the prefect, it was ordained that Augustine would go to the emperor's court at Milan. There, Symmachus hoped, he would come to the notice of Ambrose the Bishop.

Part Two

TAKE AND READ

Chapter Nine

With barely a trickle of smoke, the lamp went out.

In the sudden darkness, Augustine sighed and faced the nightly question of whether to light it once again. For all the magnificence of Italy, for all the excitement and splendor of the emperor's court, the cost of lamp oil was a perpetual annoyance.

Augustine had grown up surrounded by olive trees, so he knew the connection between the trees and the oil that let him work into the night. Not until coming to Italy had he thought, however, about the connection between the price of that oil and how far it had traveled from the trees.

He rose and took the few steps, by now familiar even in darkness, to the shelf where he kept the oil jar. As he reached for it, a recognizable hand laid over his. Augustine turned his palm up and entwined his fingers with Titrit's, pressing them gently. "This is an oration for the emperor, and it must be finished in two days," he said.

"Then you have tomorrow night for it. Give me tonight," she said softly.

"I cannot," Augustine replied. "My mind is full of words with which I can make no order. And I am too tired."

"Sleep, then."

This he could not refuse. With her hand still in his, he left his study for the bedroom. In the darkness, her head found its comfortable place against his shoulder. The words continued to tease him, shifting and fading and reforming in his mind never quite as they should. But after a time, Titrit's even breathing guided his, and he slept.

When he awoke, the words were in no better order in his mind, but he was greatly refreshed, to Titrit's satisfaction. The rest of the household had not yet stirred. Promising he would return for breakfast, Augustine dressed and stepped out of the house for a walk. Sometimes, the words he needed fell in line with the rhythm of his steps.

At the corner of the street, Augustine approached a bubbling fountain. To his surprise this morning, a cheerful, round-faced fellow rolled himself out of the water and onto unsteady legs.

"God give you good fortune, sir!" the wet man cried. "And God give me whatever of your fortune you can spare!"

Augustine laughed with him and tossed him a handful of coins. It was so early yet that no one was about, so Augustine lingered. "How is it that you are swimming at this hour, and not in the baths?" he asked.

"I meant only to dip in my head, which had grown hot," the man replied jovially, "but where the head went, the rest of me followed."

"It sounds as if you have had an excess of good fortune."

"Now, how could that be? How could there be such a thing? Good fortune brings us happiness, and what man alive has ever said, 'No, this happiness is sufficient. I want no more'?" The man wrapped the coins Augustine had given him in his palm. "You have provided my next round of happiness, and for that I thank you. God give you as much as I, and no more dearly bought!"

The man tried to bow, and Augustine grabbed his arm to steady him, then watched as he stumbled off in search of a wine shop that opened early.

Augustine sat on the edge of the stone fountain and ran his fingers under the stream of water, reflecting that one man could gain happiness from passersby with a blessing and a quip, while he was a professor of rhetoric who must earn money by burning expensive lamp oil in order to shape beautiful lies about Emperor Valentinian II, a thirteen-year-old boy who had been emperor since the age of four.

True, Augustine sought a happiness of a higher sort than could be found in wine. He was chasing a glory higher than the accolades and the comforts it brought. Glory was a name that would live after him, assurance that he had achieved greatness. But doubt nagged him. Had Augustine ever been as happy as that simple man who had just pulled himself out of a public fountain? Augustine splashed water on his face, as if to absorb some of the man's joy.

Augustine remembered little of the next two days. His oration had been written. In that time, he knew he had eaten, for Titrit would have seen to that. He assumed he had slept, for the lamp oil had to run out sometime. Yet he was not conscious of having done either.

Augustine was consumed by the work, but when it was done, it was as if it had never been. The work was only so many words that might just as well have remained unspoken. He began to wonder about the point of words—an inconvenient question for a rhetorician.

The day after he delivered the oration, and heard it fulsomely praised, Augustine paced the garden as Titrit watched, standing near a garden table. If he wished to speak, she would listen. If not, she would tend her jasmine. She had coaxed her vines to wind around the columns so that, if she closed her eyes and was guided only by scent, she could be in Carthage.

She heard his footsteps, but she did not turn. She loved the feel of Augustine nearby, his warmth spreading over her like the sun, unseen but all-enfolding. He reached around her, grasped one of the vines, and pulled on it. At that, she did turn. "If you break them, how can they grow?" she said.

He twisted a length of the vine in his fingers. "They have grown long enough to serve their purpose. Who could ask for more?" He set the circlet on her hair, then planted a kiss in the center of it.

As a child, Titrit had always tried to ask for more, but she had learned quickly that little was gained by asking. Still, she believed in asking. Today, she settled for a jasmine crown.

"I am going out for a few hours. I will return for dinner," Augustine said.

She was not surprised. His pacing was longer than the limits of the garden. "Where are you going?" she asked.

"To see a man who still believes his own words."

Ambrose the Bishop's skill as an author was debatable. Jerome, the celebrated ascetic and controversialist, once commented about his literary efforts that "since he is alive, I will reserve my judgement, lest I be blamed either for flattery or for speaking the truth."

Ambrose's skill in speaking was not in debate. He was not a trained theologian, nor was he a philosopher—in fact, he distrusted philosophy, considering it a questionable path to salvation. And he did not care for intellectual speculation. Ambrose's primary concern was to live his daily life as a Christian in the world, and his books were the Holy Scriptures.

Augustine, now a brilliant and increasingly famous young professor of rhetoric, liked everything he'd heard about Ambrose. Ambrose was known as an inspired preacher and a compassionate leader—constantly addressing the needs of the poor—which made him popular. By now, Augustine had been finally disillusioned by the "great teacher" of the Manichaeans, Faustus. In Ambrose, Augustine sensed a gentle courtesy, combined with an iron conviction and a searing love that Faustus could never have imagined, much less understood.

Ambrose of Milan knew his God, longed for him, and longed to bring others to him. As it happened, the force of that longing attracted and held an audience. It certainly attracted Augustine. At first, he didn't quite take in the bishop's understanding of

God, but he enjoyed listening to him orate. As he listened, he found the bishop knew his God well. He was reminded of the Scriptures, those messy, fragmented, all-too-human books he had dismissed as the works of men . . . and Ambrose showed him how they might all be the work of one hand.

"It does not matter," Ambrose said, "that the books were written by many different men, so many years apart. Is God subject to time? And do you think he spoke only in words?" Augustine had to think about this concept. "Surely, the creator can speak through his creations, shaping the natural world and the very deeds of men to bring about and to foreshadow the salvation he prepared."

The wind had picked up shortly before sunset. When dark came, it kept rising. Late into the night, the rain began.

Navigius had never been on the sea before. He would have been happy not to be rocking violently on it now. He was uneasy from the moment he set foot on the ship. He was almost grateful for the rain, for it confirmed his mood, and a reason to be miserable is always some comfort when one is in misery.

He did not argue when Monica announced her intention to follow Augustine to Rome. As soon as he learned Augustine had sailed, he knew what their mother would do. All the same, it took time to put aside the money and to set the farm in order so he could leave it on the other side of the sea for an indefinite period. He knew this time that they would not return until Monica could be assured of seeing Augustine safely home from Rome.

The wind and waves pushed the boat fiercely, tipping the

angle of the deck, which had been made slick by the rain. Navigius clung to the wooden siding and looked to the sailors for reassurance. Surely, they had been through worse. Now was the time he wanted them to tell a sea story with impossibly high waves and a safe ending. But the sailors were in no humor to tell stories as they focused their attention on the work of the sails. They kept an eye on the bow, where the tiny, still figure of a woman held on with both hands, facing forward calmly into the storm, in the sure and certain hope she would see Augustine again.

The bishop's account was a good one, but was it good enough? It did hold together. Accept the premises, and the conclusions followed. But was it true?

Augustine would have been relieved to determine it was not true. The God of the Hebrew Scriptures might be the father of his people, but to Augustine, he seemed too much a father like Patricius, raging and punishing. Still, the search for truth was not a search for comfort.

As he walked down the wide street in Milan, he took a deep breath, inhaling the scent of fresh bread coming from a high window. He stopped for a moment to take it in and feel the sun's warmth on his neck. Yes, he had given the Manichaeans nine years. He could give the Catholics some part of that time, especially as it would be one way to atone to his—

"Augustine!" a voice interrupted his thoughts. He was only a few paces from the cathedral when the cry stopped him in his tracks. He should have been surprised, but he was not.

There are certain fixed laws of nature. My mother is one of them, he thought.

He turned in time to catch her hands so she would not engulf him in an embrace. They were still in the open street. He could have said, "You have just arrived in Milan? What brings you here?" But there was so much more he could not say just now.

Instead, he said simply, "Why do you come to the cathedral? You cannot have been hoping to find me."

"You do not know much of hope," Monica said, her eyes glittering with joy. "But no, as you mean it, I was not hoping to find you here. I came to pray before I went in search of you. I learn now that a prayer can be answered before it is made."

"Mother, do not hope for too much," Augustine said kindly. He noticed Monica had aged more rapidly than the time they had been apart, and he guessed his absence was the cause.

To atone he wanted to give his mother news that would make her happy. "I have left the Manichaeans. Whatever the substance of the world is, I am satisfied that their account is not correct," he said. As he expected, his mother's face lit up with joy. He continued, choosing his words carefully. "I do not know that the bishop's . . . that the Catholics' account is correct, but I will give them time to explain it. I will become a catechumen. A catechumen only."

Monica caught her breath. For a moment she felt faint, but she restrained herself from crying out. Her eyes danced with happiness and her smile broadened as she stared into her beloved son's face.

Chapter Ten

"A wife, a wife. He needs a wife," Monica whispered to herself as she awoke the next morning.

She was deeply gratified that her prayers were being answered. Yes, Augustine had put one hesitant foot onto the rule, and he would join her in the center, just as her dream had promised.

But Augustine must marry, and it was for her to find him the proper woman who would advance both his faith and his career. A Roman, a Christian. "He knows—he must know—that he cannot enter the Church while he is still tied to his sin." She spoke into her empty room as shafts of morning light shone on the white stone walls. "But he will not break free unless I help him . . ."

Navigius looked in on his mother upon hearing her talking. He worried about her. She was more preoccupied than ever with Augustine. She barely registered that he, Navigius, had found their lodgings, that he had provided a bed for her to sleep in and food for her to eat. He watched, dumbfounded, as she rose and dressed quickly to go out.

"I must learn about Milan and its families. Augustine must

marry," she said again. She was out the door before Navigius could reply.

"The ideal wife would be an heiress," Monica said to herself as she walked down the wide street, "wellborn enough to match—and preferably enhance—Augustine's status he has achieved at court."

Of course, the wife must be a devout Christian from a family of devout Christians. Monica also added this to the list of qualifications: personable. The woman's circumstances could not be her only attraction if Augustine was expected to be satisfied with the match.

"How to find a girl who is not already promised," Monica muttered. She trusted the Lord would provide.

To commune with her God, she regularly visited the cathedral, both to pray and to observe. Navigius knew what she was doing and Augustine must have guessed, but the brothers did not speak of it.

Monica wondered if Augustine had ever mentioned to Titrit that he would eventually need to marry a Christian girl. *Surely, she has guessed*, Monica thought.

More quickly than she expected, Monica found the perfect family. They were wealthy, well-connected, and genuinely and deeply devout. Their daughter was more than personable; she was beautiful. She had her parents' piety, a fair grounding in the poets, and the wit to understand what she read. The only thing that made her less than perfect was her age: twelve. Her parents would not hear of a wedding until she was fourteen. They were amenable to a betrothal—but only if their prospective son-in-law gave up his concubine.

"I will tell her," Monica said firmly.

"I forbid you. This is for me to take care of," Augustine said. He was filled with anger, sadness, remorse—and resolve. They stood together outside the cathedral as evening fell. The air was cool and fresh.

For every other part of his life, Augustine had planned, expected, and imagined. Titrit had been there, and that was enough. He loved her and had a son with her. And now . . .

He recalled the instant he first saw Titrit in Carthage years before, negotiating the sale of the copper lantern. He remembered how he'd been helplessly drawn to her eyes, her hair, her strength. Now he would explain that there was this woman—a girl, really—who was not Titrit and was everything Titrit was not, and when this girl was old enough, he would have to marry her.

Only Adam in the Garden of Eden had had no other woman but Eve. Yet Augustine thought he felt as Adam must have felt. Eve was deceived by the serpent. Adam was not deceived. He knew that to take and eat the fruit was sin. He took and ate so as not to be separated from her, yet it was sin.

O God, these Christians claim to heal the soul, Augustine prayed. *They say you have the only remedy for everything that ails man. That may be so. I begin to believe it is so. But if it is so, it is the surgeon's remedy: the knife. You would cut away a part of me, and you say it is to make me whole. And like a patient, I see only the blade.*

The walk home from the cathedral had never seemed either so long or so short. Though the air was cool, Augustine found no comfort in it. He wondered what and where "home" would be from now on. He had lived surrounded by many different walls, but Titrit had always been within them.

And what about his son, Adeodatus? Monica had spoken of him only in passing, on the assumption that there was nothing to decide. By right of custom and by every hope of future prospects, a boy remained with his father. Augustine wondered whether Monica, in her wholehearted focus on his salvation, had thought how deeply Titrit would be wounded by having Adeodatus taken from her.

When he reached home, the villa was quieter than it should have been. Entering the atrium, he saw why. Adeodatus perched on the edge of the pool, and Titrit stood beside him. At her feet was the copper lantern.

So, she knew already what he was about to tell her. How could she not? Monica had made no effort to keep her negotiations secret. Still, he struggled to lift his eyes to Titrit. Augustine approached her with anguish.

Titrit pulled herself up to stand tall. She was acutely aware Augustine had an intellectual and professional life that did not include her, a life that could be bound by rules she barely understood. His leaving was inevitable, so why should she punish him for doing what he must? Still, she knew he loved her. Was this really what he wanted?

Augustine read her thoughts and answered her question in his mind: *I did not seek the match, but I want what follows from it. If I thought the price too high, I need not have made the offer.*

The image of his mother intruded forcefully upon his mind. He could have refused her insistence on marrying the girl. *It is my choice, and Titrit had no choice once she had chosen me. Which choice angers her more?* he thought.

"Mother says you have something to tell us," Adeodatus said.

"I do," Augustine said, forcing his eyes from the lantern to Titrit, then to his son. "I am going to marry."

These five words in one swift cut ended a life.

Adeodatus had his father's intelligence and a thoroughly Roman upbringing. He knew his father had not meant to marry Titrit. "What will happen to Mother?" he asked, his voice trembling. He gripped Titrit's linen skirt with white-knuckled fingers.

"Say it," Titrit said, her voice like a surgeon's knife. "Say it, and it will be done."

"Your mother must go," Augustine said to his son.

"Where?" Adeodatus asked, tears springing from his young eyes as he moved closer to Titrit.

Augustine's whole body contracted in anguish. He had not thought about this separation, the practical matter of where Titrit would go without him, because she had no family in Italy. But Adeodatus wanted to know this important detail—it mattered where his mother would be.

"Where she will," Augustine answered quietly.

"I will go back to Africa," Titrit said, looking down at her son. "It is just as well. This Italy . . . it is a fine place, but it was never mine. I have wanted to return home since the day I set foot here."

"What will you do in Africa?" the boy asked, holding on to her now with both arms.

Titrit almost laughed. "Right now, I have not the slightest idea. I can only tell you what I will not do."

"What is that?" asked Adeodatus.

She turned to Augustine. "I will never know another man."

She meant it to hurt, and it did, but it was what Augustine had prayed to hear. Did he pray this for her sake, that after she had sinned for so long with him, he was not sending her to sin with another? Or was this prayer for himself?

Adeodatus looked from Titrit to Augustine. "What will happen to me? Will I go with her?"

This was the question Augustine dreaded. *Father or mother? Patricius or Monica? Stay or go?* he thought. *What if I had come to this at thirteen years old? I would have stayed with my father. There would have been no question of anything else. No question either that I would have hated the decision and all that bound me to it. I will keep my son, but will this day make him despise me forever?*

Titrit was willing to spare him. It was she who answered. "No, my son," she said gently. "You would have no future with me. A boy belongs in his father's house."

As Adeodatus began to cry, Titrit kneeled beside him and spoke to him so quietly that Augustine could not hear. She stroked the boy's hair and kissed his cheek. After a few minutes, his cries subsided and he stared into his mother's eyes. She smiled at him and kissed him again.

Then the boy turned to face his father. Augustine braced himself. Though his face was wet with tears, Adeodatus looked at him with bright hope. "You will not send me away? I may stay with you?"

Augustine stared at his son, his heart swelling with a wild and burning joy. Adeodatus was his not out of necessity or custom, but by affection and free choice. Augustine had . . . won. And yet Titrit was losing the dearest person to her life. Augustine had no idea what to say—Titrit had somehow sacrificed her deepest feelings to make this possible.

Now she stood and gently turned away. Adeodatus let go of her skirt, then slowly approached Augustine, as if surrendering himself.

Augustine placed both hands on his son's shoulders. "Yes, you will stay with me. But for now, I must speak with your mother alone." He stooped to pick up the lantern. "And take this with you." Obeying, Adeodatus walked sullenly back inside their home.

For a moment, the atrium was silent.

"My love," Augustine said. "Oh, my love, I did not want that. I had not dreamed . . ."

Titrit remained still. "My son did not have a father like yours. Or a mother like yours. For good or ill."

"He loves you."

Titrit stifled a cry, but Augustine was not sure if it was a scoff or a sob. "The fact remains that he chose you," she said solemnly.

"What can be done?" Augustine said. "He is our flesh."

"Something we did not intend . . ." Titrit reflected on the happy early days of her relationship with Augustine.

"Yes, the boy we did not intend will be the child who remains of us."

"Oh, your everlasting philosophy!" Titrit said, full of anger. "For once, stop looking at what was or what might be or what should be or what it all means. Can you look simply at what is, here and now? I am losing my son."

Augustine heard a whisper of sound behind him. He looked over his shoulder and saw Monica standing at the threshold. "I do see," he said to Titrit's rigid back and bowed shoulders. "I see, and I cannot bear it."

She turned to look at him, but he was already passing Monica to step out of their home and into the street.

Titrit had been so focused on Augustine's going that minutes passed before she noticed Monica hadn't left with him. When she did, she was almost glad. Here was a target she could aim at without hurting herself.

"Is this what you want for him?" she demanded.

Monica was calm. "I did not want the beginning."

"And that absolves you for this ending?" Titrit said sharply. "How convenient!"

"It is true." Monica was unmoved.

"Will it surprise you to hear that I do not think much of your truth?"

"It is not affected by what you think of it."

A scream welled up in Titrit's throat. "You sound like him. Both of you—all of you—with your books and your rights and wrongs. Can you leave no room for happiness?"

"Is it happiness that you want?" Monica asked. But before Titrit could reply, she asked another question. "Or would you rather have love?"

Augustine did not return until well into the night. Much later, Titrit came to him. Dry-eyed, she held him while he wept.

It was the way of the world. She had expected nothing else. In the everlasting game of position and patronage, a man would be a fool not to set his marriage on the scales and weigh every advantage.

Titrit began going through her possessions to pack what she could take with her. She lived simply. Her main concern had always been her son. Tears filled her eyes as she realized she would never see him, her dear Adeodatus, grow into a man. But with a new family surrounding him, he would surely be well.

Titrit offered no advantage to Augustine. She had never dreamed he would marry her, not even in the last moments before sleep when she was folded in darkness and in his arms. Only the night after Adeodatus was born, she dreamed Augustine would not marry at all. The dawn put an end to that.

It hurt. Yes. That was the way of the world. She should not be—and was not—surprised. So, what else was she feeling?

Augustine would know the word for this; he always knew the word. Titrit frequently did not understand his words or why he worried and fussed over them into the night, but she loved the sound of his voice and the light in his eyes when he spoke them.

Was that what she felt? Not surprised she had been set aside, but surprised it was not for advantage. The advantages were there, but he was not marrying because of them. He was marrying because of the word *Christian*.

She had been set aside for a word. So, he loved a word more than he loved her. Titrit stopped packing and went to the window that looked out onto an alley. She watched two children playing with a ball as their laughter echoed off the walls.

Augustine loved her, she knew that. Even when she would rather not have known it, she knew it. Did she love him? Yes, but she really knew so little of his bigger concerns. Did it count as love if there was so much she did not know about him, about the life of his mind? Maybe he wished for a woman who knew more of him, someone who could understand all his words and ideas?

Maybe this Christian girl would give him that, once she grew up. Titrit tried to wish that for him but couldn't. She turned away from the window, sadness washing over her heart.

Was I merely a woman's flesh? she wondered. *And in the darkness, would any woman's flesh be much the same? Will hers?*

She could find out. She could try to discern whether, in the darkness, it was the flesh or the man that mattered. She had sworn she would never know a man again, and she had meant it, but Augustine would never know if she broke her vow.

This ruminating was pointless. She would keep her vow, and even though he would never know it for sure, and even if his

Christian bride became everything Titrit had been and everything she could not be, that vow would still bind her to him.

It was not enough. It was worse than nothing, but she would cling to it. She looked at the small pile of belongings she had collected for her journey back to Africa. She would not miss Monica's stern disapproval of her. She glanced out the window and, realizing the playing children had gone, she thought: *It seems I would rather have love.*

Chapter Eleven

Following his separation from Titrit, Augustine found consolation in the arrival of his friend Alypius, who had secured a post in the administration of the Empire's financial affairs. Milan could not have had a more honest administrator. The threats and bribes, even of senators, left him unmoved. He took his responsibilities seriously.

Alypius did experience one temptation, however. Due to the volume of its business, the court arranged discounted rates for manuscript copying, with an unofficial understanding that members of the administration might, from time to time, make personal use of those rates. Alypius's love of books was greater than his salary. After a brief but acute struggle, he elected to take no questionable advantage.

Augustine's second consolation was his great ally and friend Romanianus. Romanianus had business at the court and, he'd said with a grin, he had come to watch the progress of his investment. Both were true. It was also true that he was growing lonely in Thagaste.

The third consolation was Augustine's longtime friend Nebridius, who had trekked from Carthage despite worry over leaving his mother. "But there is no one there with whom I can think," he'd told Augustine.

In Milan, Augustine dedicated himself to thinking like other men threw themselves into drink, sport, or war. His mind moved more rapidly than most, and now it tried to outrun his heart.

But it could not be done. He still missed Titrit terribly.

No matter what the weather was during the day, his nights were cold and lonely. After Titrit had been gone a few months, Augustine found a woman to warm them. Livia gave what he wanted, and she wanted no more than what he had to give in return.

So, Augustine maintained two worlds. By day, he was with friends and students, fine-tuning the skill of argument and studying manuscripts. He spent his nights with Livia, and he made sure these two worlds were separate.

Alypius had much to say on the subject of chastity that spring. He did not see the need even for marriage. Wasn't the life of the mind all they sought? Augustine quickly conceded that it was, but privately he remained convinced he could not forego the life of the flesh.

"But if we could live in the mind?" Alypius persisted one afternoon as the two friends strolled through the city. It was Alypius's nature to persist.

"Oh, if we could . . ." Augustine shrugged, glancing at an open window. Inside, he saw a family sitting together by a small fire.

"Then why should we not try?" Alypius asked.

"Because it cannot be done," Augustine said. "Rather, I cannot do it."

"I did not say 'you.' I said 'we.' I mean all of us—you and I and Nebridius, and Romanianus if he chose, and anyone else who cared for it—together."

Augustine stopped to look at his friend as his meaning sank in. Alypius continued painting his picture. "Why should we not retire from the world? Find a house somewhere and give over our days to study and conversation? We would have to provide for necessities somehow . . ."

"That is simple enough. One or two of the community could be tasked with such matters. Say each man takes the responsibility for one year," Augustine suggested. He felt a tingling in his blood. This could happen. They could live for and with the truth. Not just snatch it in odd moments, but live with it, *in* it. Was this the destination toward which he had been journeying across land and sea and time? This was just how he imagined the destination would feel: easy and natural, bright with promise.

He and Alypius turned down a narrow street and headed in the direction of Nebridius's lodging. When they arrived, Nebridius welcomed his friends into his small sitting room. The three men spent the afternoon refining their new plan. Augustine contributed an outline for the first year's study. It would chiefly be the works of the philosopher Plotinus. Augustine felt it was time to explore the Platonic school, and Plotinus was one of Plato's most influential disciples.

Toward evening, the three friends set out to find Romanianus and by luck encountered him on the street. They excitedly explained the new life that awaited them. Romanianus looked at the faces before him, then he laughed.

Augustine reacted with annoyance. It was a new dream, and therefore very tender. "What is so amusing about it?" he asked.

"As a dream? Nothing," Romanianus said. "I think it's as beautiful as you could wish. But, Augustine, I am married and you are soon to be wed. Have you spared a thought for what our wives would think about the idea? I promise you, they will not hold back their thoughts."

Just like that, the fire was out, and Augustine felt colder than if it had never existed. He glanced at his companions. Nebridius's expression mirrored his own thoughts. Alypius too was downcast, but he could not quite restrain the smile that lifted one corner of his mouth. Augustine did not need to be told why, nor reminded how the entire conversation had begun.

The men separated with brief goodbyes and each walked back to his own home in Milan as a warm breeze wafted through the streets from the river.

Augustine was willing to set aside his dream of renouncing the world in order to study. After all, he could study Plotinus every day. So, every day his mind was with Plotinus, and every night his heart and body were with Livia. As the satisfaction of one appetite filled him, he found, the other emptied him.

But the most delightful company of all was his young son, Adeodatus. Worn down by years of teaching indifferent and unruly students, Augustine now rejoiced to have such a pupil: eager, curious, and quick-witted. He rejoiced doubly—triply—because that pupil was his own son, and because he was so much like his mother. It was painful to see Titrit's looks and expressions in his son's face, but she would never again be with him—this was all he had of her. Over time, the pain became a kind of consolation.

Consolation was much in Adeodatus's thoughts. He spoke little of his mother, but each night he lit the copper lantern, and each day he asked questions.

"What is it you look for in your books?" he asked Augustine one evening at dinner. The two sat at a simple table in their small garden.

Augustine reflected on the many possible answers and chose the simplest and truest one. "Happiness," he replied.

"Can you find that in books?" Adeodatus asked as he stared into his father's calm face.

"Some men can. At least, they have tried."

"But . . ." Adeodatus searched for words. Augustine never tired of watching his son do this. "But happiness is not something you read. It is something . . . something you do."

"How do you know what to do?" Augustine asked.

It appeared that was obvious to the boy. "You do whatever will cause happiness," he said, as if everyone knew this.

Augustine remembered the little boy screaming for his sword, as if the toy weapon were the answer to happiness. Then he thought of Livia, but quickly set that thought aside.

"Do we always know what will bring happiness—true lasting happiness—or do we more often pursue pleasure? Or do you think happiness is no more than the total sum of our temporary pleasures?" Augustine gestured to the fruit set out before them. "Eat enough grapes, and we will be happy?"

Adeodatus frowned, picked a grape, and held it between two fingers. "No. It must be more than that," he said thoughtfully. "But what is it?"

"That is what I look for in my books," Augustine said. The two continued eating in friendly silence.

Ambrose the Bishop was fond of reminding his attentive listeners that, as it says in 2 Corinthians, "the letter killeth, but the spirit quickeneth." Augustine was one of those listeners, and as Ambrose spoke from the stone bench in his garden, looking distinguished with his dark beard and long, narrow nose, Augustine was captivated. To Augustine, Ambrose more than earned his reputation. He was intelligent, gentle, and able to illuminate the meaning of passages of Scripture that Augustine had long dismissed as too absurd to dwell on.

In the peace of the garden filled with Ambrose's steady voice, Augustine still longed to understand the meaning of spirit itself. All he had ever known was the material world, and he considered all matter bounded by space and time. He obsessed over many questions, but he did not have the courage yet to put them to Ambrose.

Could God be infinite matter, extending throughout the world like air, existing in every part of it? No, God had to be more than that. Augustine began to think "being" was a larger concept than he had known, and he wondered how it could be known. That seven plus three made ten he knew, for he could see it. How could he comprehend what could not be seen?

He could not, so taught Ambrose. He could not see the invisible any more than a blind man could see the sun. That did not stop the blind man from feeling the sun's heat, and so believing in it. Augustine had tried to accept the concepts of the Manichaeans and found them wanting. But after listening to Ambrose speak so eloquently in his many garden talks, Augustine began to see that Ambrose's way, which admitted there were matters that could not be explained and nonetheless held them worthy of belief, was more honest, more true to a larger world beyond the senses.

The Manichaeans promised understanding to those able to understand. The Catholics too promised understanding according to the measure of a man's mind, but they promised belief to every man, without exception, if he would simply open his heart to receive it.

Augustine still flirted with that belief, as he had once turned a copper lantern in his hands, but he was quite sure he wanted understanding. Plotinus had a way of presenting him not necessarily with answers, but with new questions.

"What is beauty?" Plotinus asked. *Symmetry*, Augustine replied in his mind. *The harmonious ordering of parts in a whole.*

Is gold not beautiful? Or light itself—is it not beautiful? And isn't it true that a man's face could sometimes look beautiful and sometimes not?

Beauty must then be separate from the face. It is a quality beyond the face, somehow existing in itself. A concept unchanging in itself, though that which possesses it can change.

And more. Beauty is the order that a thing should possess. Beyond every changeable thing, there is an unchangeable measure. How else could we ever say "should"? That measure, being unchangeable, must be eternal. It must be what simply is.

"And if it is eternal, it cannot be torn away," Augustine said, reasoning it aloud later in his own garden, in quiet privacy. Here he reviewed all he'd heard Ambrose teach.

In this eternal "is," there could not be the thousand daily reminders of Titrit's absence or the sudden chill in the midst of heat when he withdrew from Livia. Where there could be no distance, there could be no separation. Where there could be no change, there could be no death.

He reasoned further, while he stared at the jasmine growing over the far stone wall, that this is the being that underlies all. From that eternal being came everything, the first being reason itself, or as Plotinus called it, the *logos*. Augustine's Greek was poor, but he could translate Plotinus's *logos* as *word*.

Just the week before, Ambrose the Bishop also spoke of an eternal word. In this, he and the Platonists stood together and, in another sense, on opposite banks of a chasm, for Ambrose spoke of a Word Made Flesh.

Augustine paced around his garden, lost in thought. Here was a philosophy both lower and higher than the concepts offered by the Manichaeans. Here was a philosophy in flesh and bone and blood. Sin was not a darkness equal and opposed to the light. Sin was a part of every man, given to him with his blood, and the need was for sinless blood to purge it.

This was the faith of Augustine's childhood. He had thought, in Carthage, that he had outgrown his mother's stories. Now, as he returned to them, he felt as if he were a child again.

Chapter Twelve

For the second time in a year, the Bishop Ambrose of Milan was besieged inside his own basilica. The chief architect of the eruptions in both instances was Empress Justina, mother of the boy Emperor Valentinian II. She was Arian by conviction and a mother by vocation, and in both capacities she detested Ambrose. She feared his fearless orthodoxy and his possible influence on her son, over whom she desired to exercise sole control. Her aim was to reduce Ambrose's influence at court and throughout the city.

Justina searched for grounds of battle and quickly found them. The churches of Milan were in the hands of the Catholics, but all places of worship belonged to the emperor. And here was her weapon: surely, at the emperor's word, one of the churches could become Arian.

Early in 385, the emperor's council had summoned Bishop Ambrose and instructed him to yield the Portian basilica, just outside the city walls.

"I offer all my worldly goods and services to be disposed as you wish, my lord," Ambrose said quietly, "but I cannot yield the temple of God."

While his outward manner was deferential to the emperor, inside he was appalled by the request. Turn over the altar of Christ to a sect that denied the divinity of Christ? It was impossible.

By Wednesday of Holy Week, Ambrose and his congregation gathered in the Portian basilica with soldiers outside. As he raised the host, Ambrose prayed that if blood were to be shed, he himself might be the acceptable sacrifice.

That day ended uneventfully, and after a sleepless night reciting psalms in the darkened side chapel, Ambrose returned to offer the Mass of Holy Thursday. His theme was the repentance of sinners. As he preached about the people of Nineveh, soldiers burst into the church. To the crowd's wonder, the soldiers ran straight for the altar and . . . bent at the knee to kiss it. When they stood, they announced the news that ended their duty there, which they declared was repugnant. The empress had yielded. Faced with a city devoted to its bishop, and with an army that showed signs of sharing the people's allegiance, Justina could do nothing but withdraw her claim, at least for now.

Not all in her party surrendered gracefully. The grand chamberlain of the court sent a message to the cathedral, threatening that if Ambrose continued to "flout" the will of the emperor, he said, "I will take off your head."

Ambrose, who considered martyrdom an easier prize than the life of a bishop, sent a prompt reply: "May God grant you to do what you threaten! I shall suffer what bishops suffer, and you will act as eunuchs act."

That had been Holy Week of 385. Now, nearly a year later in

February 386, the congregation was gathered in the new basilica, which was Ambrose's principal seat.

The scene was much the same as the year before: soldiers outside allowed in anyone who wished to enter but allowed no one to leave. Inside, a frightened and defiant congregation gathered around Bishop Ambrose.

Empress Justina was subtler this time. She proposed an edict of toleration, restoring the free right of worship to the Arian sect. Yet this tolerant law promised a penalty of death to any who disagreed, even in secret. It was not a law intended for general enforcement, but rather a choice offered to one man: Ambrose. He could agree to share his city, his churches, and his flock with the Arians, or he could leave Milan, which would amount to the same thing. Or he could refuse, remain, and take what might come.

Once the law was promulgated, Justina sought to make Ambrose's position clear beyond any doubt. He was summoned to court to engage in a theological dispute with an Arian bishop. The teenage Emperor Valentinian II would act as the sole arbiter of the outcome.

It was unthinkable to Ambrose to yield to the Arians, and unthinkable to yield the emperor authority over the deposit of the faith. But it was also unthinkable to yield by leaving the city.

The crowd of faithful followers inside the basilica was agitated in nervous anticipation of what the soldiers outside might do.

Monica made sure she was there in the midst of it all. Devotion under the shadow of death was the natural extension of the devotion that had formed her life.

In this, Augustine was on the same side as his mother. He could not have said precisely why. A sense of a son's duty toward his mother was one reason, and his admiration for the bishop could not be denied. He was also simply curious. He wanted to see for himself the people willing to fight for their beliefs, and how Ambrose the Bishop would contain the strife taking place in front of him. Whether it was any of these reasons or all of them, he wasn't sure, but he pushed past the soldiers and over the threshold.

Once he reached the basilica's cool interior, it made little difference. He waited and watched with the restless crowd. Here was the Catholic faith embodied from high to low—Ambrose himself, preacher, father, and champion, stood at the altar in his fine vestments.

Augustine noted the many old women kneeling before the altar. Surely, they couldn't tell the difference between an Arian and a Manichaean, but they prayed in silence, their eyes closed and their lips moving constantly. Staring at these old women as if seeing them for the first time in his life, it occurred to him that truth was not a question only for the philosopher. He pursued it through a tangle of definitions, evidence, and argument, but could a person who did not have skill in disputation find it? Could a person who could not read find it? Love was shared among the people here—a love willing to face swords. Where had they found a certainty that still eluded him, with all his studies of philosophy?

"What is it?" came a voice behind Augustine, startling him. He turned to find his mother's eyes on him. He felt vaguely embarrassed by his thoughts, and that they had only now occurred to him.

"How do they know?" he asked his mother. She looked at him quizzically. "All these people here . . ." He gestured to the praying women. "These people to whom philosophy is only a foreign word and to whom truth is merely that which is not a lie."

"What is it to you?" Monica replied. She saw she had sent his mind off to wander the maze of definition, and she smiled. "No, do not tell me. After all, to me, philosophy is a foreign word."

"Mother . . ." Augustine sighed.

She shook her head. "You live in a different world than most of us, my son, and your father and I sent you there. He wanted you to have everything he never did, when all I want for you is the one thing I do have myself. It is a gift worth all your books, Augustine, to know and to rest in the knowing."

"And all these people have received it?" he asked.

"Enough to be here," Monica replied confidently. "Of course, the bishop is less abstract than the Holy Ghost. Do not fill this church with the odor of sanctity."

Her eyes twinkled, and so did his. It was now the third night of the vigil and the basilica smelled of lamp oil, smoke, and sweat. "We are here, most of us, for the man."

"Because you believe this man speaks for God," Augustine said. Monica nodded. "Then I return to my question, Mother.

Where do they come by that belief? It is a gift, you say, and God is doubtlessly the giver. Why is it given to some and not to others?"

"Do you want it?" Monica looked closely at her son.

Augustine opened his mouth to tell her that of course he wanted it. For twelve years, he had dedicated his life to searching for wisdom. Here, so she said, was where it was to be found. What could be simpler?

Yet he closed his mouth without answering. He had grasped this much: What his mother, Ambrose, and the Church offered was not that he would possess wisdom; it was that wisdom would possess him. He needed to surrender himself to a God he could not see, to the God for whom he'd given up Titrit.

Monica smiled with understanding. It was a look Augustine had seen too often in the past fifteen years. The smile of hope continually disappointed but kept barely alive, like a tiny spark. Augustine knew she would weep as soon as she was out of his sight, which, this time, might not be for several days. He knew her tears came from love, but this was not the way he wanted to be loved.

He searched for other words to shift the conversation from his inadequacies without being too obvious. He was a professor of rhetoric, and this was a simple rhetorical exercise. Somehow, though, when facing his mother, all his hard-won skill deserted him.

Before Augustine could respond, Bishop Ambrose moved to the foot of the altar, and his voice instantly silenced all others in the church. "My children," he said, "let us sing."

Ambrose loved prayer expressed in music. He had studied the practices of the Eastern churches and he felt the time was right to introduce a new element to the liturgy of Milan. Before the congregation quite knew what had happened, they found themselves divided into two groups, and the bishop was putting new tones to words they knew well.

"O God, come to my assistance," sang one side.

"O Lord, make haste to help me," answered the other.

The people in the congregation sang their lines haltingly at first. The melody was strange, as were the circumstances. But soon the call and response of the two groups of singers filled the building and everyone inside with peace.

"Let all that seek thee rejoice and be glad in thee."

"And let such as love thy salvation say always: the Lord be magnified."

Monica saw Augustine was weeping. Her brilliant son, whose sensibilities were all focused on the mind, had been caught by the heart. Monica took a deep breath. This was as it should be.

Once more, Empress Justina yielded. What could she do, confronted with so many citizens willing to face death, and to sing as they did? The emperor might be the ultimate authority, but emperors had been deposed. The Roman Empire had seen enough civil war without beginning another over ownership of a church. As soon as the soldiers got word of Empress Justina's decision, they withdrew from the basilica. Soon after, the law—that tolerant law that promised death to any man who disagreed with it—was withdrawn too.

Augustine escorted Monica out of the dark basilica and into the sunlight of the day. His thoughts were now fixed on the baths and how soon he could get there.

"That ended surprisingly well," he said to his mother as they blinked at the brilliant sunshine. "Mother, you cannot have wished to remain."

"To set the world outside and live only in the moment? To hear and speak only of God? To sing of the life to come?" Monica's dark eyes shined up at her son. "It seemed that we stood on the threshold of eternity."

As bells rang out in the late morning light, they turned to leave with the rest of the crowd that dispersed though the streets of Milan.

Chapter Thirteen

I *love you. How is it that already I love you? I still do not know you,* Monica prayed. *I know only that you are, and were, and shall be, unchanged and unchanging. There is so much more I want to know.*

Augustine's mother also searched for answers. Some of the customs of the Milanese Church differed from what she was used to in Thagaste, and she had questions for Bishop Ambrose. She sent Augustine to ask them. The ruse was transparent enough, but Augustine made no complaint. If she hoped he would ask questions of his own . . . well, most likely he would.

The doors of the bishop's house were open from sunrise to sunset, and Ambrose did not require or expect visitors to be announced. The visitors arrived from the city and beyond, and Ambrose greeted and talked to as many of them as he could. Augustine had been to the house before and waited for hours without being able to speak to the bishop simply because of the press of people. Ambrose gave each visitor his full attention, treating each man or woman as the only person in the room. Augustine watched, marveling at Ambrose's obvious compassion, and thanked God such men existed. Augustine was also grateful he was not called to be one of them.

Yet bishops are only men, and men must rest. Ambrose took quiet moments of retreat every afternoon on a narrow bed set under a tree in the corner of his garden, as a crowd watched from six feet away. It was Ambrose's custom to rest with the Scriptures, and it was thus that Augustine found him on this particular day. No one would disturb the bishop at such a time, so Augustine joined the small group of silent watchers.

A bee buzzed high above, and Augustine remembered the story he'd heard about Ambrose: As an infant, a swarm of bees once surrounded him but did not sting. Instead, they flew away, leaving a drop of honey on his face, which caused his father to proclaim he would grow into a preacher with sweet words for his flock.

In the garden, Augustine was fascinated by this strange scene. The men and women watching Ambrose were utterly silent, as was Ambrose himself. Augustine had been taught to follow the written page with both his mind and his tongue. Words were to be spoken; the sound and the rhythm were part of the meaning. Yet, here sat Ambrose with a book across his knees, and he was silent. Only his eyes moved, the sole outward sign of his mind's journey. Did he think—as he surely had reason to—that if he spoke what he read, he would also have to explain it to those who heard? Was he simply resting a voice that had to fill a cathedral each Sunday, and must be ready at all times to speak to penitent, priest, or the emperor himself? Or are there some words that can only be spoken in the heart?

Suddenly, Augustine felt like an intruder. Augustine realized he cared deeply what Ambrose thought about him. How might Ambrose, so enraptured, perceive him—another ambitious young man who had decided marriage was the way to advancement, and that conversion was the way to the marriage he wanted? How could he not assume that, and how could he ever be persuaded not to?

Augustine turned away from the scene and from the silence. As he did so, an older man in the group turned and fell into step beside him.

"I am of your mind," he said, as if he understood what Augustine was thinking. "The dialogue between man and God can only, in the end, have two voices. We cannot hear what is spoken in the heart."

Startled, Augustine looked at his companion more closely. He recalled seeing this man serving in the cathedral, but he struggled to remember his name. The man again seemed to guess his thoughts. "I am Simplicianus."

Augustine had heard of him. He was Ambrose's teacher, the shepherd of the shepherd. In fact, Ambrose often called Simplicianus *father*. The older man wore this role lightly.

"I am—"

"Augustine," Simplicianus said, finishing the sentence.

"Such is the fame of the world," Augustine said, looking down.

"A master of rhetoric earns his bread by being heard and seen," Simplicianus said. "Would you rather I knew you as Monica's son?"

There was such an understanding in his face, in the comical lift to his brows and the warmth of his eyes, that Augustine did not react with his familiar mix of irritation and guilt. "Every man has a mother. Some mothers are . . . more . . . than others," Simplicianus continued. "Yours, I think, is more in every respect. Weighed in the balance, that is something to be celebrated more often than rued. Some graces have thorns—some even *are* thorns—but graces they remain."

"I know," Augustine said to this man whom he had not known five minutes. "I know she wants only my good."

"And you? What is it you want?" The two men strolled along the street, passing vendors selling oranges and other fruits. The sky was clear blue with no clouds in sight.

"The same, of course. Surely, every man—every man born of a mother," Augustine said, and they smiled together, "desires his own good." Augustine stopped to face Simplicianus.

"Not every man knows he lacks it," Simplicianus said. Then he thought a moment and said, "Shall we seek the good together, you and I?"

Augustine's eyes widened as his face lit up with surprise. Simplicianus spread his hands broadly. "You came to the bishop with questions. That was easy for anyone to see. I am not Ambrose, but I also do not have Ambrose's obligations."

"No, you mistake my . . ." Augustine paused, then took a deep breath. "Thank you. Your obligations may be less than his, but I am sure they are not small, and I am honored. But you mistake the reason for my surprise. You said we could seek the good together. Does that mean you doubt you have already found it?"

The old priest stopped and, with great deliberation, made the sign of the cross. "I have found it. I am sure I have found it, and I am sure there is no other name in heaven or on earth by which a man can be saved." He looked intently into Augustine's eyes. "It follows that I am also sure of your good, even though you are not, as yet. I did not propose a journey in any doubt of the destination." Augustine returned the man's look, taking in his meaning. "The journey does not end, Augustine. Not in this life. A man can know the good, touch it, taste it, but he must still seek it each day, just as each morning he shakes off sleep and sets his feet upon the ground." Simplicianus smiled. "And on some mornings, that is one of the labors of Hercules."

"Then how is it that your books speak so often of rest?" Augustine asked. "Or do you mean it only in the life to come?"

"There, assuredly, but not only there. Is love not a destination and a journey, both in one?"

Love. Again, he takes the word from my mind. Does he read hearts, this priest, Augustine wondered, *or does he simply . . . speak the truth?* "We were speaking of the good. Now you offer love?"

"What greater good can there be?" Simplicianus said.

A flock of white pigeons suddenly flew up from the street and circled over the rooftops. The two men parted, and Augustine headed for home with much on his mind.

Augustine was used to studying a philosophy as a true way of looking at the world that provided the key by which all its parts might be categorized, ordered, and understood. It meant using a rule and measuring the world by it.

But Augustine was aware that what Ambrose and Simplicianus offered was different. He was being asked to surrender, to embrace death. To be baptized was to die to the world. Ambrose was never clearer than he was on that point. He was equally clear that it was irrevocable, which also made it like death. To be baptized would be to give himself, as surely as he was to give himself in marriage—a pledge for which he likewise had little inclination, and less as the days passed.

Livia, a practical girl, barely concerned herself with Augustine's upcoming marriage. She simply accepted it as necessary for his career and his station. Augustine gained the impression that she assumed she would see him less often after he was wed. He had not yet found the right words to tell her he intended to be faithful to his wife. It was no great matter. There was time yet, and no doubt the words would come when he wanted them. He did teach rhetoric, after all.

Augustine did not mention to Livia the other great matter on his heart. Plato was a closed book to her—just like every other book. How could she understand the question of whether to go beyond Plato?

With his friends he spoke freely, airing his doubts and dilemmas. Yet in this matter, he found even Alypius unable to provide the help he needed. As Alypius observed, it might have been easier to do so if Augustine knew what that help was.

Simplicianus claimed to know. Augustine did not share this certainty, but it kept him coming back to the elderly priest. At least he provided answers to Augustine's many questions.

"Then what is it that holds you back?" Simplicianus asked him one day after Augustine had sought him out. They were walking on a small hill outside the city, where huge poplar trees lined one edge of the dirt road.

Augustine had allowed Simplicianus to choose the route of their meandering walk. He was guessing the priest would eventually lead him to the cathedral. He would distract Augustine with questions so he would not realize where they were headed.

Now Augustine weighed his answer. "Conversion is a great matter. A man should be sure before taking such a step."

"Truly, he should," Simplicianus agreed. "How will you be sure when you are sure?"

Augustine had to laugh. "I will know when I am. And does it make such a difference in the end? I love God, as I have told you. Of that I am sure. And you have spoken yourself of how much truth is contained in the books of the Platonists. There I read about God and his works."

"I see." Simplicianus stepped aside to allow two young centurions to pass them in the narrow road, though both his age and his calling should have given him the right of way. "How is your Greek?"

Surprised by the question and ashamed of the answer, Augustine said shortly, "Next to nonexistent."

"Then the books of the Platonists, you have read them in translation?" Simplicianus asked. Augustine nodded. "Whose translation?"

"Marius Victorinus, he who was rhetor of Rome."

"His statue still stands in Trajan's Forum, and his former pupils can still be found in the Senate. I knew him when I was in Rome. We used to speak, much as you and I are now."

"I heard he died a Christian."

"Indeed, he did," Simplicianus said, nodding. "Though if you had asked him, for many years before that he would have told you he also lived as a Christian. Mind, he still burned his incense to the old gods—a man must keep faith with his statue and all it implies—but he assured me, most solemnly, he had read our books and he believed them. I told him I would not count him as a Christian until I saw him in church, but he would only laugh and ask, 'Do walls, then, make a Christian?' For years we went on that way. Always I would urge him to come with me to church, and always he would make his joke. Then one day, at last, he came to me. He asked me to go with him to church, for, he said, 'I wish to become a Christian.'"

"What had changed?" Augustine asked, eager to hear the answer.

"He came to see that to believe our books, but not to profess them, was to lie. A man cannot live in both worlds, for each world demands all of him. And Victorinus was haunted by one of the sayings in the books he claimed to believe. Our Lord promised his disciples, 'He that shall deny me before men shall be denied before the angels of God.'"

"But delay is not necessarily denial," Augustine said.

"That depends on the reason for the delay," Simplicianus replied.

They walked on in silence. Augustine was focused on what

he thought for sure was their destination. He had been inside the cathedral before. It would seem like nothing to go inside again, except that today Simplicianus had made it a choice. Augustine disliked having no choice but to choose. For a man who believed in free will, Simplicianus seemed disinclined to trust it.

It would have happened, Priest. Are you not afraid of the consequences if you force me to make an answer? What if my answer is no? Then Augustine thought, *Do I dare say no, or is a face-saving assent enough? This is no longer the age of martyrs. The Church is respected. Respectable. I cannot be the first man to be blown in with the prevailing wind. Only I did not want—*

"Ah, here we are." Simplicianus halted at the steps of a building.

Augustine looked up. They were standing in front of the library. Simplicianus smiled—he was either the wisest of doves or the most innocent of serpents.

"Is this not where you expected to be?" Simplicianus asked. Without giving Augustine a chance to answer, he bowed and left the younger man to his books.

Augustine stared after his new teacher, marveling at his intelligence and compassion. In Simplicianus and in Ambrose, Augustine witnessed learned men living as Christians in a way he admired. His mother had been an example, but hers lacked the depth of these men.

Augustine nodded to himself, then turned to climb the rough white stone steps into the library.

Chapter Fourteen

A few days later, late in the afternoon, Augustine and Alypius found time to relax in the atrium of the house Augustine had been given as the emperor's professor of rhetoric. Sunlight crossed the floor and gradually slanted across the wall as Augustine recounted the story of Victorinus's conversion.

By that time, he had heard the coda to the story from Simplicianus: Julian the Apostate, upon ascending the Imperial throne, had banned Christians from the classroom and from the public stage. Victorinus at once renounced his career.

"Although," Augustine admitted, "to leave the classroom seems hardly a renunciation. He gave up time spent in idle words on idle subjects and exchanged it for time spent in contemplation. A small loss for an immense gain!" Augustine picked two grapes from a plate of fruit a servant had set before the men on a low table.

"You would do it yourself?" Alypius asked.

"Assuredly!" Augustine replied.

"When?"

It was a simple question that called for a simple answer. Alypius had a knack for that sort of thing. "I have obligations . . ." Augustine began, "at court, and soon more at home. Marriage comes upon us all, in the end." A moment of silence passed, then he nearly shouted. "Do not speak of time to me! You, who are now your own master."

Alypius had finished his successful third term as a court assessor and was now looking about, in no particular haste, for private clients. At his friend's outburst, Alypius merely smiled and returned his attention to the game table. They were playing latrunculi, and he had to move his king out of danger. The board was an exceptionally fine one, its squares made of marble and its pieces of silver and onyx. "I will be your master in six more moves," he said to Augustine.

That was usually the way of it. Augustine could beat him handily if he kept his full attention on the game, but to be assured of victory, Alypius had only to propose a philosophical question. Half of Augustine's mind would immediately withdraw from the board, and Alypius could generally beat the half that remained.

But today, this contest was to be left unresolved. They were interrupted by the arrival of an acquaintance: Ponticianus, a fellow servant of the court and a fellow African. Ponticianus was a tall, strong man with a fierce bearing. Augustine and Alypius stood up and greeted him as colleague and countryman. After inviting his friend to sit down to enjoy some refreshment, Augustine asked how he might serve him.

Ponticianus flushed slightly. "It is no great matter. Nothing to disturb the fate of the Empire," he said. "It is only that my family members are . . . indifferent correspondents, and sometimes a man longs for news of home, however comfortable his exile may be. I came to ask if you had received any letters from Africa."

Augustine, whose family was with him, had not—but Alypius did. While Alypius left to retrieve them, Ponticianus looked about and spied a book on the game table beside Augustine's neglected king. He took it up and examined the title.

"What is it you labor over at present? You read the Apostle Paul?" he asked with genuine curiosity.

"Not in my official capacity. It is for the satisfaction of my own mind—and heart," Augustine said.

Ponticianus's eyes lit up. "Then we are countrymen indeed! I myself am a Christian."

"I know it," Augustine said, then sighed. "But I am not—not yet."

"What is lacking?" Ponticianus could not imagine what could hold his friend back, except that he lived in the reasonings of books.

Augustine fell back upon his earlier answer. "Oh, time, freedom. It is not so easy, in this world, to put everything aside and think only about God."

"Yet there are men who do. Think of Saint Anthony." Ponticianus handed him the book, and Augustine took it by reflex.

"I do not know Saint Anthony."

"He was an Egyptian, a young man of property, and raised to be pious from birth," Ponticianus said. "One day when he went to church, he heard that Christ taught that a man should not be solicitous for tomorrow."

"Surely, he had heard that saying before," Augustine said, smiling.

"Undoubtedly," Ponticianus replied, "but this time he listened. He sold his property and gave alms, then he retired to the desert." He leaned forward to emphasize the next part of the story. "There, demons assailed him, but he conquered the flesh and the devil. Though he was a hermit, he became known far and wide—for his ascetic practices, yes, but above all for his joy. It was his exuberant joy that drew others out of the cities to follow him, so many that he had to form communities, little worlds set apart for men who had left the world."

Alypius returned to the room, letters in hand. He saw Augustine leaning forward and listening, one hand clenched on his knee, and laughed. "You will have our friend on the next boat to Egypt," Alypius joked.

"What need of that?" Ponticianus exclaimed. "The idea has spread. Why, Bishop Ambrose has care of such a house right here, just outside the walls of our own city."

How have I not known about this house? Augustine thought. *I, with my plans to retreat from the world with my friends. I, so pleased with myself for having conceived the idea. It was here all along. Why should I not grasp it?*

Augustine argued with himself silently. *It cannot be done all in a moment,* said one part of him. Another part responded: *How else can it be done?*

Augustine returned to the conversation with his friends. Alypius must have asked some question about the monastery, for Ponticianus was saying he had not visited it, though he had seen a place like it when he was stationed in Trier.

"The emperor was at the games, so he had no need of us—of myself and my comrades," Ponticianus was saying. "We went walking outside the city, in the gardens. As we were talking, we drifted apart, two and two. I cannot remember now what my companion and I were talking about. It cannot have been important, nor can it have been long that we walked, though I do remember the sun was beginning to set when we found the other two and reminded them it was time to get back. But they told us they intended to remain. There in the garden, they had discovered a small house of men dedicated to God's service. And there they had heard of Saint Anthony, and they compared the path he had followed with their own careers, so full of doubt and risk, all undertaken to compete for the emperor's favor—a prize that could be withdrawn at the emperor's whim."

Augustine and Alypius stared at Ponticianus, captivated by the scene their friend described so vividly. "So, they resolved together, there and then, to take service with a faithful king, and to work for a prize that could not be taken away," he continued. "When we had heard this, what could we do but wish them well?" Ponticianus laughed and reached for a handful of grapes. "I confess that as my companion and I returned to the city, I felt a prick of shame. I was glad there were such men in the world, even though I was not one of them."

Augustine felt not a prick of shame, but more like a gladiator's sword, driven two-handed straight into the heart. *Men do this*, he thought. *Not just one or two extraordinary men, far away by the Tiber or the Nile. Men do this, men who are living this life here and now.*

And I am not.

As if he were watching a play from the last row, he saw Alypius hand over the letters to Ponticianus and say how good it was to see him. He heard Ponticianus thank Alypius and promise to return them tomorrow. He watched his friend depart; Alypius went to see him out. When Alypius returned, he did not speak. He seemed to know Augustine would share his thoughts in his own time.

He was right, though it was not speaking so much as shouting.

"Look at us! What are we doing?" he burst out. "All that matters is what we are not doing. What good is all our learning if we still sit here day after day, while men who know far less understand the one truth that is needed and have the courage to grasp it?"

Augustine jumped up, his body energized by his thoughts, and ran out into the garden. Suddenly, Augustine felt as if he were on a ship deck again, rocked violently by forceful waves. He had hated the sea. In every moment of the voyage from Carthage, as he'd been tossed around by the waves, he had longed for firm ground. When at last he stepped ashore, he had nearly fallen down. The waves' tossing and turning seemed to have become part of his limbs.

Here and now in the garden, his limbs were under his control. They obeyed his will, but his will was in turmoil.

Alypius followed and stood silently, not knowing how to

help his friend but not willing to desert him. The sun was setting and he watched the struggle in Augustine's face and body in the shadows beneath the tall trees.

Augustine twisted his body this way and that, as if he were trying to break free of a chain. His face was flushed and feverish. He wanted release and now he knew the way. He had always told himself he waited for a certainty. Well, he had it, and he was afraid. Still, he held himself back. His own voice cried out *Yes*, and then *Tomorrow, tomorrow.*

Augustine collapsed on a stone bench and wept. Realizing he still held the book with the words of Paul, he set it down next to him and lowered his head into his hands. Then, as Alypius watched in amazement, Augustine jumped up once again and ran into the last light of evening.

Alypius was not the only witness to the strange scene of Augustine's torment. From a window above the garden, Adeodatus watched his father dash off in a seemingly mad state of agitation. *What is happening?* the boy wondered. He was not worried, but more curious and intrigued. He sensed a momentous change was about to take place in his father's life—and thus his too.

Tomorrow. Tomorrow.

Augustine stopped. Thankfully, Alypius had not followed him. Right now, he needed to be alone—that is, if a man could truly say he was alone when he stood in the presence of God.

How long, O Lord? he thought. He answered himself quickly: *Tomorrow.*

Why not now? Tomorrow was so safely near and so comfortingly far off. But God does not promise tomorrow to any man.

Augustine came to a big-leafed tree at a fork in the road not far from his home. Even through his tears, he noted it was a fig tree. *Not that it matters what sort of tree it is*, he thought, sinking down to sit beneath it.

What sort of man am I? Why can I not be rid of what I am? he prayed to God. *For years, I have asked you to give. I have asked for knowledge, for certainty, for joy. Should I have been asking you instead to take? To take away whatever in me is not yours?*

"Take. Read. Take. Read." A singsong voice floated above a nearby garden wall. It was a child's voice, chanting words from a children's game Augustine had long forgotten. The child's mother called him to come inside and get ready for bed.

Words from his last conversation swam through Augustine's mind, finally revealing the answer to him that he'd long been seeking:

"Surely, he had heard that saying before."

"Undoubtedly, but this time he listened."

"Take. Read."

Augustine stopped crying. Here was a straightforward command. A command a child could understand. He had only to obey.

He stood up and walked back to his house, passing quietly through the atrium and into his own garden. He returned to the bench, where Alypius waited. Augustine picked up the book he'd left, opened it, and looked down to read the first passage his eyes landed upon. It was from Paul's letter to the Romans. He read it silently—some words, he believed, can only be spoken in the heart: "Not in rioting and drunkenness, not in chambering and impurities, not in contention and envy: but put ye on the Lord Jesus Christ, and make not provision for the flesh in its concupiscences."

It was like the breaking of dawn, except it was evening. For years, the light had only found its way through chinks in the shutters. Now the shutters had burst apart, and Augustine stood fully in the sun. He was suddenly calm. He experienced exultation, but it felt like peace. He kept one finger in the book to mark his place—*Even though I will never lose those words*, he thought—and closed it. Then he turned to Alypius and described what he'd just felt and read.

He looked up and over the garden treetops. "I am resolved, from this hour, to belong to Christ," he said.

Alypius nodded solemnly. He received Augustine's words in silence. He was surprised, and at the same time he was not. For months, perhaps years, he had seen Augustine advance along that road. In his own mind, he had checked off the markers as, one by one, he saw the doubts fall away. He had known one chasm remained, gaping across the path. He knew well the pull of habit, once the senses had been trained in desire.

Augustine had wanted philosophy to be enough. He had wanted the will to be enough—to know the good, and to do it. That should be a man's life. Yet it had not been enough for Augustine. He had always looked farther down the road.

Alypius knew before Augustine did that the end of his road would be Christ. It was not difficult to see, knowing Augustine as he did, and knowing Monica even a little. Alypius understood the attraction. The Christ of the Scriptures was an interesting man. But the trouble was that he was clearly a man, and the Church would have him be a god clothed in a man's body. Alypius could not reconcile that idea with what he had read, so he could not take the name of Christian from the Church that preached it.

And yet . . . What would he not give, right now, to have that same glow he saw on Augustine's face, that same joy in his voice? He had been surprised it could come this way, all in a moment, from a child's command.

"May I?" Alypius gestured to the book. Augustine gave it to him readily. Alypius found the passage that had spoken to his friend, but he knew it was not the one for him. He read the next verse: "Now him that is weak in faith, take unto you." Having read what he needed, he closed the book and returned it to Augustine.

"We said—was it only an hour ago?—that I am now my own master. That is not entirely true. I am the one who is weak in faith, and I need a master to lead me in the right way," Alypius said. "I still doubt whether that master is the Church, but if you will grant it, I will take this road with you a while and see what comes of it."

"I would like nothing better!" Augustine replied. "I think you have been on the road all along, though you may not know it."

"We have hardly gone at the same pace," Alypius said with a smile.

"No, you are right—you walk and I run," Augustine laughed. "But I have run for so long, every which way except the way I should go, while you have been content to steadily set one foot in front of the other. We may not arrive so very far apart." Augustine took a deep breath, as if he had never truly breathed before. "We will speak more about this. We must. But right now, I need to do something before another minute passes."

"Of course," Alypius said, stepping back.

Augustine rushed out of his house. This time, Alypius followed.

Monica crossed the atrium on her way out to the cathedral for her evening prayers. With increasing frequency, a small voice whispered that if she truly cared about her son's soul, she would remain here and do something. Praying was the answer.

"Mother," Augustine's voice called.

She turned toward the sound and immediately took in his changed demeanor. She saw the book in his hand and the light in his eyes. She knew.

"Where you are, there am I," said Augustine. He stretched out his hands to her, but she was already in his arms.

His mother was small in stature, yet her personality was so fierce that she seemed big. Many times he had tried to escape her intense focus on his spiritual life. But now, finally, he understood her devotion, and he shared it. Monica had wanted for him only to feel the joy she felt, the same joy his father had experienced before dying.

Hugging her, Augustine realized he had always shared her intensity, and finally it had found its rightful purpose.

Chapter Fifteen

Augustine needed to make changes, and the first was to say goodbye to Livia. She took his words with little emotion—she had never expected to be part of his life for long. After gathering the few items she'd kept in his rooms, she departed Augustine's house, slipping out the door.

Augustine watched her go with relief. When he turned back to his desk, he knew another part of his life had to change: his work. To continue as a teacher of rhetoric—devoting his attention to words rather than to the Word—was unthinkable.

Augustine returned to the classroom just long enough to fulfill his obligations, but the exercises he'd set had interested him even less than they did his unruly pupils. The words sounded empty even as he delivered them to the classroom.

When the next vacation came, Augustine retired. He bid a final goodbye to his students and wished them well. Then he straightened up the classroom, took one last look around the room, and stepped out into the street.

That evening over dinner, he told Monica, Navigius, Adeodatus, and Alypius his joy at leaving his students in the hands of other, more patient teachers.

"What will you do now, Father?" Adeodatus asked. It was the question on all their minds.

"I have given it a lot of thought, my son, and I have an idea that we might all pay a visit to a country villa in Cassiacum, not far away." As all eyes turned to him, Augustine continued. "My friend Verecundus lives there and has offered his villa as a place for us to stay for a while. It has many gardens and a stream that runs through it—lots of space to explore, and peace and quiet in which to rest."

"I know Verecundus," Alypius said. "He is the teacher, a grammarian, who hired Nebridius to be his assistant here in Milan."

"That is the man. His wife is Christian," Augustine added, nodding in Monica's direction.

"How soon can we go?" Adeodatus asked.

"As soon as we can pack our belongings!"

The group settled happily in the spacious villa in Cassiacum. It was surrounded by gardens, gently sloping paths, and a wide terrace, where Augustine could read quietly. He decided to become a student again, to learn to know this God he now loved, and learn to see himself as God saw him. This seemed like an ideal spot in which to do this.

Day after day, Augustine read and reread the Psalms, and though he was alone, it seemed they enveloped him in the same way they had done in the darkened basilica, with voices responding to each other in prayer.

One evening, as the sun set, he sat with his mother on the

terrace. While Augustine read, Monica listened to the birds singing in the treetops overhead.

"Mother, when I think of the many years I spent with the Manichaeans, I am angry that I wasted so much time," Augustine said.

"Your anger should be pity, my son," Monica said. "The Manichaeans were offered the divine medicine, yet they clung to their sickness unto death. How can we not pity a blind man, especially a blind man who had no desire to see?"

"Yet," Augustine said, "there must be a way to make them see. I have been trained in rhetoric, the art of persuasion—"

"I have marveled that you have the ability to arrange words as a weaver arranges different threads on a loom so that the pattern, when complete, seems inevitable," Monica said.

"I have served the emperor with such words," Augustine said. "Now my words can be made to serve God. I will find the words to open the Manichaeans' eyes." As he declared this resolution, he stretched out his hand as if reaching for a pen lying ready nearby. There was no pen, but the Book of Psalms was still open on his knees. Evening had now arrived, and the world was growing dark as he had wrestled with the blindness of the Manichaeans.

It was time to get ready for sleep. He knew his task now, and it would be there when he awoke in the morning. He rose and bid his mother goodnight.

But in the morning, he woke with a painful toothache. It was so bad that he could not speak, let alone write persuasive paragraphs to illuminate theological truth. Adeodatus was sent running for garlic, but the household remedy had no effect. Monica sat by Augustine's side, determined to suffer with him. Alypius and Adeodatus hovered, knowing their presence was of no use but feeling it wrong to be anywhere else.

Ordinarily, Augustine would have disliked having everyone stand around him. He rolled over in bed and faced the wall. Strangely, he felt it was a bit like being back in the cathedral, where he was one voice among many voices raised together. With that thought came another, and he turned back to his family and signaled for the wax tablet and stylus Monica had placed nearby.

"Let us pray," he wrote, and he placed his Book of Psalms in Adeodatus's hands. Adeodatus recited the psalm his father had selected:

"When I called upon him, the God of my justice heard me: when I was in distress, thou hast enlarged me.

"Have mercy on me: and hear my prayer.

"O ye sons of men, how long will you be dull of heart? Why do you love vanity, and seek after lying?

"Know ye also that the Lord hath made his holy one wonderful: the Lord will hear me when I shall cry unto him.

"Be ye angry, and sin not: the things you say in your hearts, be sorry for them upon your beds.

"Offer up the sacrifice of justice, and trust in the Lord: many say, Who showeth us good things?

"The light of thy countenance, O Lord, is signed upon us: thou hast given . . ."

Suddenly, Augustine's toothache was gone. He sat up abruptly, and Adeodatus left off his reading. They were all surprised and pleased with Augustine's recovery. As he rose and began putting on his tunic, Augustine told his family and friends to get on with their day, as he was restored. Once alone in his room, he sat on the edge of his bed, his mind working.

Outside in the hallway, Monica worried. When the toothache subsided, she feared Augustine's eager resolution to write had disappeared with it.

But she had no reason to worry. Augustine would write in the days to come; however, he wanted to be sure his intentions were pure.

Let the words not be mine. Let them be yours. And the outcome will be yours, and in your time, he prayed. *I am not the light. At most, I can reflect the light. I did not open my own eyes—why should I think I could open the eyes of others? It is for you, Lord, to open their eyes, as in your mercy you opened mine. Let me speak of your mercy.*

Adeodatus, now fifteen, sat with his father on the villa's stone terrace. He had just returned from a long hike with new friends he'd made from the nearby villas. Monica, with Navigius, had gone to the village to purchase food, and Alypius and Nebridius had returned to Milan for business.

While birds flitted in and out of the shrubs, Adeodatus watched his father reading and writing quietly at the table. He struggled to understand the meaning of his father's recent transformation, but he recognized it was significant. He appreciated that his father made it clear he would not compel Adeodatus to believe—and this made him even more curious. The boy enjoyed speaking with Augustine on philosophical matters as a kind of intellectual game; he'd been watching his father work from afar with deep curiosity for a long time now.

"Why is Father always talking with his friends?" he had once asked Titrit when he was no more than six.

"He is a philosopher and teacher. That's what men like him do," she replied.

"But I don't understand what they are saying," the boy said.

"Neither do I," Titrit said, smiling, "but he does, and that is what matters."

Adeodatus frowned. "I heard one of his friends ask him a question last night, and Father said, 'I don't know.'"

"That is why he is a good man," Titrit said. "He seeks understanding, not praise as the man who has all the answers."

"He's not like my friends' fathers—his hands are never dirty from work," Adeodatus pointed out.

"Your father's work is different. He seeks . . . knowledge. He needs to ask questions and find answers to help him understand."

Adeodatus frowned again but let his mother's words sink in.

As he grew older, Adeodatus learned from Augustine that asking questions was important, and seeking the right answers mattered. Sometimes, talking about the answers could take hours or days, but it was always an interesting pursuit. The goal of speech should be to expound truth. As his beloved mother had expertly guided his first steps, his father had expertly guided his mind.

Adeodatus was becoming a quick thinker, to Augustine's great pride. It was as natural for Adeodatus to seek truth as it was to put one foot in front of the other. He did not think about the doing of either one; he thought only of where he wanted to go.

"What is happiness?" Augustine set the question before his son as a way to open a discussion about truth.

It was the question he posed again and again in those months at Cassiacum. Happiness must be that which could not be taken away, he said. If a man could lose something, he feared to lose it, and then he was not happy. That much was obvious. Then happiness could not belong to the body, for anything that was of the body could be lost. That left the soul. The man—the soul—that possessed God was happy, for only God was or could be eternal.

This much the teenage Adeodatus was able to follow. The question of which god was God, and how one could possess him, was less clear. In this, he had followed his father, but not in the way his father might have thought.

For all of Adeodatus's life, his father had spoken of philosophy. Whatever his father thought or believed, there had still been a woman in his life who was not a wife. No philosophy had changed that, until now. Adeodatus did not understand all the claims of Catholicism, but he knew that in order to become a Catholic, his father had changed not only his way of thinking, but his way of life. This church had a power that nothing else had.

"I'm going for a walk next to the stream," Adeodatus said, standing and stretching his long arms. "Would you like to join me?"

Augustine looked up at his son and noticed how tall he was getting. "Yes, I would like that very much," he said, setting down his pen and closing his books. "Perhaps we can find a new path to explore together."

Approaching the villa in her return from town, Monica stopped at the sight of her son and grandson walking down to the stream together in the distance. They were deep in conversation, obviously enjoying each other's company. She smiled, her heart filled with love. What would she ever do if she lost either one of them? She shrugged off the thought.

"Do you see now?" Augustine asked.

Alypius turned around quickly in the cold December morning air at the sound. He had been awake since dawn. In fact, he had not slept at all the night before. Just a few minutes earlier, he'd slipped out of the villa and discovered the ground frozen hard with a light covering of snow.

To set one foot in front of the other, and then to do so again. The point of making a journey was to reach a destination. The point of asking a question was to receive an answer. The Church provided answers, but Alypius didn't even know the right questions.

All night he'd contemplated this conundrum: A man who was God, a God who was man. It seemed like a contradiction, but grant that one contradiction and everything else fit, with Christ as the center and keystone.

So, somewhere in the night, Alypius had surrendered to Christ. He could not fix the exact time, but he had done it at last. His next task was to tell Augustine and the others. Then he had to submit his name as a candidate for baptism. But he had to confront himself—the self he had been, the self he still was. So here he was, on the frozen ground.

When the sun climbed a little way into the sky, enough to soften the snow, Alypius returned to the villa. Noticing his friend was gone, Augustine had been on the lookout for him. As Alypius drew nearer, his friend smiled.

"You see now?" Augustine asked again, quietly. He'd sensed Alypius's struggles in the previous weeks and purposely left him alone.

"I see God. And in seeing him, I see everything I need to see," Alypius replied.

At sunrise on Holy Saturday, Bishop Ambrose finished morning prayer, then entered the baptistery. The catechumens waited, standing around the edges of the shallow, octagonal pool that signified death and life. Among them were Augustine, Alypius, and Adeotatus.

Ambrose was about to offer these people their final instruction, and it was his last chance before the Sacrament to explain how both were real: the death to sin must be a true death, and the life . . . was Life Himself.

The ceremony was simple. Any basilica priest or deacon could have told the catechumens what to do and what to expect. A young subdeacon had once spoken that thought aloud, in curiosity rather than disrespect. Ambrose had happened to hear, and he had answered calmly that these souls were about to be reborn, and he was their bishop.

The inscription on the wall of the baptistery had been written by Ambrose years before. It was a reminder that the eight sides of the pool represented the eight days of creation: seven, and then the day of the new creation in Jesus Christ. Under the old law, circumcision was done on the eighth day, that the covenant with Abraham might be written in the flesh of his people. Now there was a new law, a new covenant, a new eighth day.

First, he explained, they would make a renunciation. They would renounce the devil and his works, the world and its pleasures. Then, having faced the father of lies, they would turn to the east, to the Son of Truth. They would come to the octagonal pool, and there they would see only water, but they must discern the invisible aspects of God through the visible aspects he had made.

"So it had been from the beginning, when the Spirit moved upon the waters," Ambrose said. "The grace of the Spirit is turned away by the impurity of sin, unless it be washed clean in the water. And as Noah sent out two birds—the raven that did not return and the dove that did—so their sin must be sent out from them and the Spirit be welcomed in. The Egyptians were swallowed up in the Red Sea; the Israelites passed through to the other side.

"Consider also that Moses cast wood into the bitter waters of Marah and so made them sweet," Ambrose explained simply. "The water is of no avail without the wood of the cross of the Lord."

Ambrose scanned the faces of the small group in front of him, wondering, as did they, what their own crosses would be.

~

That night, the moment finally came: Ambrose baptized Augustine, Adeodatus, and Alypius one by one with quiet words and a gentle touch of the cool water.

Augustine walked home afterward in the golden sunlight of Milan, looking at the familiar streets with new eyes. He felt a profound peace, his soul unified in a way he'd never experienced before. He was happy.

Chapter Sixteen

For the first few weeks, it was enough just to be. Augustine was free of his past life and was surrounded by his family and friends in a beautiful villa near Milan. He was able to study in peace and write for hours. It was more than enough—he was in the present, and this was good.

But sooner or later, he mused one night after everyone else had gone to bed, he would have to make decisions for his future.

It was winter and the evenings were dark and cold. He thought of Titrit. He had decided he would not marry the girl his mother had found for him—he had no interest. He had set down the desires of the flesh on a garden bench and had no wish to take them up again, even in a licit form. If a desire always took just a little more room than it was given, it was best to give it no room at all. Perhaps there was one such desire for each man. Augustine knew this was the way it was for him. So much for what he would not do.

As for what he *would* do, one obvious step was to return to teaching. Augustine paced the villa's atrium, imagining how he could teach again. Perhaps now he could teach the Word of God instead of the words of men. Yet teaching meant he would lead a public life in which the measure of success was public praise. A man who earned a living by words must, to some degree, speak words for which people were willing to pay. It was then a dangerously small step to believe that words for which people were willing to pay must be good words.

He strolled through the garden, enveloped in evening shadows, and sat down on a bench. He let his mind wander to the dream of leaving everything behind, all the more now that he knew men who did just that. Suddenly, an idea came to him. Since he had turned away from marriage, he was now free to pursue the monastic ideal. He rose and returned to the house as details formulated in his mind. He climbed the steps to his bedroom, telling himself that if the idea persisted the next morning, he would share it with his family.

"Please join me this morning. I need to speak with you all," Augustine told them. The morning had brought new clarity to his vision—he wanted to make it real. "I have an idea of creating . . . a new community, a monastic community," he began. He proposed that they find a location where they could study, write, and teach. Others of like mind would be invited to join them.

"My answer is yes," Alypius said immediately after Augustine described the plan. "I have thought of a similar idea—it is a natural step for you and for me."

"I want to be part of it," Adeodatus said with a sincerity that surprised and pleased Augustine.

"For myself . . . I must return home to Thagaste," Navigius

said. "The olive trees need tending more than any philosophy." Augustine smiled at his brother and nodded with understanding.

"I will go with either of you," Monica said, looking from one son to the other.

"And I must go back to Carthage to be near my mother, who still lives there," Nebridius said.

"I see we are coming to a decision," Augustine said. They would return to Africa to establish a new home of study and prayer. It all seemed beautifully easy, and so it might have been, were it not for the civil war.

Once again, Empress Justina's influence bore down on all of them. Augustine warily followed her activities as much as he could. For four years, while Theodosius I reigned unchallenged in the East, the West had had two de facto emperors. Valentinian II might wear the purple, but he was still a boy, and many people—beginning with soldiers in Britain but not ending there—preferred the successful commander Magnus Maximus. Maximus had been content to share for a time, keeping to the North in exchange for recognition from Theodosius and Valentinian.

But Justina's Arian sympathies lost her the love of more than Bishop Ambrose. Magnus saw his chance and marched on Italy; Justina and Valentinian decamped to Thessalonica, where Justina pleaded for Theodosius's aid and offered her beautiful daughter, Galla, as an inducement. Now, shipping throughout the Mediterranean was thrown into disarray.

Augustine and his party left the villa near Milan and

journeyed south to Rome, but the ports were blockaded, which meant for now they could travel no farther. They settled down at Ostia, in sight of the sea, and awaited the outcome of royal whim and divine will.

"Death is an evil for the evil and a good for the good," Augustine declared.

Today, he and his friends, brother, and son carried their conversation into a cook shop, just to have somewhere different to go. Monica had chosen to remain behind in their rented villa, to spend her time in prayer. They walked there past the dust and the noise of construction. An old apartment building was being gutted and rebuilt as a coastal villa for a knight or senator. By comparison, the cook shop seemed a haven of peace, and they were glad to come in off the street.

They were talking about the contrasting ends of the wicked and of the just. Augustine and Alypius took the lead, while Adeodatus carefully followed the conversation and put in a question whenever it lagged. Nebridius weighed each opinion he heard and matched it against what had already been said and what he already knew. Navigius set himself to listen. He wished he could be elsewhere, but he was unable to hit upon anyplace better.

"Death is not a good," Adeodatus objected.

Alypius smiled. "Not death itself, perhaps. Distinguish the state from its effects."

"The state of death?" Augustine asked, caught by the word. "There hangs a question. When can a man be said to be 'in death'?"

"Anyone can see when a man is dying," Navigius grumbled. "It does not require philosophy."

Augustine threw up his hands. "Hear my brother! If anyone can see when a man is dying, then it follows that the judgement also does not require a physician. Whereas it is the mark of the philosopher, because he loves wisdom, to acknowledge there is wisdom he does not possess. I would not claim to make a judgement about a man's illness, or to be able to reason him back to health."

"You could reason him out of it," Alypius said. Before Augustine could answer, Alypius took up the question again. "To be dying is not to be in death. We only say a man is dying while he is still alive. To be dying is to be approaching death."

Augustine laughed. "Then when is a man not dying? From the moment we are born, we are set on the road to death. The only thing we do not know is the length of the journey."

"It would follow that we are all, all of us and at all times, both in life and in death." Alypius frowned as he spoke, but he could draw no other conclusion.

Navigius shook his head—he was impatient with this kind of talk. Augustine glanced at him, and at that glance, Navigius's shoulders fell and he shifted his eyes away from the group.

Augustine watched him a moment before speaking. "I think my brother may have been right." Navigius snorted quietly, but Augustine continued, "In speaking of the moment of death, we may do well to abandon philosophy and return to common usage. After all, if we take any moment, not just the moment of death, we know perfectly well what it is until we try to define it.

As soon as we speak of the present moment, it is past. And let us recall our original topic was the fate of the soul after death. In regard to the body, it does not matter how we arrive there. When we have arrived, we shall be eternally in life or eternally in death. There is no *and*; there is a simple *or*. It is a choice we must all make, philosopher or not. And common usage may guide a man no less surely than philosophy."

With those last words, Augustine watched Navigius, and Navigius did not return the look. Augustine followed his gaze and realized he was staring at a man seated in a nearby corner, his back to the wall. Augustine felt he should know him. As soon as the man smiled, Augustine realized he did.

"Evodius." Navigius spoke the name first—it was a name from their younger days from home, found here on the other side of the sea. He had not been a close friend to either brother. Unlike Navigius, he had desired from an early age to see the Empire of which Thagaste, and even Africa itself, was a part. But unlike Augustine, he desired order, stability, and the pure light of day. He had gone away to serve the Empire. Augustine wondered how much of it he had seen.

Evodius jumped to his feet and came toward them. The brothers greeted him, introduced him to their friends, and poured wine as everyone shifted to make room at the table.

Evodius asked pardon for not having made himself known sooner. "I wanted to be sure it was really you, Augustine of Thagaste, sitting in a cook shop in Ostia and holding forth on life and death and the soul. How is it you are here, so far from home?"

Augustine caught Alypius's eye. "There is no brief answer to that question," he said.

"Then make your answer as long as it needs to be," Evodius said. Nebridius, who had been watching and weighing this new arrival, nodded in approval.

Augustine told the tale in its full length, while the cook shop owner watched the movement of the sun in the sky and wondered if he would ever get his table back, or if at least this strange group would order supper. Evodius listened in attentive stillness. He asked the occasional question, but for the most part he allowed Augustine to tell the story, including several digressions. His expression gave little indication of his own thoughts. Only when Augustine reached the moment of his conversion in the garden did Evodius smile.

"I too," Evodius said.

Augustine's face lit up, the soul shining through the flesh at this discovery of unlooked-for brotherhood. "God be praised!" he cheered. "Tell us how it happened." The cook shop owner sighed and calculated the hours until closing.

Evodius took a moment to arrange the facts in his mind. "I had spent too much time in places like this. I served the emperor, and my task was to find those who were less willing to serve him. So up and down Italy I drank and dined, and with everyone I spoke to, sooner or later I spoke against the emperor. I remembered the names of everyone who agreed with me, and I reported them."

He looked down at the tabletop. "I know," he said grimly, though no one had judged him. "I believed the Empire was the best, if not the only, guarantor of peace and common good. Every civilization builds palaces and temples. What other civilization has built roads and aqueducts? Rome not only protects its citizens but gives them life. Peace is needed to preserve that life. I thought peace was an ideal worth serving, even at the cost of my own disquiet. We are Romans, are we not? What is our own private good compared to the good of the state? To sacrifice my life would be a small thing. Yet, somehow this felt much greater, and I could not understand why. I told myself it did not matter. I should have the courage to say yes to any sacrifice. So I continued to say yes, until the day I summoned enough courage to say no."

"What happened?" Adeodatus asked. To a boy of fifteen, this was a good story that neared its climax.

Evodius shook his head. "It is on the other side of the river of life. I will not bring it to this side, not even in words. I decided peace could not be bought with blood."

They all reflected in silence. Then Alypius asked, "What will you do now?"

"I intended to return home. It seemed the proper place to begin life over again, and Thagaste is far enough from any seat of government that I could leave behind the temptation to try to make heaven on earth. That plan has now been . . . somewhat delayed."

"I think I know why," Augustine said, leaning forward. As the cook shop owner had somehow known he would, he said, "Let me tell you everything that is in our minds."

~

Evodius agreed to join them in the community they planned to establish in Africa. They were overjoyed at his decision. For Augustine, it was also a quiet rebuke. While traveling the many miles south, he had been dreading the voyage to come, but when they had reached Ostia and discovered they would have to wait indefinitely, it felt like more than he could bear. Why could the journey not simply be done? He had so many plans for the destination.

Through our delay, you gave us Evodius, he said to God. *What else will you give, if we stop cursing the delay and praise it instead as your gift?*

Ostia was a port town, known for ships and salt and, more recently, the villas of the wealthy who wanted to breathe sea air. Forced to accept the delay, Augustine and his group decided to explore Rome, only a few hours away.

Augustine's memories of Rome were dominated by sickness, fog, and frustration. Alypius's memories were filled with the law courts and the amphitheater. Now they looked for a different Rome. In contrast to the splendid palaces and temples, the tall columns and the statues, they wanted to see its less visible treasures. Some of it, in fact, lay underground, in catacombs that wound beneath the streets and the gardens of the living.

From the outside, the most notable feature of Rome's churches was the crowd of beggars clustered around their doors. When Augustine saw them, it struck him that the beggars truly were a part of the building. It seemed as if the coins given to them on the threshold opened the great doors, and that was not far from the truth.

Inside the doors, Augustine and his group were greeted first by a latticework screen at which, during the sacred celebrations, a door-keeper stood guard, ensuring only those who had accepted the sacrifice could participate in its offering.

Beyond the screen, the basilica's nave stretched to the choir and finally to the altar. Between them was another screen, this one of columns, joined by a balustrade. In the temple, only the high priest could enter the holy of holies and only once a year. Here, every day was a day of atonement, and here, the man consecrated to be the voice and the hands of the great high priest entered into the presence of God.

Augustine liked churches best at night, when candles that hung from chandeliers and clustered about the altar made the marble columns and the mosaics gleam, drawing flashes of fire from the golden votive offerings placed on the balustrade. He felt this was the true world, or at least its antechamber, and everything outside was its shadow.

On the road back to Ostia from the center of Rome, Augustine insisted they make a stop. Here on the bank of the Tiber was the spot where Paul of Tarsus rested, having finished his race. The Tiber was a slow-moving river with heavy, old trees leaning over the water from the banks. Paul's body was held at the center of a construction site. The small church Constantine built there had been completely redesigned only the year before, and now the structural supports of the beautiful basilica that was to take its place arched toward heaven, cradling Paul's undisturbed tomb.

It was a peaceful afternoon when they found this spot. By instinct, they stopped talking and simply sat in the soft grass on the riverbank, each one lost in thought about Paul: Paul and his conversion, Paul and his teachings, Paul and the beginnings of the Church.

The group traveled back to Ostia, to the simple single-story home where they were staying. As with most Roman homes, this one featured a small but lush garden.

One afternoon, Augustine returned early from the baths feeling restless. He'd left the other young men of the group to continue discussing the topic of the day because it all began to feel pointless—he wanted solitude.

Finally back inside the house, he wandered through the rooms, not quite sure what he was looking for. As soon as he entered the back of the house, he saw his mother sitting at the windowsill, looking out peacefully at the garden. Without a word, he joined her on the small bench with embroidered pillows. He too gazed out at the pretty garden with blossoming trees and shrubs.

"In Thagaste," she began, without greeting him, for sometimes speaking to her son was a natural continuation of her thoughts, "I could name every plant I saw from our windows. In their familiarity, they spoke to me of God. I do not know the names of so many of the plants here, yet I find that their strangeness speaks to me of God. They tell me I am far from home, but that here he will still provide a garden."

"And why should he not? He meant us to live in a garden. We are faithless; he is not," Augustine said.

Monica turned to him with a laugh. "Then in heaven, will there be more flower names to learn?"

"There is nothing to learn there. The blessed do not learn. They know," Augustine said quietly.

"What must that be, to know?"

"I . . ." It was his turn to laugh. "I do not know."

But he wanted to know, and so did she. Mother and son spoke quietly together about knowing, about the senses and created objects as they were known by the senses. Now that they were on the same side of faith, they understood each other perfectly. Everything before them—the trees, flowers, shrubs, even the heavens themselves—would pass away, they agreed, but the cause of them would not pass away, for that was wisdom, and wisdom is eternal. For wisdom, there is no past, present, or future.

Monica and Augustine stopped speaking, feeling these ideas wash through their hearts. For an instant almost too small to be counted part of time, Augustine thought he could taste the knowing—not on his tongue alone, but in his whole body. He could taste with his fingertips. Yet as soon as he had the thought, he was aware of it. As soon as he was aware of it, he tried to grasp it with his reason. And it vanished.

There was salt in the air, as there always was at Ostia, and this reminded Monica of the ocean journey from Africa to Italy. The thought of the return voyage made her ask, "My son, what should I do? I am still here, but I do not know why. I have lived my life in hope, but today I have the fulfillment of it beyond even my prayers, here before my eyes. What should I do?"

Augustine simply held his mother's hands and smiled.

Sounds of the others returning to the house made them turn toward the door. Adeodatus went from room to room, seeking his father to ask him a question that had arisen as they walked. He found Augustine and Monica sitting together in silence at the window, and he knew without being told that they were looking upon things the eye could not see. He turned and left the room.

Part Three

A LAMP IN THE WIND

Chapter Seventeen

His earliest memories were of olive trees, his favorite being the times when he and Navigius had gone out with their father to watch the turning of the press.

Now here he stood, decades later, at the same spot, watching the same press. Augustine doubted it was the same mule in the harness, but he could not tell by looking. No, the real difference in this scene was himself.

It was a hot day, and sweat covered the workers' faces. Olives disappeared beneath the slow turn of the grinding stone. Then olive pulp was stacked in the press on fiber disks that would allow nothing through except clear, flowing oil.

Augustine observed the age-old process, but his mind wandered. He'd just received devastating news: Nebridius, the trusted friend with whom he shared every question, every doubt, and every discovery, had died.

The letter Augustine held in his hand was the most recent correspondence that had reached him from Italy across the sea. Long before, he and Nebridius had begun the search for wisdom together as young men, and they had continued it together even when they were on different continents. All he had left of Nebridius now were many long letters and fine memories.

Nebridius too found wisdom in the end, Augustine thought. *He died in the Catholic Church. He died in hope. The life after death is the life for which we pray and work. It is the life that matters.*

To mourn him is not to mourn for him, but to mourn for myself. Is that the action of a friend? My sorrow is nothing if he has found joy.

Augustine smiled as he recalled when he and Nebridius were boys in Carthage. They had felt themselves alone in the middle of a crowd and were content to have it that way. He could almost hear Nebridius telling him, "Be content, right now." If he was alone, was he not alone with God?

Only a few months ago, he had written to Nebridius of his need to set himself apart from the toil and confusion of this life in order to prepare for the life to come. Perhaps there were some men who could do both—men who could both be Christ's shepherds and remember all the while that they were still sheep themselves—but he needed tranquility and solitude.

I did not mean this much solitude, Augustine thought.

Losing Nebridius hurt deeply, but this was just Augustine's most recent loss. A few months before, Augustine's mother had died just as they were preparing to leave Ostia. Monica had taken to her bed with a fever, telling her son this was where she was to rest. Navigius, who had been with her at the passing of her husband and who knew of her hope to lie beside him, thought to cheer her and expressed a confidence, greater than he felt, that surely she would return home.

She had looked past Navigius to Augustine, who stood silently beside his brother and discovered a different meaning to the word *home*. What did it matter where her body lay? She would never be distant from God. It was the disposition of her soul on which she dwelled, and about which she made her only request to her sons: "Wherever you may find yourselves, remember me at the altar of the Lord," she had said to them.

Augustine promised he would. Now Monica, like Simeon in the Temple, had seen what she had been promised, and God would let her depart in peace. For the sake of that certainty, Augustine had restrained his tears, even as he watched her draw her last breath. He had reached down to close her eyes. The cry in his heart was expressed out loud by another voice: Adeodatus, kneeling at the foot of the bed, had let out a wail. Alypius had placed his hands on his shoulders and whispered to him, and he was quiet.

Evodius, who'd had the psalter ready, began to chant: "Mercy and judgement I will sing to thee, O Lord."

"I will sing, and I will understand in the unspotted way, when thou shalt come to me," the others answered him.

"I walked in the innocence of my heart, in the midst of my house."

"I did not set before my eyes any unjust thing: I hated the workers of iniquities."

Later, when the house was full of people who gathered to

help make funeral plans, Augustine stepped out into the garden. Exchanging a glance, Alypius and Evodius followed him. They waited for him to speak, and he directed the conversation, as was only fitting, to the glories promised to the just in their true home.

But as he spoke with his friends, he also spoke silently to God: *They think I should not be left alone. They marvel that I have not wept, and they think I should be encouraged to speak my grief in order that it might bring me the release of tears. But, oh, my God, why should I grieve? Should I not rather rejoice? She has conquered. She has been faithful in small matters and in great, and now your arms have opened and invited her to share her master's joy. What is there in that to grieve? Nothing. Only this: In coming to you, she has departed from me. There was a single life made up of our two lives, and because she is gone that life is also gone, and that life was my life. The wound is fresh. It is my wound, so I feel it more than I feel the joy that is hers.*

Now Augustine returned to the most painful loss of all. His beloved son, Adeodatus, at the tender age of sixteen, had died suddenly of an illness.

Adeodatus had been taken by fever at the same age Augustine was when he had first gone to Carthage, ready for adventure. *At the age when so much of life began for me, you chose to give him an ending,* Augustine prayed to God. *I do not ask why. From my great sin you fashioned my great gift, and shall I now complain if I must render that gift back unto you?*

Augustine wondered how he could reach Titrit to tell her of

their son's death. *For all I know, she already knows,* he thought. *When my mother died, I felt the pain that the living feel. In this, I feel only darkness. Darkness has no existence in itself. It is the absence of light. How can I feel an absence? How can that absence be more real to me than anything I see, hear, taste, smell, or touch?*

You are a father, he prayed to God. *You gave your son for mine, and from all eternity, you knew it would be so. Your word is eternal, and eternally speaks everything that was and is and will be. Because all that is created comes to be and passes away, your word speaks when they will come to be and when they will pass away. You know the times and seasons that are best for each man. Your purpose may be hidden, but it can never be unjust. If it is your will that I know the justice of this, thy will be done. If it is not your will, thy will be done.*

Each of Augustine's losses somehow made the others more vivid. Augustine reflected that no relationship is only between two people. Each bond creates multiple bonds, stretching through society—indeed, creating society. Society begins with kinship, and to break one bond is to break every bond that had been formed from it. So it is to love what is born to die.

Yet the answer would never be not to love, even if that were possible, he thought. *The trick is to see every human being as one of infinite worth, and at the same time as nothing in comparison to God. And whenever we contemplate a particular man, and the balance tips to one side or the other, we must level it off—or, I think, it will be leveled for us.*

Suddenly, Navigius was standing beside him, watching the workers at the olive press. He ran the oil production now and supervised the workers' movements closely. But he knew the contents of the letter in Augustine's hands and understood how deeply his brother was suffering. So, he did not question him, but instead dipped in a finger to taste the oil. He had always preferred to do the pressing early, when the olives still had a flush of green. More was lost to pulp and they yielded less oil, but that oil was purer and more highly sought. Navigius lingered over the flavor as another man might test wine. He nodded.

Augustine watched his brother with admiration. He'd never thought seriously about Navigius's work before, but he had a new respect for it now. *What must it be like to taste the fruit of one's labor and to find it good?* Augustine wondered with envy.

He always believed Navigius was content with his life—possibly more resigned to it than truly satisfied. But now Augustine wondered, *Or is it that he was placed, from the first, where he was meant to be? And if that is so, then why have I, for all my wandering, not yet found where I am meant to be?*

On an impulse, he went to join Navigius at the press. "I have been thinking . . ." he began.

Navigius smiled a little. "You do not need to tell me that."

Augustine laughed. "I need to tell you what I am thinking. I am glad to be home again for many reasons, but for one, perhaps, above all."

"Augustine, there is no need . . ."

"Here there is enough oil for me to work through the night. I thank you."

Navigius met his eyes. He was surprised, and he made haste

to turn the emotion into a different kind of surprise. "You are returning to writing your book?" he asked.

"It is agony," Augustine said, "but writing the book also makes the agony possible to bear."

Navigius shook his head. He did not understand his brother, but this time it did not matter. Augustine left him to his work and returned to the house where they had grown up. He and his friends were staying there for a few months while they considered locations for their monastic community. And it was a peaceful place for Augustine to concentrate on the book.

Augustine's book was a distillation of conversations with Adeodatus on the role of the teacher. It had been nearly complete when Adeodatus died. Now Augustine was revising it. He needed this work, though at first he did not understand why. Contemplating the loss of Nebridius helped him to understand. It was not Nebridius's presence he mourned, for they had so often been separated. He had delighted in his friend's company when he could have it, but when he could not, he had his letters. And while Augustine had the letters, he had Nebridius.

Someone with whom I could think, that was Nebridius, and that was Adeodatus, he thought. *That was the love of friendship, as distinct from the love we owe to all mankind. And that love can continue in the work of thinking. I cannot write about my son's death, so I will write about his life.*

With new energy, Augustine returned to working on the book.

Here was Adeodatus, puzzling over the meaning of the word

nothing, because words are signs, and a sign cannot point to something that does not exist.

Here he was himself, moving the discussion along in the worry that nothing should delay their inquiry. For in such a context, there could be use even for a pun.

Here again was Adeodatus, now arguing that some signs were greater than the things they signified, for the word *vice* was not itself vicious.

And here he was himself, pointing out that the understanding of the thing itself was greater than the sign.

And here were they both together, agreeing that the role of the teacher was not, in the end, to teach. No one can know a thing from another's words. At the most, he can believe it. To absolutely know a thing is true, that must come from the light of truth within each man—and that light is Christ. Each man teaches himself through Christ, who is the only teacher.

We have nothing that we have not received. And what we receive, we do not receive from other men, except insofar as you use them to direct us toward yourself, Augustine prayed to God. *How do you mean to use me? Let me not hinder it.*

Augustine smiled as he reviewed the writing. He sat back and looked out the window, spotting Navigius far off, talking to one of the olive press workers. From another room in the house he could hear Alypius speaking to Evodius in a cheerful exchange. A horse whinnied as its rider passed the house on the way to town.

Augustine took it all in. *Life continues*, he thought. For the first time in months, his mood lifted.

Chapter Eighteen

"Does the town have a bishop?" Augustine asked.

"It does," Evodius replied. "His name is Valerius, a Greek. He has little Latin, they say, but he is undoubtedly a bishop. My friend Cornelius explains it all here." Evodius handed Augustine the letter he had just received. They sat in the atrium of the house in Thagaste.

Augustine took the letter because it had been offered, not because he doubted Evodius. He had asked the question out of a newly formed habit of self-preservation. The Church in Africa reminded him of their stay at Ostia: for the blockading ships of Maximus, substitute Manichaeans, Donatists, and the uncountable pagan gods. Besieged by such forces, faithful people were constantly in search of true champions. Augustine would make a formidable champion of faith, and many people knew it. To his mind, far too many people knew it. He had left Africa as a teacher and a Manichaean and returned as a former court professor of rhetoric and a convert of Ambrose, Bishop of Milan. The news of Augustine's return had spread, and his reputation as a man of eloquence and devotion grew.

His friends were less surprised than he was. It was a simple fact that if anyone—man or woman, slave or free, consul or child—asked Augustine a question, he would answer it with eloquence. Now people came to Augustine with questions wherever he went. Many others sent letters seeking his advice and words of wisdom.

With good reason, Augustine was in constant fear of being called to ordination when he traveled. If the city of Hippo Regius, just north of Thagaste, already had a bishop, it would be safe enough to go there.

The idea of the monastic life still animated Augustine and his friends, and they still searched for a suitable spot upon which to establish their monastery. Along the way, they had been looking for more companions to join in the adventure. Now a trip to Hippo Regius, all the way to the edge of the sea, offered the possibility of both.

Evodius had asked his friend Cornelius, who lived in Hippo Regius, about the town's suitability for a monastery. Cornelius was a former member of the emperor's secret police. He shared Evodius's doubts as to whether service in the secret police was honorable, but he had not yet made the decision to renounce his career. In his letter, Cornelius answered all his questions and expressed joy at the prospect of meeting the great teacher Augustine in Hippo Regius.

"Another journey seems clearly indicated," Augustine said, handing the letter back to Evodius. "It will be, God willing, one step closer to rest. Let us leave tomorrow."

Hippo Regius, the great port of Numidia, sat on the northern part of Africa on the Mediterranean Sea. It was called royal because the ancient Numidian kings, the men who had ruled before there was an emperor, had made it their chief dwelling. Now the kings were gone, but the word *royal* still applied, for the harbor was the most direct link with Rome for this province. As a port, it was well guarded. The walls were strong.

The town was also a convenient meeting place, as it was situated halfway between Carthage and the Numidian capital of Cirta. Within those walls dwelled about forty thousand citizens, and though they called themselves Christian, most kept an amulet close by, just in case.

The priests said that Christ would have them consider the world to come. That was fine to consider in church on Sunday, and if facing death, when of course eternity would matter. But during the six other days of the week, a man might need rain to save a crop, or a woman might need help when she felt the pangs of childbirth coming on. It was common sense, they thought, to bring these matters to gods whose primary care was this world here below.

The dominant strain of Christianity in Hippo Regius was represented by the Donatist sect, whose bishop had forbidden the bakers to bake bread for the Catholics, and the prohibition was largely obeyed. "But here and there," Cornelius said, explaining the situation to Augustine after he had arrived in the city, "one of the bakers takes pity on us. Or he reasons that the same coins pass through the hands of the just and the unjust alike. Whatever the reason, I have bread to offer you."

Cornelius had invited Augustine to dinner at his house,

which was small and simple but appointed with a tasteful harmony that spoke eloquently of its owner. That was why, when they entered the dining room, Augustine's gaze was drawn immediately to the one ugly object present. A short sword, its grip cracked with age and its blade notched, hung prominently on the wall in a place of honor.

"It was my father's," Cornelius said, noting Augustine's interest. "It is the only item of his I have left. I have carried it with me through all my postings."

They sat down to a lavish dinner of fish, figs, roast peacock, and plenty of wine. Cornelius was a gracious host, clearly eager to spare no effort in service to his famous guest. He was also anxious to waste no time, and as his hands were busy with platters or flagons, he asked Augustine question after question, listening attentively to each answer.

Finally, when Augustine told him of the planned monastery, silence fell. Cornelius peeled a fig. "Where will it be?" he asked.

"I do not know as yet," Augustine answered. "Perhaps somewhere here in Hippo Regius. We are still searching and praying."

"Then it will be some time before your plan becomes real."

"It may be," Augustine replied. "Is that any reason for you not to make an answer now?"

Cornelius set down the fig he had peeled. He took up another and began peeling it. "Is there anything wrong with my present life?" he asked.

"Nothing I can see, except that it is yours rather than Christ's," Augustine said.

"I once gave my life wholly to a man. Or rather, to an idea embodied in a man. I don't know if I can do it a second time. I feel there is no service I would not do, and do gladly, if it were only—"

"If it were done only on your terms?" Augustine smiled.

"Yes." Cornelius abandoned the fig and the fruit knife. "Is there anything left in you that remains only you?"

"Far too much," Augustine replied solemnly.

"And you intend to defeat it by retreating from the world?" Cornelius asked with a look of consternation.

"It is the only way I can see. I am not strong enough for anything else."

Cornelius rose. "Will you allow me to think before I give you my answer?"

"Of course," Augustine said, also rising from his chair. He sensed the evening had come to an end. "Thank you for your welcome and for your hospitality."

Cornelius slowly walked with him to the door.

As Augustine strolled back to his lodging, he reflected that he completely understood Cornelius's hesitation. Who could understand it better? But God was mighty, and Augustine knew he had been brought here to this city for a reason. What reason could there be, except a yes from Cornelius?

The following day was . . . the sixth day of the week. Augustine refused to refer to the days by their Roman names. Why should he, even in name, give to the gods what God had created?

Least of all should the day upon which the Lord had suffered be honored as the Day of Venus. Love Himself had supplanted the goddess of love.

In his morning prayer, Augustine offered the day's fast for Cornelius. He began the morning in the great Basilica of Peace. Others noted his presence as a stranger and welcomed him. Augustine had just begun a pleasant conversation with several men when Bishop Valerius happened by and greeted him.

"Excuse me, kind sir, I don't think I know you," the bishop said, extending his hand to Augustine.

"I am Augustine, from Thagaste," he replied, bowing his head.

"Why, Augustine. Yes, of course it is you!" Bishop Valerius said, his old watery eyes bright with happiness. "I did hear you had arrived a few days ago, and I meant to find you. Please, will you dine with me tonight? I would like to welcome you properly."

"That is very kind, but I'm afraid I already have an engagement," Augustine said. He had promised to meet Cornelius again.

"Very well," the bishop said. "Perhaps another evening. I hope to see you again soon."

After the two men parted, Augustine spent that day and the next exploring Hippo Regius. As he breathed in the salty sea air, he could almost imagine he was back in Carthage, though he knew that in size there was no comparison.

I fell away from you by the sea, he prayed to God. *I buried my mother by the sea. I feel ill when I remember being on the sea. I do not wish to live by the sea.*

Hippo Regius hardly seemed to be a city where he could leave the world behind. It might be smaller than Carthage, but it was still a bustling port, a destination for goods and men from all over the Mediterranean. Augustine knew almost no Greek, but understood its sounds, and there was no mistaking sailors' cursing in any language. How could he and his companions find monastic peace within these walls?

Outside the walls, it was even worse. True, this was beautiful country, where the mountains met the sparkling sea. A man might think himself happy to dwell in the cleft of the rock or to settle on one of the estates that dotted the plain. But let a Catholic take one of those estates and he would, sooner or later, find himself at war, trapped in a siege with no walls.

The Christian sect of Donatism defined itself by persecution. The true Church was the church of martyrs, said its bishops, pointing by way of contrast to the Catholic clergy, who dined with civil officials and dwelled securely beside their churches.

This viewpoint resonated with many people. Some truly looked to heaven as their only home, knowing nothing but oppression on earth. Others believed earth could be made a heaven—if only enough of the oppressors' blood were shed. It was an intoxicating idea: to wield the sword against the powerful, and to do it in the name of God.

This attracted peasants, who had worked the land of others

for too long, as well as disaffected soldiers, who could turn their desertion into a proud refusal to serve a rival god. For these reasons and many more, armed bands now roamed the African countryside. Sometimes they contented themselves with plunder and spoilage, but they were also known to burn churches, and Catholic clergy who fell into their hands could expect rough treatment. Reprisals from the Catholics were not uncommon, and these fed the story of persecution the Donatists told, both to the world and to themselves.

As Augustine and his friends knew, such violence was not confined to Africa. In the year 391, citizens of the Empire had been granted the right to bear arms. It was a practical measure, taken so the common people might defend themselves against brigands of all varieties. It was also a tacit admission that the Empire could not defend them.

Hippo Regius, though, located at the center of dispute, was relatively peaceful at present. Augustine knew that could change at any time, and he was eager to be gone.

On the eve of the Lord's Day, he went, as agreed, to dine again with Cornelius. One look at his host's face told Augustine his decision was no. He was disappointed. *I was so certain my coming here was your will*, Augustine thought to God. *Was it your will that I leave with nothing?*

Augustine said, "Will it be uncomfortable if I stay to dine? If you prefer, you may give me your answer now, and I will take my leave."

Cornelius flushed, but he quickly shook his head. "I owe

you a meal, at the least, for your travels and your labor. And I want you to understand."

"I do understand, but I will hear anything you wish to tell me."

They went inside the house to dine, but Augustine could not hide his disappointment.

Bishop Valerius wished, as he did every Lord's Day, that the Donatists would not be so loud. He had grown used to thinking of himself and his flock as men on an island. The Basilica of Peace was theirs, but it did not seem well named, for nearby stood a larger basilica, and the Donatists' voices and music drifted from it constantly, disrupting their prayers.

Abutting his own baptistery wall was the wall of a villa with a floor mosaic of the Nine Muses. It reminded him in stone that the pagans were not yet defeated.

Then there was the perpetual unrest in the countryside. And it was still not uncommon to meet a Manichaean on the streets outside his door.

But mostly, he wished the Donatists would not be so loud. He was an old man. Latin did not come easily to his tongue, and Punic not at all, and each week it was more difficult to make himself heard in any language.

He recognized that members of his congregation were becoming frustrated also. He could feel it when he preached; their patient forbearance was obvious as he hunted for each word. They needed so much more than he could give them, beset as they were by constant threats to their faith. They needed a shepherd capable of providing stronger food.

Knowing this was in all their minds, on this Lord's Day he spoke about it. He told his congregation he intended to seek another priest to serve with him, and one day, God willing, to inherit his responsibilities. He would try to find someone for them who could . . .

"Here is the man!" shouted a voice from the heart of the nave. There was a stir, a confusion of voices, a cascade of exclamations, and then a small knot of people pushed forward. In the midst of them, pushing back as if for his life, was Augustine of Thagaste. The crowd surged right into the apse, to the great chair where Valerius sat near the curved benches on either side—the spot they wished Augustine to sit.

Augustine pleaded with them, but his fine orations could not be heard above the shouts echoing through the basilica. There was now only one word he could speak that would matter, and Bishop Valerius sat and waited for it.

Augustine wasn't sure what he was saying, but in his heart he spoke to the one he knew would hear:

Not this. This is not my place. I have not sought the place of honor or the command to come up higher. Truly, if a man seeks it, you would give him a just punishment by bestowing it. But I have not sought it. All I have sought is to serve you in peace, by . . . by my own will. Does the slave obey only when it pleases him? If I have made myself your slave, there can be only one master.

It took me so long to let you master what was evil in me. For so long, I ran from you and tried to hide myself in the flesh. You showed me how wrong, how wretched, I was. You poured your oil over me and scraped away the dirt with it, and the loss of the dirt was freedom. I knew that. What I did not know was that there are other ways to hide. I thought that, so long as what I chose was not evil, I could make any choice I wished. I did not see that I must let you master what is good in me, no less than what is evil. I did not see that choosing even the good can be a way of hiding, if it is chosen according to my will rather than by yours.

I hid because I was afraid. I am afraid. You rescued me from the world, and will you now throw me back into it? And this time, you would give me the care not of mere minds, but of souls. How can any man make answer for souls? Will you remake me, unworthy and unable as I am?

He thought of his friend Laurentius, baptized while his mind and will slumbered alike in fevered dreams. Laurentius had not chosen it, yet he had been remade.

Forgive me, Lord, my light, he prayed. *Your commands are good, and you do not command anything you cannot accomplish. You can accomplish even this, even in me.*

Augustine became aware that the people around him were reassuring him, promising that he should be made a bishop soon. They had mistaken his tears for disappointment that he was only to be ordained a priest. *Only.*

There is much teaching to be done here, he thought.

Then, looking up at Valerius, he handed over his spirit. "Be it done to me," he said, lowering his head in submission.

Chapter Nineteen

He did not sleep well that night, nor in the next few nights. Finally, on the third night, he fell into an exhausted slumber.

"Father . . ." Augustine turned in his bed at the voice and saw his beloved son enter the dark bedroom. Behind him stood Monica and Nebridius, smiling. In the doorway was Laurentius, also smiling. Augustine threw off his covers and sat up in bed.

"Father, here is a truth—you are a new man," Adeodatus said playfully, pulling up a chair next to the bed.

"Augustine, my son, I am pleased beyond measure," Monica said, coming forward to kiss him on his forehead.

"But I don't know how to begin. Everything is different . . . I am afraid," Augustine said.

"You've become a new man at least twice before and on two different continents," Nebridius laughed. "In Carthage, you became a father at the birth of Adeodatus. In Milan, you became an adopted son of Bishop Ambrose."

How good it was to look into the face of his old friend Nebridius! "Yes, and those changes were complete and irrevocable, yet I was still Augustine of Thagaste. But now . . ." Augustine slumped against the bedroom wall.

"Now you are a father to these people, in this city," Laurentius said.

"You are Augustine of Hippo now," Adeodatus said. He stared at his father with pride.

Augustine looked into his son's eyes, then to Monica and Nebridius and Laurentius. "You've all come to help me, haven't you?" he asked. "I fear I have taken on too big a responsibility."

"You have wandered for years and miles," Laurentius said kindly, "and now you know what you are and what you will always be."

Augustine reached out to touch Laurentius, but he was already fading, like a cloud dispersing in the sky. He turned to Monica and Adeodatus, but all he could see was their bare outlines. He wanted to call them back.

He shook himself awake and looked around the room. They were still close; he could feel them. Rubbing his eyes, he got out of bed and dressed.

"This is my duty," he said to the empty room. Somehow a new resolve and confidence had taken over his mind. He needed to walk and think, and as he stepped onto the street and into the morning light, he faced his worries.

By the laying on of the bishop's hands, Augustine was now responsible for every soul in the diocese, Catholic and Donatist, Manichaean and pagan. At the Judgement, he would answer for every word and action done or not done on behalf of every one of those souls. The weight of it was enough to drive a man mad.

Still, if a man is to be given the impossible power of summoning God in the guise of bread, it is as well that he realizes the human impossibility of the task he is set. Else he might go mad in another way.

His other worry was that he had no idea how to begin his task, the salvation of souls.

"I lack everything except the will for the work," he muttered to himself. He suspected it was likely his work as a priest would soon become the work of a bishop.

"I will learn everything I can," he said out loud to no one. He knew his priority.

Bishop Valerius had given Augustine a command: He was to preach. The order had taken him entirely by surprise, even though he was an experienced teacher and famous orator.

Preaching belonged solely to the office of the bishop. That was not the case throughout the Church, but in Africa it was a custom of long-standing and universal application.

Augustine knew why the custom was now to be overturned in Hippo Regius. He was a far better speaker than the elderly Greek. The entire population of the town knew this and none more deeply than the bishop himself.

Augustine accepted the logic of the command, and even if he had not, he would have accepted the command itself. He would preach—as soon as he knew what to say.

The teacher must first and always be a student. That was true of the study of Cicero. How much more true—how much more infinitely true!—of the study of Christ. And how particularly true for Augustine himself, who had only begun to study Christ.

He was quite clear that he could no longer direct himself according to his own inclinations, so he wrote to Bishop Valerius. He set his request down in ink, rather than making it in person, in case others wanted to know how their famous new presbyter saw his duties.

"My duty is to study with diligence all the remedies the Scriptures contain for such a case as mine, and to make it my business by prayer and reading to secure that my soul be endued with the health and vigor necessary for labors so responsible," he wrote. "This I have not yet done, because I have not had time, for I was ordained at the very time when I was thinking of having, along with others, a season of freedom from all other occupation, that we might acquaint ourselves with the divine Scriptures, and was intending to make such arrangements as would secure unbroken leisure for this great work."

He felt a small pang for that dream of a life of pure leisure. Quickly, he set the pang aside and put pen back to paper, asking for a smaller season of leisure, until Easter, in which to prepare himself to set his hand to the helm.

It was a blessed idyll, and much needed. His ardor for teaching was rekindled—he feared it had been lost forever—after a year of the rowdy schoolboys of Rome. And now he had a subject that was truly worthy of being taught.

He came into the basilica and stood on the steps of the apse in front of the great chair of Valerius, who had commanded him to this service. There, with a copyist diligently taking down his words, Augustine preached.

This was not the schoolroom; he could not assume the congregation had any prior levels of education. He could not even assume their literacy. It was not an easy adjustment, but the people themselves kept it ever-present to his thoughts. They were not timid about responding to his sermons. They called out answers to rhetorical questions, which he employed more frequently once he saw how it engaged them. They laughed, cheered, or even applauded when a point took their fancy. When a point did not, he saw either the restless, shifting feet and wandering eyes of boredom, or he saw sullen, guilt-haunted eyes turned resolutely away from him. He did not try to avoid these gestures and expressions. In fact, Augustine reminded them frequently that he preached above all to satisfy his own conscience, that he needed to share with them the necessary truths.

But he did work to hold their interest. When he didn't know what to say, he remembered the old women who had prayed through the siege in Milan. That usually helped.

While he learned to keep his patience with the congregation, he had more difficulty with the clergy.

"Not in rioting and drunkenness, not in chambering and impurities, not in contention and envy: but put ye on the Lord Jesus Christ, and make not provision for the flesh in its concupiscences." This was the passage from St. Paul's Letter to the Romans that had led to his own conversion. In warning of these sins, St. Paul might as well have been speaking of the clergy of Hippo!

Chambering and impurities, his own sin that had been nurtured with such care for so long—yes, that was still regarded as a sin and would cause a man to lose the respect of his peers, as well as divine favor. So the clergy avoided it, or at least tried not to let it be seen.

Rioting and drunkenness—how could a universal practice be considered a vice? He had already decided that one day he would reform the celebration of martyrs' feasts. Those holy men and women had mastered the flesh, so they did not fear death itself. What could be more absurd than to "honor" them by forfeiting control over the flesh? *Wine and psalms, and a woman's hand in the torchlight*, Augustine thought. In this, the clergy were no worse than the people they served, and not a few of them were better.

Contention and envy, or to call these words by their root, the single word: pride. There was the vice that seemed to follow the laying-on of hands. He feared pride in himself. The clergy of Hippo were doing the work of God, and they were doing it while surrounded by schismatics . . . and they wanted the credit for it.

True, Bishop Valerius had a pure heart and pure motives. Augustine chafed at his slow and limited speech and sensed he had little to learn from him. Most of the men with whom Augustine now spent his days were unlearned, untraveled, and some illiterate, but they claimed a preeminence based not in what they were, but in what they had been given.

The simple fact was that Augustine was lonely. He sorely missed the long philosophical conversations he'd had with his old friends.

The people of Hippo had claimed him, and they were so

enamored that they would not allow him to leave, for fear that some other community would snatch him away. When Augustine came into church at the Feast of the Lord's Ascension, he felt a new kinship with the apostles, bereft of their friend and staring longingly up into the sky.

On the eve of Pentecost, he rose early and went at once to work on the sermon he would give the following day. He was interrupted by a deacon, who knocked on his door with a message that he had visitors. Augustine sighed, but he intended to be a bishop like Ambrose, available to any who sought him. He set down his pen and stepped out into the atrium, where Alypius and Evodius awaited him.

Augustine could not speak. Evodius sized him up in one glance, then turned to Alypius. "I do not think he received your letter," he said.

"Very well," Alypius said with a laugh. "I concede that you were right to doubt the courier."

Augustine rushed forward. "Alypius, you are here! How good to see you, my friend . . . Do you have news?"

"Yes, of sorts. We have a new idea. If your bishop will allow it, our old project need not be abandoned," Alypius said.

"It would simply be . . . redirected," Evodius said.

"We wanted to escape the world entirely, of course," Alypius continued. "What if instead we prepare together to bring God to the world? A monastery not for hermits, but for the training of priests."

"Yes!" Augustine exclaimed. "There is a need for exactly this. I will ask for Bishop Valerius's consent at once."

Suddenly, the same deacon approached Augustine once again. "A letter has just arrived for you," he said, and the three friends burst out laughing. It was in Alypius's handwriting.

So began four happy years. Valerius gladly gave his assent to the plan and offered a portion of the property adjoining the basilica as the site of the monastery. Men arrived from throughout the province eager to join the monastery, and many of the city's own priests became spiritual brothers to Augustine and his friends.

Meanwhile, far from Hippo and from Africa itself, the Empire was changing. In 395, Emperor Theodosius died. His sons Honorius and Arcadius received the thrones of the Western and Eastern Empires, respectively. There was logic in the decision: never again would one man rule over a united Rome.

The boy Honorius was left in the care of the emperor's favored general, Stilicho. This general was not universally acceptable to the Romans, for half his blood came from the Vandal tribe of eastern Germany. Yet his early military successes had convinced Theodosius that Stilicho was the man to safeguard his son's inheritance. The next decade would largely vindicate that judgement, at a time when military successes were sorely needed. While Augustine contended with the Donatists, Stilicho contended with another barbarian tribe: Alaric and his army of Goths.

But in 395, the people of Hippo had more pressing concerns. Valerius, his health failing, wished to secure the future of his flock beyond a doubt. He wrote to Aurelius, Bishop of Carthage, who was first in authority among the bishops of Africa.

Valerius asked for Augustine, now forty-one, to be consecrated bishop while his predecessor was yet living. Augustine would be coadjutor during Valerius's life and would succeed immediately upon his death. On the day the letter granting permission arrived, the Basilica of Peace reverberated with the echoes of the acclamation of many people.

The only Catholic in Hippo who was not overjoyed was Augustine. He yielded with reluctance, for even though he had long known the consecration was inevitable, he had no desire to trade the comfortable imprecision of *someday* for the solid finality of *now*.

But yield he did, and once he had set his hand to the plow, he did not look back. As soon as he could, he delegated the financial affairs and the administration of the Church's property to others. He desired to spend all his waking hours on the care of souls, and there was more than enough of that work to keep any man busy.

In that busy year of 395, Stilicho proclaimed a general religious amnesty, undoing many of the laws against heresy and once again sanctioning the celebration of pagan festivals in Africa.

Augustine now had to compete with these, as well as with the theater and the games. And the Manichaeans. And the Donatists.

Months passed in this way. Then came the turn of the year, and then another Easter.

Valerius knew more than he let on. That Easter, he took to his bed, sensing he would not leave it. The rest of the household knew it as well, with one exception: Augustine refused to face it.

Every moment he could, he sat by the old bishop's side, praying. Valerius was seldom conscious now, so Augustine's vigils were silent. But one night, when the rest of the house was asleep, Augustine chanced to look up and saw Valerius's eyes open.

"What is it you pray for with such concentration?" the dying man asked.

"That you will not go," Augustine replied.

"If I were never to die, it would be well," Valerius conceded. "But if I am to die, why not now?" Soon after, he drifted again into sleep. Augustine continued watching him, reflecting that, after all, he did have something to learn from the unlearned Greek.

When no one could find Augustine in the morning, a deacon went in search of him and discovered them side by side— the body of Valerius on the bed; the Bishop of Hippo asleep in the chair beside him.

Chapter Twenty

"Jerome will have to be answered." Augustine realized he had spoken this thought aloud to an empty room.

He was alone and it was night. He was still not accustomed to being alone.

Augustine needed to confront Jerome before leaving Carthage. Jerome had been born in Italy and studied in Rome. He was a celebrated translator of the Scriptures, famous for his asceticism and his biting sarcasm. He had settled in Bethlehem to be a hermit and to gather a monastery about him. From there, his words traveled throughout the Empire.

In the summer of 397, Augustine had come to Carthage to consult with Bishop Aurelius, his friend and superior. While Augustine was there, he had received an account of Jerome's exposition of a contested passage in Scripture, specifically in the Letter to the Galatians. The issue between Paul and Peter had been the question of circumcision for the Gentiles, and Peter's inconsistency, as pointed out by Paul: "If thou, being a Jew, livest after the manner of the Gentiles, and not as the Jews do, how dost thou compel the Gentiles to live as do the Jews?"

The public dispute between the two apostles was difficult

to resolve for many people in the Christian Church. How could Paul have challenged the rock upon which the Church was built? What did that do to the unity of Christ's body?

Jerome asserted it did nothing, for in reality there had been no dispute, rather only the appearance of one, contrived by Peter so that Paul, in seeming to rebuke him, might in reality rebuke those who held the erroneous opinion that Gentile circumcision was necessary. But Peter was not truly among those who held that opinion. In public, there was a useful facade. In private, all was amity. It was a simple solution, a pretty story . . . and it struck at the very lifeblood of the Scriptures themselves.

Jerome maintained that the apostles had lied. And to allow one lie, any lie, into the sacred books was like allowing in a moth, whose larvae would shred the whole as quickly as they would the pages of any physical book.

It would be a thousand times better to admit that the apostles could disagree, to admit that even Peter himself could be mistaken, than to preserve their wisdom at the expense of their truth. The apostles were still men. Men could err, and men could disagree in public. The Scriptures were the Word of God. How could they not mean what they said?

Augustine shook his head at Jerome's tangled argument. He would have to answer Jerome immediately. He was aware of the irony that Jerome would have to be answered in public.

Augustine was not looking to stir up controversy. He'd already had enough of that as it was, and he was still getting over one of his most notable controversies that had occurred years prior.

In the summer of 392, as he, Alypius, and Evodius organized their monastery, Augustine had been approached by a delegation of citizens made up of Catholics and Donatists. The Donatists were willing to descend from the heights to make common cause against a common threat.

The Manichaeans had a formidable spokesman in Hippo, a priest by the name of Fortunatus, who had made many converts. Would Augustine, with his gift of rhetoric and his intimate knowledge of the Manichaean creed, challenge this man to a debate?

The Catholics were eager to show off their new champion, and the Donatists, by their presence at Augustine's door, acknowledged that for such a contest they had no one who was his equal.

Augustine agreed to do it. Fortunatus knew of Augustine's reputation from his Carthage days, and he was persuaded to consent. The debate took place on August 28 and 29.

As the two men readied themselves, a small crowd gathered to listen with interest. Young scribes sat at the side, prepared to record the event:

Augustine: "I have arrived ready to discuss the question of our divergent creeds . . ."

Fortunatus: "I wish first and above all else to have the witness of the famous ex-Manichaean brought to bear on the slanders that had been spread about the Manichaeans' way of living."

Augustine: "In what I have seen, besides the fact that they rejected the truth, the Manichaeans behaved morally."

Fortunatus: "But—"

Augustine: "I was never one of the Elect, and thus I never witnessed their behavior at their private ceremonies. I will not speak of that which I do not know. . . . Can we move to the substance of the debate?"

Fortunatus: "The Manichaean doctrine revolves around the world's two powers—the good and the evil, eternally at war. God, incorruptible and untouchable, sent his son to deliver men from the evil into which they had fallen as a result of the war."

Augustine: "If anything can injure God, he is not untouchable. If he cannot be injured, then what was this power of darkness going to do that made it necessary for God to wage the war in which we have been ensnared? It is a cruel God who would create souls for such a purpose. No, God created all things, and he created them all good, save only sin. That is of man, and it comes from his own free will, which God gave to us so we might be able to acquire merit, doing the good by our own wills and not by simple necessity. For how can we have merit or guilt if we do not act by our own will? If, as you assert, there is an evil power that compels us, then why did Christ have to die—was it to save us from something that was not our fault? Again, I say this—your God is a cruel one."

As the scribes noted, Augustine returned to that point again and again during that day and the next. Why would God create souls if he knew they must be acted upon by evil? And why must he redeem them if they had no choice?

At last, on the afternoon of the second day, Fortunatus spread his hands wide. "What am I to say?" he asked.

"That is a question I used to ask myself," Augustine answered, "when I was a Manichaean."

Fortunatus departed to seek counsel with his superiors. Shortly after, he departed Hippo.

The outcome pleased everyone except Augustine, who had hoped for the true victory of converting Fortunatus, rather than him simply retreating.

But it was at least a blessing that Fortunatus's leaving diminished the Manichaean presence, leaving Augustine free to confront the Donatists, whom he regarded as the more serious threat. The Manichaeans professed a belief in Christ—though a Christ merely imprisoned in the flesh, which to them could not be other than evil—but they did not claim to be part of the Church. The Donatists partook of the body of Christ, the great sacrament of unity, yet they divided the body that was God's Church. How could they not see that schism was a greater wound than any individual sin? Augustine would not tolerate individual sin, neither among his clergy nor among his flock.

When he ascended to the bishop's chair, he extended his small monastic community to all the priests, deacons, and sub-deacons of the city, inviting them to renounce property and the cares of property, and to dwell with him in poverty, simplicity, and continence. At the same time, he sponsored and encouraged the formation of similar houses for women, building up communities of prayer within his diocese.

The bishop and his monks dressed simply, and when they went out, each took whatever cloak happened to be within reach. Their table was set with vegetables and grains, but there was wine—Augustine's answer to the Manichaeans. The number of times a man could fill his cup was strictly counted, and if any man swore, he lost a turn. Augustine gave them better subjects to talk about; together, they studied the Scriptures and the writings of the saints, cultivating their minds as they denied their bodies.

These were the shepherds Augustine intended to spread across Africa. In teaching, he set the example. His sermons expounded not only on the meaning of the Scriptures—with particular care given to the Psalms, for Ambrose had taught him how much more accurately words are remembered when they are sung—but on the parts of the liturgy, down to the smallest greeting and acclamation. Men should understand what they spoke at all times, but above all when they were speaking to God.

When he was not teaching, Augustine met with the petitioners. At the time the Imperial administration accepted Christianity, it also accepted the authority of the Christian bishops to resolve disputes. Because the judgement would be binding in civil law either way, many people preferred to submit to the bishop—especially when that bishop was the thoughtful and just Augustine.

He spent his mornings listening to pleas, complaints, arguments, and tirades, with scribes taking down each point. Both parties were made to promise that they would abide by his judgement—a promise the winning party invariably kept.

Though he did not say it, Augustine felt this part of the work would be easier if the parties involved had any skill in rhetoric. So often he sat and listened, waiting for the kernel of an argument he could have made more skillfully and in half the time. When he found himself editing for style rather than listening for the substance, he reminded himself that all earthly eloquence was but a clanging cymbal when set before the Word of Heaven.

When the petitions were done for the day, then he faced the letters. They came to him from throughout the Empire: from Jerome, conceding the argument about Peter but contesting certain linguistic conclusions; from Simplicianus, Augustine's old teacher and now the successor of Ambrose in Milan, asking questions that would require a thorough exposition of the Epistle to the Romans; from a young Greek who fancied himself a philosopher, asking elementary questions that were apparently not elementary to him; from an aristocratic widow, a woman of both education and virtue, asking how she should pray; and more. Always more.

When the letters were done, then at last he could turn to his own writing.

~

Through it all, he often thought of Milan. He thought of Ambrose, of course, as his model for a bishop. But as time went on, he thought more of his own younger self, that Augustine with so many questions, who had been unable to approach the bishop because of this same press of business. How many young Augustines were there that he could not reach?

"If a man desire the office of a bishop, he desireth a good work," Saint Paul said in his first letter to Timothy. A man should not desire the office for itself, but for the sake of the work he could do. What was that work, except the reconciliation of man to God? Not of men; of man—each man, one by one.

He pondered this sometimes when he walked through the basilica. For the most part, it had little decoration, but its floor was a vast mosaic tapestry. As tradition dictated, families gave sections of mosaic as a gift to the church, and inscriptions duly recorded how many square feet had been paid for by each house.

So many stones, so many souls.

Augustine returned to his work: to hear another case, to prepare another sermon, or to answer another letter from Jerome.

Chapter Twenty-One

It was late, and Augustine did not know or care how late it was. He was engaged in work he enjoyed and found useful—a happy combination rarely found in his official duties. He was working on an exposition of the principles by which a preacher should interpret the Scriptures, allowing him to combine his rhetorical training with his joy in speaking about the Word of God.

The scribe with Augustine also did not know how late it was. He might have cared, but his pen was kept moving too swiftly for such thoughts. Every now and then, though, a yawn forced itself in.

Then came a pause as Augustine searched his memory for the perfect passage to use in illustration. "Shall I fetch more oil for the lamp?" a voice asked.

Augustine nodded his assent before he realized the voice did not belong to his scribe. He looked up to see among the shadows of the doorway the solid figure of a man. He needed no light to recognize this friend.

"Alypius!" Augustine cried.

He was a bishop now, since his consecration in 394, formally called Alypius of Thagaste. Augustine dismissed the scribe to get his deserved rest and set Alypius in his chair. He noticed his friend had gray hair at his temples. "It must be news of grave importance to bring you here in person," Augustine said.

"Not all of us hate travel as much as you do," Alypius replied. "But I grant that I would not leave Thagaste on a whim, or solely on a private visit. I come as a messenger, though it is more true to say I am here on my own behalf."

He explained that he had been in correspondence with Paulinus of Nola. Augustine knew the name. The story of the Roman prefect and his wife who had renounced their great wealth for the treasures of heaven had traveled throughout the Empire. Paulinus too had been seized and ordained. Now he was working to establish a monastic community and to avoid consecration as a bishop.

In his most recent letter, Paulinus had asked Alypius for an account of his own life and his conversion. "I do not wish to refuse such a man," Alypius concluded, "but . . ."

"But you do not wish to tell your own story," Augustine said.

"So, instead, I came to the man of words." Not wanting to be misunderstood, Alypius leaned forward and spoke quickly. "It is not a tribute I would ask you to write. This is not Milan, and I am no emperor. I came to you because you will not lie, either in what is said or in what is left unsaid. You will not omit my visits to the amphitheater years ago."

"No, I would not," Augustine said. "But it is not easy to tell the story of another man's soul and its journey to God. We can only fully know this ourselves. Though it may be the best way to come to know God."

"Then why not tell your own story, while you are at it?" Alypius asked.

They both laughed. Then they stopped laughing as the idea took hold in their minds.

The next morning, when Alypius awoke, he went to search for Augustine. He had been up early, but not early enough— Augustine had already left the house. Alypius found him walking by the sea.

"I came to ask your forgiveness," Alypius began.

"For what?"

"I should not have suggested you add a task to all those you have already on your shoulders."

"For me, to think is to write," Augustine said, stopping to shake off sand from his sandals. "One follows the other, and then the other follows the one. It is the way I make progress, so while I think—"

"Which is always," Alypius said.

"Which is always, yes. While I think I will write, and while I write I will think. You have asked me to think and to write about God, which is ever my study."

The two men walked along the beach in silence for a few moments as small waves edged near their feet in a mesmerizing rhythm. The sky was a rosy pink. The rising sun warmed the air.

"But your pen is needed on so many battlefields," here

Alypius spoke as a lawyer, "and a work such as the one I proposed might leave you open to attacks from your enemies."

"I would stand convicted by my own words, do you mean? But that is precisely what has made me decide to undertake the work." Augustine looked out over the wide expanse of water. "The story of my life is not the story of excellence or perfection of my own. It is the story of God's unlimited and unsearchable mercy. Let God increase, and I decrease. Only in this way can I render an account of the souls in my care." Augustine stooped to pick up a pebble. "And there is this: Last night in my dreams, I returned to the streets of Ostia. Do you remember the request my mother made?"

Alypius nodded. "'Wherever you may find yourselves, remember me at the altar of the Lord,'" he said. "I recall her words clearly."

"I have fulfilled it," Augustine said, turning over the pebble in his hand, "first as a layman and now as a priest. But imagine if it were written—and read. Imagine the prayers that would rise then, not only for my mother, but for my father as well, and for my son. And in addition to all of these, prayers for myself, prayers that might accompany me to the Judgement."

"I am persuaded," Alypius said, "and I withdraw my apology. But with a condition."

"Yes, I will send you a copy." Augustine sent the pebble skipping across the surface of the water, and the two men turned to walk back to Augustine's study.

After leaving his friend, Alypius strolled through the streets of

Hippo toward his own lodging. He passed a market of vendors selling ripe produce and stopped to admire the colorful displays. He enjoyed Hippo's warm climate.

"No man's life is his own story, but the story of what he has received," he said quietly to himself, thinking of Augustine and his book.

"What's that you say? You wish to buy that apple?" said the vendor, an old man with a wrinkled brown face.

"No, no, sorry, thank you," Alypius said. He continued walking, thinking about how intertwined his life and thinking were with Augustine's.

"Our story is the story of the God who came down to us, a story that is shared and yet unique for every man." When a passerby stared at him, Alypius realized he'd muttered these words aloud; he picked up his pace to head for home. It was better to think in private. And he was excited that Augustine was willing to write his life—it would be a story many men would find inspiring.

Back in his own study, Augustine contemplated these very same ideas. What would he write? And then the bigger question: What is a man's purpose? This was exactly what he wished to explore.

John the Baptist knew it well, Augustine thought. *He was not his own—he was a lamp to shine a light on the God who would come after him. It is perilous to be a lamp. The flame is so small, and the wind of pride so strong.*

Augustine shrank from ordination out of fear of pride. He'd seen it distract many fine men. Now, with so many eyes upon him, he had chosen to write about himself. Yes, many people would condemn him, but many would praise him too.

It is easy to desire praise, and fatally easy when what is praised is good, he reasoned. *A man should desire virtue, whether it is praised or not, but can man discern when the desire is for virtue and when it is for praise?*

"He who does truth comes to the light"—so says Saint John the Evangelist, Augustine prayed to God. *Let it be your light and not my own. I will not write about myself. I will speak to you. I will tell you what you know, so that others may know it—and perhaps so that I may know it myself.*

Ever since he'd been ordained, Augustine had discovered the great number of people who lived their entire lives as catechumens and never took the last step to baptism. To receive baptism would mean they would have to make a significant change of life. Remaining a catechumen meant putting off that change to some vague point in the future. Perhaps tomorrow, perhaps next year. Augustine knew that state of mind, and he also knew no man was promised tomorrow or any time at all.

When I had the fever in Rome, I nearly died. If I had died then, I would have been lost, he thought. If he could explain the danger he had accepted—even embraced—for so many years, he might awaken some souls to the danger in which they now stood. *I will be called to account for all the souls in Hippo, including the soul of its bishop.*

So many seemed to think they knew his story. He had been lost, then he had been found. The prodigal had returned and had gone in to the banquet. Conversion was the end of the story.

CHAPTER TWENTY-ONE

If only it were so. If only the choice could be made once.

For the martyr, perhaps, it could. A man could fix his will at the point of death. The convert knew that moment, the ecstatic freedom of being possessed by his choice. That feeling might last for a considerable time, but there would come a morning when, at the hour when he should rise, he would linger in bed, preferring the darkness behind his eyelids to the glories of the day. It had been that way since the Garden.

Madness to set the will against what we know to be good. Our first parents spoke with God. They knew him for their creator, yet they turned from the Creator to that which he had created. In the man's case, to the woman, Augustine thought, recalling that the jasmine would be blooming now in Carthage, *and in the woman's case, to the fruit of the Tree of Knowledge.*

And in my case, to the fruit of a pear tree.

When Augustine had at last turned to God, he placed his lusts before him. Then, with greater difficulty, his pride. One by one, he gave up the sins of a lifetime. He could hardly bear to look upon one incident, the one he'd tried to hide from Titrit so long ago: the story of the pears.

He had been sixteen. It was the year before he went to Carthage, and a year is a long time at sixteen, especially with nothing to do and time to spend with the same friends week after week.

They were not good pears. There were better trees, with better fruit, on Laurentius's own land. But late one night, when the two teenagers had nothing to do, Laurentius had suggested stealing these pears, for no reason other than that they hung on someone else's trees.

Augustine agreed at once. It was ridiculously easy—there was no moon and no guard, no difficulty to overcome. They stole the fruit and gave it to the pigs, laughing and giddy with the knowledge that they had taken something that was not theirs.

I loved my own will, even though it was not yours, Augustine thought. *No, I cannot claim even that much excuse. I loved my own will because it was not yours. I did not sin for the sake of some good. That time it was not for Titrit, or for professional renown, or even to fill my belly. I sinned for the sake of the sin itself. Oh, Lord, my life—to trade away everything and not even expect anything in return!*

It was a sickness, caught from those with whom I kept company. Yet it is in sickness that we come to know the physician. And the graver the sickness, the more grateful we are for the cure. You opened your side and poured out the only true and lasting remedy, the remedy of your blood.

Now he would write of his own nothingness. He would write of, and to, the God who is everything. Augustine took up his pen.

Great are you, O Lord, and greatly to be praised; great is your power, and of your wisdom there is no end. And man, being a part of your creation, desires to praise you . . . You move us to delight in praising you, for you have made us for yourself, and our hearts are restless until they rest in you.

Chapter Twenty-Two

On a late summer day in the fateful year of 410, Augustine rested in a friend's country villa, where he had been ordered to go for the sake of his health. As it happened, getting there was the difficult part, and now he sat in the villa's garden, grateful to have arrived at last. His beard was long and white, and his eyes were filled with kindness for his host and for the host's family. He was especially happy to be surrounded by peace and quiet.

Meanwhile, the world outside the villa was in turmoil. Stilicho fell in 408, and the Empire's administration had been thrown into chaos, thus emboldening the old bands of Donatist outlaws. They mixed lime and vinegar and threw the solution into the eyes of priests to blind them—a fitting punishment, they believed, for the blindness of error. Naturally, the Bishop of Hippo was a sought-after target.

This particular journey to the country had been accomplished without disturbance, yet Augustine had been frustrated when his guide had taken the wrong road and gotten thoroughly lost. By the time they reached their destination, Augustine's patience was worn thin by sickness and hours in the saddle. He was hard put to speak calmly to the guide.

But within two days, Augustine had already established a daily rhythm of activities at the estate. His version of resting included offering Mass daily for the household, answering letters, reading new books that had been sent to him for replies, meditating on Scripture, and working on a book about the Holy Trinity. At least there were no petitioners here, though he suspected his host had turned some away at the gate this morning. So quickly had news of his arrival traveled.

In the afternoons, he sought solitude in the garden. One day, the steward of the house found him there, though he hesitated to approach until Augustine beckoned him forward. "Do you bring a message?" he asked.

"No, Your Grace. At least, it is something I heard, but I speak for myself. I am a good Catholic."

"Christ be praised," Augustine replied. More than by the man's protestations, he was pleased by the automatic dip of the steward's head at his utterance of the holy name.

"Amen. But, you see, my cousin, who works a small plot near here," the steward said, "he is not a good Catholic. He is a Donatist, or at least he allows them to stay in his house. And today, when I was out on the master's business—for I do not idle with such folk, and I would not have you think it—I saw him with some of his guests, and I heard them talk about an ambush that had not come off. It was to have happened the day you arrived here, Your Grace, and I thought . . . Well, it is only that I beg of Your Grace to go home, when you go, by the same road you took to get here, and not to tell anyone in the meantime what that road was."

"I thank you, and I shall do so," Augustine said. *If any of us can retrace those wanderings he calls a road*, he thought.

He blessed the steward and dismissed him. Later, he spoke of it to his host, who joked that Augustine should now recall his guide and thank him.

Augustine shook his head. "It was a simple mistake, made with no ill intent," he said. "As such, there is no fault, and I do not blame him—at least, not now, when I am no longer sore. But, equally, there was no good intent of the kind that would deserve praise. He did not know he was saving me. God works through us as he wills, whether through our virtues, our faults, or even our sins. The praise or blame of our actions accrues to us in the same way whatever the outcome may be, for the action is ours, while the outcome is God's. So, I thank God for my preservation, but I think of our guide exactly as I did before."

Later, Augustine reflected on the recent events as he watched a raven soar over the villa. He wished for a bird's-eye view of the dramatic battles for power of these years, so he could make sense of it all. He went over the facts in his mind:

The Donatists were not the only ones invigorated by Stilicho's fall. The savage plunderer Alaric, king of the Visigoths, also saw an opportunity.

After years of fighting the Goths, Stilicho had lost the love of the Roman people by negotiating with Alaric. A new enemy had appeared on the horizon, a pretender to the imperial throne in Britain, and Stilicho had judged him the greater and more immediate threat.

Alaric had fought for Rome once, and he had done so with distinction. He dropped hints that money could make him do it again. This seemed like a reasonable bargain to Stilicho, but Emperor Honorius, now a young man and increasingly touchy about the fame and success of his guardian, saw the situation differently. When his brother, Arcadius, died, leaving a seven-year-old son to rule the Eastern Empire, Honorius listened to counselors, who suggested Stilicho had grown too powerful and was plotting to supplant him—to put Stilicho's own son on the throne.

It was enough. Stilicho and his son both died—though Stilicho cast some doubt upon the rumors by refusing to allow the army, a considerable segment of which was still loyal to him, to start a civil war to save him.

Understandably, Honorius would not bargain with the Goths. Alaric took the news philosophically. He was a bold and unpredictable man—he had invaded Italy before and he could do it again.

Augustine knew well that toward the end of 408, Alaric did just that. For nearly two years he moved about the region, disrupting African grain shipments, menacing Rome upon two occasions, withdrawing when Honorius—or rather, the succession of advisors who replaced Stilicho—offered to discuss terms, and marching again when the discussions came to nothing. In the summer of 410, he attacked Rome again. In this third assault, one of the gates was opened.

Treachery? The threat of starvation? The knowledge that Honorius was unlikely to save the city in time? The why and the how were worthy questions Augustine considered, but they made little difference to those inside the walls in the pre-dawn hours of August 24.

During the next three days, the Gothic army took its reward for the hard labor of the past two years. Alaric was a curious kind of Christian. He was an Arian, Augustine knew, and believed Christ was not equal in dignity to the Father. Though he diminished Christ, Alaric still revered him, and he commanded that the churches be spared—thus, people found their way to them as true sanctuary. For the rest, he had no interest in punishing the city with utter destruction. He was there merely to teach a lesson, to set an example for future negotiations.

So, Augustine realized, the ruin could have been much worse, yet it was still devastating. Attacks on palaces and people left some in ruin and some intact. Alaric died not long after his triumph, but he had ensured his place in history. He had taught the eternal city that it was mortal.

As we all are, Augustine thought, rubbing his knees. Recently, they had begun to keep him up at night, a painful reminder that he was aging.

In the months that followed, refugees streamed into Africa. They arrived at Carthage, the wealthier among them settling there. This African city was most like Rome.

Augustine left his friend's villa and returned to Carthage early in 411, when he was fifty-seven years old. He was surprised to see so many new faces there—a large number of the exiles were pagans of the old world: educated, cultured, traditional. They regarded Christianity as irrational, a religion of slaves. Even more, they thought—and were not afraid to say out loud—that Alaric's triumph had not been his, but a punishment visited on Rome for deserting the ancestral gods.

One evening, just as the first stars appeared in the sky, Augustine took a walk through the Forum. He never tired of exploring all the places he had loved as a young student. The square was mostly empty. He passed two men—the elder, an official in his mid-forties, held the younger, a lad of perhaps twenty, by the wrist. The boy stared at the official. "Do not the holy books say it is better to live maimed than to die? That we should be willing to cut off a whole hand, if we must?" he asked.

"They do not say 'to live,'" the official retorted, "but 'to enter into life.' The saying is not about this life. And it is about avoiding sin, not shirking duty."

"Are you a priest, to tell me how to read the holy books?"

"He does not need to be," Augustine interposed. "He is correct, and that is all that matters. And I am a priest," he added to prevent the next question.

By now, even in the dim starlight, he saw the cause of the argument. The official held the boy by the right wrist, and that hand was missing its thumb. Such a sight was not uncommon. A hand missing a thumb could not hold a sword. A man who could not hold a sword could not be pressed into the army. There were men who thought this maiming worth the price.

The boy shrugged. "Well, it has been done. Are you really

going to bother the judges with an event that happened months ago and cannot be proved?"

"No," the official said. "You are . . . free . . . to live the rest of your life with the consequences of your fear." He glanced down at the boy's sandals. The lacing was crooked.

The boy looked down as well. "What else can I do?" he asked, still defiant.

"Repent," Augustine said.

"Does repentance grow thumbs?" the boy asked.

"No. But even if a man is maimed, he can still hope to enter into life."

The official released the boy's wrist and the boy took off at a run in his crookedly laced sandals. The official bowed to Augustine. "I am in your debt," he said. "The lad is perfectly right that I cannot do anything, but that particular trick is one I despise. I thank you for your help. May I know your name?"

"Aurelius Augustine."

The official's face suddenly animated. "Then you are one of the men I have come to seek! I am Flavius Marcellinus, tribune of the emperor. He sent me to inquire into the claims of the Donatists. I am calling a conference of the best minds on each side, and I have been told it would be impossible to represent the Catholic side without the Bishop of Hippo."

"I will take part with good will," Augustine said, smiling. As a priest, he had to ask the next question, but he hoped it would not be taken in the wrong way. "Are you . . . ?"

Marcellinus understood and put up his hand. "I am a Catholic, by God's grace. I endeavor also to be a just man."

Augustine shook Marcellinus's hand. "I am glad to know you, Tribune Marcellinus."

The two men walked together for an hour, enjoying each other's company. When they parted, each felt grateful for the happy surprise in meeting the other.

The refugees told stories of what they'd seen and experienced in Rome. Augustine sought them out to hear their accounts and learn all he could. He read what was available, including a vivid account by a Briton called Pelagius, who wrote of "all ranks and degrees leveled and promiscuously huddled together. The slave and the man of quality were in the same circumstances, and everywhere the terror of death and slaughter was the same, unless we may say the fright made the greatest impression on those who had the greatest interest in living."

Since his conversion to Christianity, Augustine never mistook this world for the next. He had seen more of this world in thirty years than most men saw in their entire lives, and his eyes had been opened. He looked to the world that was to come.

But Rome was this world, and if Rome could fall, then it might be that this world was coming to an end. Why was Rome being punished?

Marcellinus had pointed out that the accusations of the pagans should be answered, lest men return out of fear to worshipping the ancient gods. He visited Augustine at his lodging to discuss the upcoming conference, where this topic was sure to be discussed. "The pagans have their Jupiter, but we know Rome is under the protection of the blessed Peter and Paul. Yet they did nothing," Marcellinus said. "Some men wonder what their protection is worth. For that matter, some men wonder what God's protection is worth."

Augustine tilted his cup, letting the wine swirl gently. "Do you ask your wife to love you for what you can provide, or for yourself?"

"Yes, I see." Marcellinus paused to refill his own cup. "I am not the one asking the questions."

"I know it," Augustine said.

"Only . . . I would like to know the answers. I cannot be the only one who would like to see the errors refuted and the truth explained. Is it wrong to ask, if I ask in that spirit? Such suffering cannot be willed by God."

"No, it is not." Augustine's dreams lately had been full of images from stories he'd heard about Rome. Just the night before, he'd dreamed about orphaned children wandering with tear-stained faces through streets of fire while he searched for help fruitlessly. "And it is not wrong to ask in order to understand. I will think on it, I promise you. For now, let us pray for the Donatists."

The great conference was only weeks away.

Augustine often missed Adeodatus. He fondly remembered how they used to walk for miles in conversations covering a wide range of topics. He imagined the questions his ever-curious Adeodatus would ask now. Surely, he would want to know more about the followers of Donatus and what they really believed.

"And God saw the light that it was good; and he divided the

light from the darkness," Augustine recalled from the Book of Genesis. He smiled at the thought of how he would explain to his son that to the followers of Donatus, it was simple: The light was divided from the darkness. A man could belong to only one.

When the dispute between the Catholics and the Donatists began early in the fourth century, it was based solely on religion. The Donatist schism bound up the purity of the Church in the purity of the priests—a thrilling, if dangerous, enterprise. It threatened to fracture the African Church, and with it, a good bit of Africa itself.

Emperor Constantine could not afford to have Africa—which fed Rome—fractured, so he stepped in to lead his empire. Constantine was also a Christian, the Church's most famous and influential convert, and in the Donatist controversy he saw a chance to define what a Christian emperor should, or could, be. So, Augustine would have told Adeodatus, Constantine intervened in this dispute.

The Donatists were happy he did—until they discovered he was not going to take their side. His ruling, in their eyes, set the Catholics on the side of the world, while they kept to the side of heaven. They built their own church, built their own buildings, and established their own sacraments, priests, and bishops. In towns throughout Africa, one sect or the other claimed ascendency, depending on popular sentiment and which side had shed more blood.

In this fashion, a hundred years or so passed.

Now, as the fifth century had succeeded the fourth, another

emperor decided this dispute must end. In June of 411, Catholics and Donatists were commanded to send their champions to Carthage, where Flavius Marcellinus, as the emperor's representative, waited to begin the great conference.

Augustine wished Adeodatus were alive to attend the conference with him.

The day of the conference arrived. Both sides accepted Marcellinus as moderator, and he felt no need to push his influence. The roster of Catholic bishops was quite enough to set a faithful mind at ease: Aurelius of Carthage, Alypius of Thagaste, Possidius of Calama, and others equally learned would all be there.

And towering above them by a common recognition was Augustine of Hippo. Augustine's gifts were famous, and his spiritual care extended throughout the province, bringing him often to the region's capital.

Marcellinus, a tall, dignified official, was easy to see among the other men listening, and Augustine noticed that Marcellinus paid keen attention to every word. Marcellinus was fascinated by theology, and whenever he could, he came to listen to Augustine, who could make ideas clear so that any audience understood why they mattered. Through listening and conversation, and by asking many questions, the Bishop of Hippo and the military commander had become friends. So, as Marcellinus took the moderator's chair in the wide rectangular room at the start of the conference, he silently dared the Donatists to bring any argument they could. They would be answered.

During the first two sessions, the participants argued about procedure; Augustine observed but had little to say. Marcellinus, anxious to be and to appear just, conceded every point he could to the Donatists. He was the picture of reason and civility, with his gray hair and great height.

To ensure the accuracy of the official record, Marcellinus agreed that every word should be written out fair in longhand, and that the transcript would then be approved by both sides. For the sake of the stenographers, a six-day delay was granted so they could write up all that had been discussed thus far.

During those six days, Marcellinus scrupulously kept away from his friend, devoting himself to other business. But as the day of the third session dawned, the two men found themselves arriving at the conference together. It was a warm morning, the sun already beating down on the dusty streets, creating sharp shadows.

After a few pleasantries, Marcellinus could not resist asking Augustine the question that had kept him awake for a week of nights: "Should not the Church be pure?"

"Should be, must be, will be—but not on earth," Augustine replied. "Here, none of us is entirely what we shall be, and we do not know what that is. The glass is dark, and I think we will all be surprised when at last we see." After a moment, he added, "I confess, I do wonder at times. The Donatist creed has never crossed the sea; it remains on our shores alone. Yet they never doubt they are the church universal. Do they think Christ's blood was enough to only redeem Africa, or does anyone else matter, if only Africa is redeemed?"

"I think . . ." Marcellinus began, but there was no time to continue talking. Side by side, the bishop and the soldier stepped into the day's battle.

Chapter Twenty-Three

The Donatists were defeated in their arguments at the Conference of Carthage. As soon as Marcellinus declared the Catholic party as the victors, the Romans began to suppress the Donatists with a violence that Augustine would never condone but was helpless to stop.

As he journeyed back to Hippo, he thought of the conference and the question Marcellinus had put to him privately: Had Rome fallen because its citizens had deserted the ancestral gods, or had it fallen because the Christian God was unable to protect his people?

Augustine thought back to calamities that had befallen those who were faithful to their gods, or to God. No man escapes suffering, no matter his faith. And no man died who was not destined to die.

Augustine's guide, on the horse in front of him, suddenly slowed down and pointed to a shady spot with huge leafy trees. The two men led their horses to it and dismounted. They pulled out some food and water and sat on the dry grass to rest.

The guide was silent, lost in his own thoughts, as was Augustine.

The Roman gods could not be on the same footing as the true God, equally incapable of shielding their adherents. Augustine turned this thought over in his mind, stepping from one bit of logic to the next. He took a long drink of water and looked out over the dry mountains. Insects buzzed in the heat.

There would have to be a refutation of the gods themselves, from Apollo, Saturn, Juno, Minerva, and the rest, all the way down to Aesculanus and Argentinus, the gods of bronze and silver coins, he thought. His reasoning went like this: If Apollo were the great foreknower he was named to be, why did he labor to build the walls of Troy? Did he not foresee that the king of Troy would, when the work was done, refuse to pay him? And how did the great warrior Ulysses, as the poet told, seize and carry away the image of Minerva? He did it by first slaying the guards—so who had been the protector and who had needed protection? But when the false gods were put to flight and the true God remained sole victor in the field, the question of why had to be answered.

A line from the Book of Matthew came to Augustine's mind: "God maketh his sun to rise upon the good, and bad, and raineth upon the just and the unjust." Why? Both wicked and just men had perished in the sack of Rome. And both wicked and just men had been spared. Why?

To Augustine, the answer was simple: As it was in a man, so it was in the world. Rome stood in splendor, with all its treasures and joys that could be touched, tasted, and seen. It was easy to love this city. But this city would pass away. Of the spirit and flesh, only the flesh was visible. The City of Man was visible, but entwined with it was the City of God. That—the true Eternal City—was the city that mattered.

It pleased God to bestow earthly gifts on the just and the unjust alike, so that it would be apparent these were not the gifts most worth striving for. Likewise, he bestowed affliction according to no earthly law, so that it might be apparent that earthly afflictions were not the dangers that should most be feared. Let a man love God and fear sin, rather than love honor and fear the fire. Men should set earthly joys and sorrows at their proper value, and so work for joys—and shun sorrows—that had no end.

Augustine suddenly identified the answer of why the destruction of the earthly city had happened. When a person was no longer dazzled by the City of Man, he could see the City of God.

He sighed. In order for people to see both cities for what they were, Augustine would have to describe them, explaining their origins, histories, and futures.

The guide stood up to prepare the horses to continue their journey. Augustine stretched his limbs.

The writing of this explanation would be an extraordinary undertaking, but could there be any task more worthwhile? Besides, Marcellinus had asked it of him.

Augustine enjoyed writing and refining his ideas, but he was continually aware of how little influence he had on the violence in the world around him.

The Donatists wanted revenge for their defeat. In 408, the

provincial governor named Count Heraclian, had been rewarded for his murder of Stilicho, for doing so removed a potential rival to the throne. In thanks for this deed, Heraclian was granted governorship of the Province of Africa. In 412, he himself threatened the throne from Africa. He proclaimed himself emperor and invaded Italy, but he was swiftly routed and forced to flee back to Carthage, where just as swiftly he was put to death.

In the aftermath of Heraclian's revolt, rumors and accusations flew fast among the survivors. An official with Donatist sympathies accused Marcellinus of having conspired with Heraclian.

Augustine rushed to Carthage to intervene. His efforts were tireless, but futile. At dawn on September 13, 413, Marcellinus was beheaded.

Marcellinus was dead. But Augustine's promise to his friend remained, and he continued to write. In a sense, it was the same work Augustine had done at Alypius's request, in the book that had become his confessions to God. In it, he told how God had operated in the life of a single soul. Now he was tasked with tracing the hand of God through the history of the world.

But always it was really God's story. Woe to the man who made it his own—that was a danger that had been on his mind more than ever before.

Augustine was in his study in Hippo—one of his favorite places. Here he could work in peace, sorting out his ideas with little interference. Through his long rectangular window, he could look out into a courtyard, where boys from a nearby school sometimes played an elaborate game with a ball. Today he saw about six of them, all teenagers, playing. He thought of Adeodatus—how he missed his son.

He turned back to his desk. While he labored to answer the pagans and fired occasional volleys at the Manichaeans and the Donatists, Augustine recognized a new threat: Pelagius, that same Briton who had written so eloquently of the sack of Rome. *If only he were not quite so eloquent*, he thought. *If only he had accepted my invitation.*

Pelagius was a theologian and Augustine had heard of him for years. In fact, they were the same age and had arrived in Rome at about the same time, though their paths had never crossed. And when Augustine returned home to Africa, Pelagius had remained at the crossroads of the Empire, writing, debating, and listening to ideas from north and south, east and west.

Pelagius briefly found his way to Africa with the other exiles, and when he landed at Hippo, he sent word of his arrival to Augustine. Augustine had been in Carthage on business and replied courteously that he hoped a face-to-face meeting could be arranged sometime in the future. In truth, he was already troubled by some of what he had read in Pelagius's writings.

Augustine returned to Hippo, but Pelagius was gone, finding his way in the following year to the Holy Land. Augustine had permitted himself the momentary hope that Pelagius, if he were to be a problem, would become Jerome's problem—not his own. But he did regret the lost chance of meeting him, and he came to regret it more deeply as the letters and the tracts multiplied. It could be difficult to remember the man behind the written word, especially when the writings were so terrifying. Pelagius was horrified by sin and by the widespread acceptance of it as an inescapable part of human nature; he believed it was something to be rooted out.

A loud thwack, followed by the boys shouting in awe, made Augustine look out his window and smile. He didn't understand their game, but he watched as two boys raced in a wide circle and the others cheered.

Augustine tried to boil down Pelagius's beliefs: God commanded perfection, which man could achieve of his own will. For how could God command the impossible?

As the boys' shouts got louder, Augustine put his hands over his face. He needed to concentrate.

Pelagius's proposition did not impress Jerome, who knew how far the human heart was from perfection. But many others were impressed, both by the challenge to make of themselves a new creation, and by the example of the man who issued the challenge. Pelagius preached nothing he did not practice, and his ascetic lifestyle earned him many attentive listeners. Through his friends in Rome, and their friends, his message spread.

Augustine turned to the reports, the copies of letters, and the books he had gathered. The day before, he'd read of debates about infant baptism. He read the testimony of formerly lukewarm Christians who had been kindled to flame. This morning, he read stirring calls to obedience in the First Letter of John: "For this is the love of God, that we keep his commandments: and his commandments are not heavy."

Now he stood in front of his desk and laid all these items side by side. It was as if he were putting each brightly colored tile into this mosaic of the mind. And then he saw a danger so great that it nearly stopped his heart.

Pelagius is saying we can earn heaven, Augustine thought. *He believes, in effect, that we can buy our salvation. But our salvation has already been bought, and at a price we could never have paid. Take away the need for redemption and you take away the need for a redeemer.*

"What hast thou that thou hast not received? And if thou hast received, why dost thou glory, as if thou hadst not received it?" Saint Paul had put that question to the people of Corinth. It was as much as to say, "Everything is grace."

Augustine sat down and wrote. He defended that statement with Scripture and with remorseless logic, but beyond that, he knew the truth of it—he had lived the truth of it. He wrote so furiously that he did not notice the boys outside his window had ended their game. They now lounged on the stone wall, talking amiably as the sun started its descent.

His own life, reflected Augustine, was the story of a man who had fled salvation, and of a God who had pursued him in spite of himself. He feared it would be a terrible thing to surrender himself into the arms of God's mercy. Only after he did so could he begin to grasp how much more terrible it would have been to stand alone and upright before God's justice. To kneel or to stand: That was the choice each man had to make, and if he did not choose right, no other choice mattered.

Pelagius, in words that stung because there was so much

truth in them, was telling the old lie of the Garden: "You shall be as gods." *To counter that lie, every effort must be . . .*

"Your Grace!" A young deacon burst into Augustine's study, jolting him out of his thoughts. "You are needed at once," he said.

Taking up a cloak, Augustine followed the deacon out into the now-darkened streets. They carried no torch; the deacon knew the way, and their feet knew the stones.

As they walked, the deacon whispered, "Some of our people had word of another ship owned by Galatian traders. Our men assembled a band of their own and raided at first darkness, rescuing more than a hundred, all told. I have heard that Camillus is among them."

"God be praised!" Augustine said.

In recent years, the slave traders had become bolder and more numerous. Hippo, as a port city, saw more than its share of them. Some of Augustine's congregation had decided to meet force with force. Tonight, it appeared they had rescued Camillus, one of Augustine's own monks, who had disappeared two days before.

The deacon led Augustine to a warehouse amid shadows near the harbor waters. It belonged to a merchant who dealt primarily in the popular fish sauce called garum. As they walked through the rows and rows of amphoras, the smell of spiced fish overpowered Augustine's senses. And there, gathered at the back of the vast room, tended by Augustine's flock, were the victims. They were not shackled, but they trembled in fright. Because of the danger of reprisals from the traders, these people would be scattered throughout the city, hidden in faithful houses, until safe routes could be found to return them to their homes.

Augustine saw Camillus among them and put up a hand in greeting, but he did not immediately approach him. Huddled almost at the bishop's feet was a Berber girl of nine or ten. He kneeled beside her and tried to summon words in a language he had last used a lifetime ago. "I am Augustine. Will you tell me your name?" he asked.

"Tidir," she replied.

"Will you tell me what happened to you, Tidir?"

As the girl began to tell her story, Augustine's stomach clenched in anger.

"They come at night," Augustine explained to Alypius the next week, recounting the little girl's story. "They will surround an isolated farm, kill the men, and drag away the women and children—free Romans all. I have heard of a woman in Hippo who lures other women to come with her on the pretext of selling them wood, then binds them over to be sold. There is talk that some men sell their own wives—simply through greed, and because It is so easy to find a buyer. And it grows worse every year."

"I have heard some of this too," Alypius said, steering Augustine around a street vendor with piles of fruit on display. When Augustine was well launched on a subject, he sometimes forgot his surroundings.

They had met up in Tubunae, a town along the route to Carthage. The two men had much to discuss as they headed to the residence of Boniface, a Roman official and friend of Augustine's who had asked for his counsel on some private matter he was to disclose to them here.

"Then," Augustine continued as they walked, "when some of the victims are freed, some traders will bring a legal action to recover them. Horrible though it be to say it, they have supporters in this. There must be new laws, and better enforcement of them. When you next go to Italy, will you look into this matter?"

"Be assured I will." Alypius, the lawyer, was also the traveler. Augustine remained in Africa, but Alypius would carry Augustine's words across the sea.

They had reached the inn where Boniface was lodging. He had been watching for them, and after calling for wine, he led them up to his room. It was a small rectangular space with a low table and chairs. A window opened up over a courtyard with pink bougainvillea shining brilliantly over the rooftop.

"My wife has died," Boniface began. Augustine and Alypius simultaneously began to speak, but Boniface cut short their condolences. "It is my grief, and I will bear it. I do not wish for your sympathy; I ask for your counsel. She was everything I loved in this world, and now that she is gone, I wonder whether I should not leave the world also. I do not mean by the sword," he assured them, seeing their looks of alarm. "I mean by the razor. To shave my head and throw away my sword . . . and live for God. To become a monk."

He leaned forward, eager to share his excitement with his guests. Apparently, he did not see in their faces what he had hoped. He answered them as if they had protested his idea. "And why should I not? Is there any higher calling?"

"No," Alypius said.

"It is a calling both of you embraced."

"One we accepted," Alypius said. Augustine smiled at the lawyer's choice of the word. *A calling we ran from, nearly as hard and as far as we each, in our own ways, ran from God*, Augustine thought, *until we realized, yet again, the futility of the chase.*

"You accepted wholeheartedly," Boniface said.

"We are not quite such fools," Augustine murmured, "as to give God only half a heart."

"Then why do you tell me I should not do the same?"

"We have not told you anything, as yet," Alypius reminded him.

"I thought you would be overjoyed. Shouldn't a man pursue the highest calling?"

"A man should pursue his calling," Augustine said, leaning forward. Now it was Alypius's turn to relax. "In your case, it seems to me that the state of the Empire, with thieves and bandits inside and Goths and Vandals pressing on the borders, is your calling. While this world endures, some men will have to bear the sword."

"But when I think of the monk's life, I feel such elation . . . such happiness," Boniface said dreamily.

Augustine shook his head. "Look for peace. Sometimes happiness will follow." He thought of his mother's face, lit by the sunset at Ostia. "Sometimes it will not. But whether it does or not, if the work is your work, then there will be peace in the doing of it. When you drive back the barbarians, is there happiness in that? In the blood and the screams and the stench?"

Boniface considered this. "No, but there is honor, a duty done, brotherhood." He stared down at his clasped hands as memories played across his face, almost as clear as they must have been in his mind. After a time, he looked up. "And that is my peace."

Augustine and Alypius remained for two more days in Tubunae. They walked and talked, enjoying each other's company like a fine meal. Augustine felt free to express all his ideas, as he felt more at ease with Alypius than anyone else. They talked about the Pelagian controversy—Alypius wanted to be sure he fully understood his friend's arguments. Then the two men parted ways. Alypius journeyed on to Carthage, where he would sail to Italy. Augustine returned to Hippo.

Upon reaching home, Augustine discovered several letters had arrived from Evodius, who was now the Bishop of Uzalis. He took them to his study and opened them one by one, smiling as he read. Evodius had questions about the nature of the soul, and he asked for copies of the completed books of *The City of God* and Augustine's treatise on the Trinity.

Although he could not see them for months or years at a time, Augustine deeply enjoyed indulging in theological speculation with his friends. To contemplate the nature of the Trinity was the closest he came to true rest. Letters from Evodius always reawakened this longing, and he remembered that some men spent their entire lives in contemplation.

But he was not one of them—at least not now, in the midst of a war. Not many men had the will or the mind to pursue abstract speculation, and, as he reminded Evodius in his first reply letter, "if Christ died for those only who with clear intelligence can discern these things, our labor in the Church is almost spent in vain."

Augustine's task as a bishop was to speak for and to the rest of the people, to the merchants, coppersmiths, and sailors who did not know or care whether one, two, or three persons had spoken to Moses on Mount Sinai, but who did need to know what they must do to be saved.

Augustine had received another letter he must answer. He got up and paced around the study for a few minutes. Then he settled into the comfort of his chair and took a deep breath.

The letter was from Deogratias, one of the deacons of Carthage, who had an excellent character and a pleasing manner. Bishop Aurelius had his hands full with administering that diocese, so it often fell to Deogratias to give new converts their first instruction in the faith. It fell to him so often that he had begun to feel his program was dry and his delivery was worse.

"I need your advice and beg of you to share your experience with me," Deogratias asked in his letter. "What should I teach and how should I teach it so that I inspire others instead of putting them to sleep?"

Augustine answered with a book. It was short compared to

the ever-growing *City of God* and the stacks of paper expended on Pelagius. Yet it was a book. Augustine sympathized with his correspondent's frustrations—he had felt all of this himself. But looking at the dilemma from outside, the situation did not seem so dire. Augustine began to write a return letter.

"Is your presentation really dry to people who have never heard it before?" he queried his friend. "And if you are so inadequate to the task, why are you constantly being selected for it?"

"You must not be discouraged," he continued. He understood the vast distance between what can be known in the soul and what can be expressed in words. "Give what you are able to give, and think less of doing your own thoughts justice than of offering Christ to those who come to seek him."

Thinking of his own work, Augustine asked Deogratias, "Is your greatest frustration being constantly interrupted? To be torn away from your own work at the request of another frustrates anyone. I beg you to ask yourself, Deogratias, what is more profitable—the task you've set for yourself or the task set for you by God?"

As to what he should teach, that was a simpler matter. "You must tell the story," Augustine wrote. "Give particular weight to the points at which the City of God can most clearly be seen breaking through into the City of Man."

He stopped to look out the window to the empty courtyard. "Tell of the garden, and of the fall permitted by the God who loved men enough to make them free, even if they would do themselves deadly harm.

"Tell of the wood of the Ark, and of the wood of the cross to which we must cling, or we drown.

"Tell of the lamb that was sacrificed, and of the Lamb who made himself the sacrifice.

"Tell of the Bread of Heaven, who took hunger upon himself so that we might be fed.

"Tell of Christ, who walked the earth as man and God, and who established his Church to be pruned by the knives of the persecutors and watered by the blood of the martyrs.

"Tell of the two ends of the two Cities, to one of which every man must go.

"Tell a man what he should flee, and what he should desire.

"And tell him that if he remains faithful, then as the light dawns on the seventh day, he shall have his rest."

Chapter Twenty-Four

The lamp still burned, but Augustine put his pen aside. He was nearing the completion of his long book. Hours before, he had sent his scribe to bed and was content simply to watch the flame of his lamp alone in peaceful silence. He was seventy-six years old—he should be tired, but he was not. He had not done enough, he felt. He never could. This feeling came back to him again and again.

I found you late—not too late, I pray, but late, he prayed to God. *What we might have done can never be done. We spend our lives chasing it, and it only grows farther away.*

We spend our lives chasing rest. We pursue that which comes when we are still. We think we pursue, when in fact we are pursued.

What we desire is you, yet we run from you. We know, even before we know it, that before we can rest in you, you must rip and tear away anything else in which the heart might wish to rest. That means even the good, if we prefer the gift of God to the Giver.

Augustine thought that perhaps, at long last, everything else had been torn away. He had lost his treasured friends. In 425, five years earlier, Evodius had died. All his questions now had answers. Then, in this very spring of 430, Alypius died too.

Augustine did not doubt that a better advocate than he had pleaded his case. And so, Augustine was alone. And he was old.

In 426, he had done his best to provide for his people. In three decades as a bishop of Hippo, he had seen many cities disrupted by the sudden death of their shepherd and the resulting struggle for power. So, he took careful thought for his own congregation. After much prayer and thought, he publicly proclaimed—to acclamations that filled the Basilica of Peace—one of his priests, Eraclius, as his successor. Augustine asked Eraclius to immediately take over much of the diocese's administrative work, as he had done for Bishop Valerius. This left him time to complete the work only he could do. *Or as much of that work as I am granted time to do*, he thought.

He was grateful Pelagius had been expelled from Rome in 418, by edict of the emperor himself. Yet the man's heresy continued to surface in towns and cities, manifested in different forms. At one time, Augustine had exchanged verbal barbs with one of Pelagius's disciples, Julian of Eclanum, in a public square before a small crowd.

"You are simply a Punic quarrel-seeker. Alypius is your lackey," Julian had sneered, pleased to have caught Augustine by surprise.

Augustine stared hard at Julian but did not respond.

"And Monica? Your mother was a drunkard. That is well-known," Julian had said, laughing.

"It is small wonder, because you reject grace, that you cannot see the grace that rescued Monica from her early vice," Augustine had responded evenly. The crowd was quiet as he continued.

"I praise God that while my own mother died knowing I was a Catholic, your parents did not live to see their son turn heretic."

Julian had lunged forward as if to strike Augustine, but Alypius pulled his friend away from the crowd, so Julian turned away.

As weeks passed, Augustine realized the painful conflict had served a good purpose. It actually helped him refine his thoughts about the soul's place in relation to the two Cities. The idea required time to clarify and expound upon, but it came down to one simple but all-encompassing notion: Everything is grace.

If God is omnipotent, and if we have nothing we have not received, then even the first impulse by which the will turns to him is his gift. How many will be saved? That is not for us to know. But Augustine feared, as he considered the state of the empire, that it could not be many.

He'd recently been spending time reviewing and correcting his own writings. A man's words lived after him, and Augustine wanted to make very sure he'd chosen the right words. But he had been a prolific writer and he did not know how much time he had left. Would his books survive? The books were contained in his library, and his library was contained in the city of Hippo.

It was the summer of 430, and the city of Hippo Regius was under siege.

Augustine was not alone in wondering how much time was left. Twenty years before, Africa had witnessed the invasion of Italy. Now it too suffered an invasion.

The tribune Boniface—the man who had once poured out

his wish to escape to a life of contemplation to Augustine—was now Count Boniface, military commander for Africa. In the past three years, Boniface fought more with allies than with foes. That was just what the Empress Galla Placidia, regent for her son Valentinian III, wanted. She encouraged rivalries between the senior army commanders, hoping to prevent any one of them from becoming too powerful.

In 427, Flavius Felix, who commanded in Italy, had sent forces to Africa to engage with Boniface. Boniface prevailed, but the campaign distracted his attention, forcing him to look east instead of north.

To the north of Africa, separated at its tip by a narrow strait, was Iberia. Across this strait, in 429, came the tribe of the Vandals—not just their warriors, but old men, women, and children as well. They intended to stay and quickly moved east, keeping to the coast. They also kept contact with their ships, which matched their rapid progress.

Count Boniface confronted them at the border of the province Africa Proconsularis. It was a complete and glorious triumph . . . for the Vandals. Boniface and the remainder of his army retreated along the coast and took shelter inside the walls of Hippo Regius.

The Vandals settled in to learn the ways of siege warfare. Fourteen months later, they mastered it, and Hippo became their king's first capital in their brave new world.

The danger was close—Augustine and his clergy received word that the Vandal army approached. Bishops of other cities sought refuge in Hippo. They told Augustine how the Vandals raped women and burned all structures, and that they had tortured and killed bishops within sight of their walls. The Vandals came as conquerors. What they could not use, they would destroy.

Still, Hippo's clergy remained with their flock. Other bishops reminded Augustine that the Lord himself had commanded his disciples, "When they persecute you in one city, flee to another." But Augustine believed that phrase applied to particular individuals when the Apostle Paul had made his escape from Damascus, knowing others would carry on the work. No, when the danger threatened everyone, it should be shared by everyone. And the chief danger to any man was always to his soul. The clergy had a duty no one else could fulfill.

As the Vandals encircled the city walls, the Basilica of Peace was filled with lifelong catechumens who suddenly decided their baptism should be delayed no longer. And people of faith also crowded the basilica, seeking penance for sins they had been willing to live with but were not willing to die with. Fearing imminent death, others came for consolation that could only be found in Word and Sacrament. So, Augustine baptized, reconciled, and preached. All around him was the desolation of the City of Man. He prayed God would save the city from its foes or give his servants the courage to endure what he would allow them to suffer. Augustine reminded himself and his congregation that every man is born to die.

Then, in the midst of the siege, and in the heat of an August afternoon, Augustine fell ill with a fever.

~

His deacons took him to his bed. As soon as his head touched the soft pillow, Augustine sensed he would not rise from it again.

He called for his scribes. He had one last task for them: Copy the penitential Psalms, in letters as large as they could make them, then nail the words on the walls around his bed, so that wherever his eye fell, he would read of man's need for the great mercy of God.

The deacons stood by his bed, trying to hold back their tears as they fanned his face. Though their Bishop of Hippo was seventy-six, they were not ready to lose him.

For four decades, he had served God and his Church. For four decades, he had given himself as completely as the martyrs gave their lives in a moment. For four decades, he had prayed, "May I not be my own life."

Yet, as Augustine constantly reminded his clergy, no man should presume his reward. None knew better than he the weight of his sins. Whatever time he had left, he would spend it in penance.

He asked his priests and deacons to leave him alone for a time. This included Eraclius, who kissed his hand with a look in his eyes that Augustine remembered well. He felt that same way the night Bishop Valerius had died. They left him to his prayers, alone with his God in the gathering dark.

He prayed, from the Psalms:

Have mercy on me, O God, according to thy great mercy.

And according to the multitude of thy tender mercies blot out my iniquity.

Wash me yet more from my iniquity, and cleanse me from my sin.

For I know my iniquity, and my sin is always before me.

To thee only have I sinned, and have done evil before thee: that thou mayest be justified in thy words, and mayest overcome when thou art judged.

For behold I was conceived in iniquities; and in sins did my mother conceive me.

For behold thou hast loved truth: the uncertain and hidden things of thy wisdom thou hast made manifest to me.

Thou shalt sprinkle me with hyssop, and I shall be cleansed; thou shalt wash me, and I shall be made whiter than snow.

To my hearing thou shalt give joy and gladness: and the bones that have been humbled shall rejoice.

Turn away thy face from my sins, and blot out all my iniquities.

Create a clean heart in me, O God: and renew a right spirit within my bowels.

Cast me not away from thy face; and take not thy holy spirit from me.

Restore unto me the joy of thy salvation, and strengthen me with a perfect spirit.

I will teach the unjust thy ways: and the wicked shall be converted to thee.

Deliver me from blood, O God, thou God of my salvation: and my tongue shall extol thy justice.

O Lord, thou wilt open my lips: and my mouth shall declare thy praise.

For if thou hadst desired sacrifice, I would indeed have given it: with burnt offerings thou wilt not be delighted.

A sacrifice to God is an afflicted spirit: a contrite and humbled heart, O God, thou wilt not despise.

Glossary

Arianism: A heresy that says that Jesus Christ is not co-eternal with God the Father, but was created in time by the Father. This would make Christ subordinate, not equal, to the Father. The heresy was named for its creator, the priest Arius of Alexandria.

Donatism: A schismatic movement led by Donatus, an early fourth-century bishop of Carthage. It was a response to the behavior of many priests and bishops during the Emperor Diocletian's persecution of Christians. These priests and bishops had apostasized out of fear, burning incense to the pagan gods, informing on their fellow Christians, and in some cases even handing over the Sacred Scriptures to be burned. The Donatists believed that such men were no longer really priests or bishops, saying that the minister must be pure and faultless, or the sacraments are not valid.

Manichaeism: A religion founded in the third century and named after its founder, the Persian Mani. Mani claimed that his was a religion of pure reason, as opposed to the mysteries of

Christianity. He taught that there are two equal powers in the world, the light and the darkness, and that they are perpetually at war with one another. Every person has both of these elements in himself. Everything is material, even the soul.

Pelagianism: An early fifth-century heresy started by the monk and theologian Pelagius. Pelagius believed that it is possible for a man to fulfill the law of God by his natural strength, without the need of divine grace. He believed that we can "earn" heaven on our own merit, by our own good works.

ALSO FROM THE MENTORIS PROJECT

America's Forgotten Founding Father
A Novel Based on the Life of Filippo Mazzei
by Rosanne Welch, PhD

A. P. Giannini—Il Banchiere di Tutti
di Francesca Valente

A. P. Giannini—The People's Banker
by Francesca Valente

The Architect Who Changed Our World
A Novel Based on the Life of Andrea Palladio
by Pamela Winfrey

At Last
A Novel Based on the Life of Harry Warren
by Stacia Raymond

A Boxing Trainer's Journey
A Novel Based on the Life of Angelo Dundee
by Jonathan Brown

Breaking Barriers
A Novel Based on the Life of Laura Bassi
by Jule Selbo

Building Heaven's Ceiling
A Novel Based on the Life of Filippo Brunelleschi
by Joe Cline

Building Wealth
From Shoeshine Boy to Real Estate Magnate
by Robert Barbera

Building Wealth 101
How to Make Your Money Work for You
by Robert Barbera

Character is What Counts
A Novel Based on the Life of Vince Lombardi
by Jonathan Brown

Christopher Columbus: His Life and Discoveries
by Mario Di Giovanni

Dark Labyrinth
A Novel Based on the Life of Galileo Galilei
by Peter David Myers

Defying Danger
A Novel Based on the Life of Father Matteo Ricci
by Nicole Gregory

Desert Missionary
A Novel Based on the Life of Father Eusebio Kino
by Nicole Gregory

The Divine Proportions of Luca Pacioli
A Novel Based on the Life of Luca Pacioli
by W. A. W. Parker

The Dream of Life
A Novel Based on the Life of Federico Fellini
by Kate Fuglei

Dreams of Discovery
A Novel Based on the Life of the Explorer John Cabot
by Jule Selbo

The Embrace of Hope
A Novel Based on the Life of Frank Capra
by Kate Fuglei

The Faithful
A Novel Based on the Life of Giuseppe Verdi
by Collin Mitchell

Fermi's Gifts
A Novel Based on the Life of Enrico Fermi
by Kate Fuglei

First Among Equals
A Novel Based on the Life of Cosimo de' Medici
by Francesco Massaccesi

God's Messenger
A Novel Based on the Life of Mother Frances X. Cabrini
by Nicole Gregory

Grace Notes
A Novel Based on the Life of Henry Mancini
by Stacia Raymond

Guido's Guiding Hand
A Novel Based on the Life of Guido d'Arezzo
by Kingsley Day

Harvesting the American Dream
A Novel Based on the Life of Ernest Gallo
by Karen Richardson

Humble Servant of Truth
A Novel Based on the Life of Thomas Aquinas
by Margaret O'Reilly

The Judicious Use of Intangibles
A Novel Based on the Life of Pietro Belluschi
by W.A.W. Parker

Leonardo's Secret
A Novel Based on the Life of Leonardo da Vinci
by Peter David Myers

Little by Little We Won
A Novel Based on the Life of Angela Bambace
by Peg A. Lamphier, PhD

The Making of a Prince
A Novel Based on the Life of Niccolò Machiavelli
by Maurizio Marmorstein

A Man of Action Saving Liberty
A Novel Based on the Life of Giuseppe Garibaldi
by Rosanne Welch, PhD

Marconi and His Muses
A Novel Based on the Life of Guglielmo Marconi
by Pamela Winfrey

No Person Above the Law
A Novel Based on the Life of Judge John J. Sirica
by Cynthia Cooper

The Pirate Prince of Genoa
A Novel Based on the Life of Admiral Andrea Doria
by Maurizio Marmorstein

Relentless Visionary: Alessandro Volta
by Michael Berick

Retire and Refire
Simple Financial Strategies to Navigate Your Best Years with Ease
by Robert Barbera

Ride Into the Sun
A Novel Based on the Life of Scipio Africanus
by Patric Verrone

Rita Levi-Montalcini
Pioneer & Ambassador of Science
by Francesca Valente

Saving the Republic
A Novel Based on the Life of Marcus Cicero
by Eric D. Martin

The Seven Senses of Italy
by Nicole Gregory

Sinner, Servant, Saint
A Novel Based on the Life of St. Francis of Assisi
by Margaret O'Reilly

Soldier, Diplomat, Archaeologist
A Novel Based on the Bold Life of Louis Palma di Cesnola
by Peg A. Lamphier, PhD

The Soul of a Child
A Novel Based on the Life of Maria Montessori
by Kate Fuglei

What a Woman Can Do
A Novel Based on the Life of Artemisia Gentileschi
by Peg A. Lamphier, PhD

The Witch of Agnesi
A Novel Based on the Life of Maria Agnesi
by Eric D. Martin

For more information on these titles and
the Mentoris Project, please visit
www.mentorisproject.org